George Alfred Townsend

Poems of Men and Events

George Alfred Townsend

Poems of Men and Events

ISBN/EAN: 9783337406622

Printed in Europe, USA, Canada, Australia, Japan

Cover: Foto ©Andreas Hilbeck / pixelio.de

More available books at **www.hansebooks.com**

GEORGE ALFRED TOWNSEND'S

POEMS OF MEN AND EVENTS

1899

Gath

POEMS

OF

MEN AND EVENTS

BY

GEORGE ALFRED TOWNSEND

GAPLAND EDITION

E. F. Bonaventure

NEW YORK

1899

PREFACE

I HAD devised a publication of all my verses; but upon arraying them for this edition, with its limited page-type, found that the printer's nicety had overreached me, and I believed that my noble friends, the subscribers, would be better satisfied with a selection of representative compositions than with quantity. I therefore omitted the *Poems* in my book of 1875, and those published in "Tales of the Chesapeake," and "Bohemian Days," and "Poetical Addresses," and set to the front my latest pieces, not till now published, and added to them particular reproductions bearing out the title of this book, or in line with my present preferences and ideas. Forty-three years have gone by since I printed my earliest verse. Although the newspapers have been my bulrushes, holding me up, Poesy has been Pharaoh's daughter, raising me.

GAPLAND, MD., March 6, 1899.

SUBSCRIBERS

(To May 1, 1899.)

CONTENTS

CONTENTS.

CONTENTS.

ILLUSTRATIONS

AUTHOR'S BIRTHPLACE, GEORGETOWN, DELAWARE

POEMS

BIRTHDAY THOUGHTS

JANUARY 30, 1899

KING CHARLES'S soul took flight
  This day from his cabal:
I am no Jacobite,
  My date is radical.

Our place is in the van,
  We move before the facts;
The blood of Milbourne ran
  For antecedent acts.

I know not if his name
  And type were in my dam,
Our phantoms seem the same
  And as he was, I am:

Stern to perceive and say,
  Though not officially,
And quit the humble way
  From vaulting sympathy;

An English partisan
  To swell our kingdom big,
My christening Georgean
  And all my color Whig;

Nor yet from landed dower
  To reason and to speak,
Impetuous for power
  To help the faithful weak;

My quill drawn from the goose
  I hissed the cautious sense,
And wrote to be of use,
  And for my audience.

Events were all my Muse,
  They warped my wish more pure
And dried the fresher dews
  Of morning literature.

Imperfect everywhere
  As is the cannon cast,
Small time did I forbear
  To touch it into blast,

Nor loaded on my heart
  That hungered to be free,
The convoluted art,
  The printer's factory.

Strong manhood justly wrecked
  I took my arms between,
Nor harmed the eagle pecked
  By tits of concourse mean;

Nor would with herds unite, —
  The small peccary band:
I was the last Free Knight,
  Goetz of the Iron Hand.

To this withdrawing pride
  From daws and choughs and rooks,
I owe the countryside
  And company of books,

Preferring to be blind
  And silent lines pursue,
As Milton's lonely mind
  The light of Eden knew.

A few strong friendships kind
  My castles did maintain, —
The conquests of the mind
  To have its causes gain.

How blessed to have seen
  And known wide Freedom's day!
Whose generations lean
  The forests hid away,

Since Indians lost among
  Beneath the cypress firs,
My fathers learned their tongue
  And were Interpreters.

Now almost lost again
  Amidst a mighty race,
Amidst the teeming men,
  My art is like the chase;

My bow is well outclass'd,
  My arrows shoot to err,
But to a forest Past
  I was Interpreter.

POEMS OF MEN

JOHN PARKE CUSTIS

To Boucher's school I will not go
  If Nelly's gate I must go past !
At school, I learn so very slow ;
  From Nelly I learn twice as fast.
Sweet Nelly Calvert, are you there ?
  Blue jacket, boy's hat, riding whip?
Mount Airy has not too much air
  When swells my heart to Nelly's lip.

Turn from the road ! the pines are green,
  Our teacher shall be the wood dove ;
Stepfather Washington is keen
  And thinks that school-boys should not love.
What did he know of love, I ask,
  When in my mother's gate he turned?
Love is the most delightful task
  That two together ever learned.

Here is a hazel-berried sprig,
  I'll set it in your fillie's fore.
Kiss me if I am not too big !
  Reprove me not if I adore !
This budding spring is perfect bliss ;
  Who would not rather on thee look
Than dawdle at Annapolis,
  Or at Mount Vernon hug a book ?

At Nottingham my boat is moored
    I sent it round Potomac way,
We'll put our hunters both aboard
    And canter on to Herring bay;
So far our guardians won't pursue
    But let us have an all-day freak
And I will bathe you in the blue,
    Sky-feathered wing of Chesapeake.

Or sail you down the golden roads
    Patuxent's ships are lost within,
To dream more love than Ovid's odes
    Sighed to your high mysterious kin;
Thy grandam surely was a queen,
    I feel her sceptre in thy moods,
Thy government is as serene
    As Pocahontas in her woods.

There flashed a fox! She's like a bow
    And arrow on her courser's stride.
Sweet mistress — *Yoricks! Tally ho!*
    The way to take you is to ride.
Like a hawk's shadow see her flow!
    To horn and hounds her strain is bred.
She's galloped into Marlboro':
    Nelly, we're found out: let us wed!

JUDGES' GRAVES

PRETTY EDENTON! dreaming on the Sound,
In thy level cotton-fields is a burial ground

Near a planter's dwelling, past a miller's creek:
(Hold the foxhounds back whilst the tombs I
　　seek!)

To the States and province both of foreign birth,
Guests of courteous Johnstons even in the earth,
Iredell and Wilson like water oaks of gnarl
Sleep, as often in one bed, by shining Albemarle.

Washington's own Justices on his bench supreme,
Here fortuitous they meet in everlasting dream,
Young in years, in wisdom deep and mutual
　　　　partisan,
They lie like David in the cave, asleep with
　　Jonathan.

How the rigid cedars grow, drinking of their skulls!
As the lawyer from their minds unknowing of them
　　culls.
How the cotton lint is blown on their rusted grill!
How the bluebird sings to them and they a cen-
　　tury still!

As their court in robes is bowed to the bench recess,
While the bar stands to the sound sudden of " *O
　　yes !* "
These preceding in their shrouds that God-visaged
　　one,
Cried unto the final Judge their caller, Washington.

Ye who dream that passions quit Justices divine,
Pause and read Iredell's memoir by Wilson's un-
　　marked shrine!

He who Independence signed, on the Bench grew
    pale,
Lest the Sheriff drag him down to the debtors'
    jail.

Knightly Raleigh who, hard by, planted Roanoke,
Harried to the axe and block by abusive Coke,
No more wantoned in career than this Scottish
    chief
On whose breast the humid light twines the myrtle
    leaf.

Broken-spirited he hid where he might not dwell,
By the wealth-untroubled home of his friend
    Iredell,—
He of Ireton's Cromwell race, of his name un-
    done,
Followed Wilson on the bier, out from Edenton.

As they rode their circuits round, till the General
    Term,
They assemble where the Chief Justice is the
    Worm;
In the air their Institutes like a shedding tree
Annually blossom forth greenest Liberty.

    1887.

WILLIAM B. ALLISON

THE talent nature gives of Graciousness
    Ambition most perverts, but it outlasts
Wide combinations and august address,
    And at its table gentles and outcasts

Holy Communion take, like Christ's repasts.
　　Allison! framed to give, not to refuse,
By grace is made refuser of the state;
　　He sayeth "no" the heart not to abuse,
He smooths the suppliant not in vain to wait,
　　His largess falls where needful like the dews
That o'er the chilly zone precipitate —
　　And freshening influence on the land diffuse;
Like Providence his years we do not count,
　　Nor see the frost around the living fount.

BLAINE

(BY GAIL HAMILTON DODGE)

A WISTFUL spirit sensitive
Whose onset ended in "forgive!"
And who was timid not to live;

He seemed a ruler of affairs
But pined away with little cares,
His port the hound's, his heart the hare's.

Inspiring love, hate echoed it.
He was uncautious in his wit
And wounded men of savage grit;

They kept him from the diadem,
They stabbed the steed which trampled them.
The people kissed his garment's hem.

He did not have the moral might;
He had the leman's tender light
That greatness visits in the night.

A transport still thou didst bequeath:
That thou wert only underneath,
Take, Blaine! the white Camelian wreath!

This book it also is thy tomb;
Two women watched it, one to doom,
A light of Maries fills its gloom.

So is thy end as thou didst rise;
Not with a sword thy sculpture lies;
The pen for penmen must suffice.

1897.

PLANTA GENISTA

PRETTY *bonne* of black Angers,
　　Sweeping daily in my room!
Do I from you breathe the airs
　　Of the yellow-flowering broom?
Plant that the crusaders set
　　In the helmets of Anjou
And were called Plantagenet
　　From the broom that busies you?

Fleurs de lis have made me tire,
　　Stale the French camelias bloom,
But my homesick thoughts inspire
　　Tender memories of your broom:
How the housemaids, o'er the sea,
　　Ran my boyhood round the room
And the broomstick fell on me,
　　When I fought them for the broom.

Could I be a boy again,
    Would I have that struggle o'er? —
While I see you, pretty wren,
    Hopping on my sunlit floor
With your high cap's snowy lace,
    On your cheeks a rosy bloom,
While your instepped slippers chase
    Waltzes round the flashing broom?

Now I see how Geoffrey's son
    Was the Queen of France's groom!
Round his whisking youth she spun
    Like the spirit of your broom;
Swept his mind up like the floor,
    In it one cool vision set,
Till there were but Eleanore
    And the bold Plantagenet.

Your forefathers came to harms
    By Plantagenetic arts
Rifling for concealèd arms
    All too near Sicilian hearts,
In my heart your hand is deep
    And my blood runs like a flume, —
At your masthead you do sweep
    Up its river with your broom.

Would you give me but my due
    If I grew a moment gay?
As the red Fulk of Anjou
    France's Northmen drove away?

Or like Anjou's Margaret
  In the Roses' wars of doom,
In your widowed helmet set
  All the terrors of the broom?

René's knightly orators
  Gave not sweeter tunings vent
In the tilts of troubadours
  Than your household implement;
I can see the bright-skinned slaves
  Dusting in my fever room,
Like the cool tree shadows' waves,
  When your white arms move the broom.

You are of King Robert's race
  And his daughter's romance owe —
Fiammetta's bending grace
  To a lone Boccaccio;
Lean your broom by me in trust,
  I can tell you tales as fair;
You have swept my mind of dust
  With Griselda's light and air.

One sweet kiss that shall Angers
  Ever on my spirit bloom!
On my heath of barren cares
  Plant the blossoms of the broom!
Hyssop with your lips my sins!
  For the lists my courage whet!
And among your Angevins
  Crown one more Plantagenet!

DANTE

LIKE some bronze statue rust the more restores,
Dante! thou standest in the junk of old:
Armor and crosiers, catapults and oars,
That make thee Pluto in a hell of mold.
All that hell was thy bony features hold,
Death and imagination, monkish stern!
A savage Christ, thou Virgil's hand did fold,
Mild pagan company in hell's sojourn, —
Poet who might'st in thy dark age have told
The light of Friar Bacon, Bannockburn!
Letters melodious in a barbarous tongue
Thy banished genius turned thy age upon,
And feudal night with acclamations rung
As when in Florence wheeled her gonfalon.

READING GIBBON

SOME penance for my father's wrong,
　In purgatorial cell,
His son would do that memory strong
　They named an Infidel;

He who, exiled from sire and home
　For his credulity,
Made of the mighty tale of Rome,
　Homerian history.

The pulpiteers they did instil
　Aspersions partisan,
I bought his book and kept it till
　I read it when a man,

Then Koran, Talmud, Testaments,
  Old Moses or his scribes
Like whimseys seemed in Arab tents
  Took down by savage tribes.

The vast procession of mankind
  Like some great circus seemed
In his kaleidoscopic mind,
  Metempsychosed or dreamed.

Still, in the terms of them who pray,
  I thought his book so wise
He seemed like Christ on judgment day,
  Who held the great assize.

He wove the bad with so much glad,
  In my astonishment
Haroun al Raschid in Bagdad
  Was less magnificent.

By night or day in cave or camp,
  His touchstone had such skill
Aladdin with the burning lamp
  Was Edward Gibbon still.

No creedsman and no mountebank,
  Nor of his soul afraid,
He had the instinct of the Frank,
  And was the last crusade.

Nor in the literary life,
  His gallantry was sunk ;
His love was Necker's noble wife,
  For her he was a monk.

He left the gates of faith ajar
 For science yet to hope :
A gentleman, a warrior,
 An Emperor and Pope.

CALVIN BRICE

" I HAVE been everywhere,"
 Said Calvin Brice,
" In battle and affair,
Society and snare :
If there's anything up there, —
 Purgatory, Paradise, —
I would like to go and see
For curiosity ! "
 Said Calvin Brice. *

The spirits in the air
 Heard Calvin Brice ;
They knew how he would dare,
So seeing and so fair,
Country-hearted, *débonnaire*,
 And with never avarice :
" He shall have his wish and come !
Play the dead-march on the drum
 For Calvin Brice ! "

From the dead line, *sans* care,
 Stepp'd Calvin Brice,
Topographer to dare
And with gods to pay his share,

* Spoken by Mr. Brice to Hon. Edward Wolcott.

Or with apparitions fare, —
   However fall the dice.
He has gone beyond the goal,
The pioneering soul
   Of Calvin Brice.

And if they keep him there, —
   Our Calvin Brice —
With his Absalom hair,
And his nose large and square,
'Tis because that everywhere,
   He is without artifice.
Hell and heaven must delight
In a soul so apposite,
   As Calvin Brice.

SOPHIE

ALBERT GALLATIN TO LAFAYETTE
MAY 28, 1825

LET me sit by Sophie's grave
Where the hemlock woodlands wave
Far above the river's rave —
   My tender Sophie!
She was all I had to bless
In the savage wilderness ;
Brief the time of our caress,
   My angel Sophie!

O'er the mountains following
Like the leaping fairy spring,

How she made the young birds sing,
    To see my Sophie!
Folded on my breast so tight,
Round us fell the Indian night:
She was hidden morning light—
    My bride, my Sophie.

It was spring she brought with her;
Summer's precious loiterer,
Autumn dug her sepulcher,
    My darling Sophie!
O, my heart was like the stone,
Lettered only with my moan!
Earth and I were here alone;
    The winds wailed, " Sophie ! "

Then I quit my shaggy glen,
Plunged into the strife of men;
Glory was a wild beast's den
    Without my Sophie.
Cruel seems it to achieve
And her dear mould here to leave;
Can she suffer as I grieve,
    My lonely Sophie?

Though she sent a sister down
My sad life of man to crown,
I am dreary with renown —
    It is not Sophie;
The wild laurel on her breast
Of all my laurels is the best:
Leave me here to sob and rest
    By what was Sophie!

Let me weep on Sophie's grave! —
Life is timid, death is brave —
I go mad to think how clave
　　To me, child Sophie.
Blessings on thee, little wren!
Though I never come again
To her mound, I'll hear thee, when
　　I think on Sophie.

New Geneva, Pa.

TO JOHN SHERMAN

Thy blue eyes look from thy unguileful mind
Like the boy orphan's in thy mother's brood,
Or tender on the wife thy manhood wooed,
Who now is speechless though her look so kind:
The violets are not more freshly dewed
Than thy bright eyes and country heart behind.
Industry, Freedom, Solvency thy heirs,
They have marched on beyond the old frontiers,
Clean are their wheatfields thou hast cleansed of
　　　tares,
And their remembrance thy retirement cheers.
I think how oft that million-blessing palm
Has crossed my hand with no official fears
And seem to talk to Nestor in his calm
When Homer knew him in the vale of years.

October 24, 1898.

KIDNAPPED PARSEE

In Leitersburg along the mountain line
I fed my horses while I stopped to dine

Amidst the gravestones by a blood-red church
That like a red bird in a tree had perch
Upon a summit near the wagon-stand,
Where flows Antietam into Maryland.
The fleeing slaves here watched by bloody men
Unto their slavery were turned again
Just as they saw salvation's bright'ning day
Upon the sill of Pennsylvania.

A generation since then had gone by,
And all the landscape laughed in liberty:
Free schools and railways, factories and roads,
And on the mountain chateaus and abodes,
Orchards of fruit and never-tiring wheat
Made Freedom's evolution thrice complete.

Here Jacob Leiter in the West so far
Had pitched his town just after Braddock's war,
When southward moving o'er the mountain crown
The Germans like a bursting dam streamed down
And spread their hamlets o'er the valley thick
And made a Germany of Frederick.

Joseph, his heir, near three score years dwelt here
And died not till Emancipation year.
I read on slender monuments the life
Of Joseph Leiter and of Ann his wife
And drowsy in that summer noon I lay
Between their graves and dreamed this dream away.

"What sort of nigger is this we see
Riding a horse like a white man free?

Come show your pass ere you go that way!"
The man said only, "Parsee.   Bombay."

"He's a Indian nigger but he will sell;
Virginia niggers are bred too well:
We'll cross Potomick with him 'fore day!"
He sobbed and muttered, "Parsee.   Bombay."

They pulled him down and they took his horse,
The fierce kidnappers without remorse;
They chained his feet as they hid him away
And gagged him, mocking, "Parsee.   Bombay."

He drew a drug from his straight, black hair
And swallowed it with a gurgling prayer
To the Sun that was setting, fiery red,
And he fell in the shamble stony dead.

They found him there whom they meant to sell
Cold as a clapperless, copper bell
In the shop on the undertaker's lot, —
Joseph Leiter, who knew it not.

Joseph Leiter had born a son
That day as the light was almost done;
At night he came to his carpenter's shed
To finish a coffin for some one dead;

His lantern fell on the sulphur face
Of a stranger of some alien race
And the dead lips bubbled or seemed to say:
"Me poor Parsee from me home, Bombay."

Joseph Leiter the dead man put
In the coffin; the lid he shut.
Thus to his wife his pity ran:
"They'll steal a coffin who steal a man!"

Two days passed and the dead forgot,
Light one night was in Leiter's cot;
Soft he looked and the dead man stood
Out in his kitchen cooking food.

Thinking he saw a ghost or witch,
Leiter's heart had a deadly twitch:
"*Guebre fire,*" did the dead man say,
"*Ormuzd raised me! Parsee.　Bombay.*"

Panther men through the window pane
Watched the Parsee living again:
"Where is he?" they asked his host.
"He is dead and ye saw his ghost."

In his coffin at noon they saw
Him still dead who had found no law;
In the churchyard his pit was dug,
He had swallowed a second drug.

Their dead neighbor the clods immerse,
While on the undertaker's hearse
O'er the mountain, the midnight through,
Leiter drove with the dark Hindoo.

Still in the West the dusk of night
Covered the vale from the mountain's height;
Gettysburg in its East repose
Bloomed with the sunrise like a rose.

Rose from stupor the tranc'd Parsee ;
Worshipp'd the sun on his bended knee ;
Cooled in the West his eyeball far,
Shuddering, " *Ahriman!* SLAVERY! WAR!—"

Bathed in the summit's springs with bliss,
Gave unto Leiter a freeman's kiss,
Slipped a ruby his finger upon
Saying " *Keep it for little son !* "

" Nay," spoke Leiter, whose greed was strong,
" We have treated a stranger wrong.
You that are risen like Lazarus
Owe no present, like that, to *us !* "

Putting the jewel back in his hair,
Gorgeously glowing a planet there,
The Parsee like a Prince did say :
" *Iran will give to thy son*, BOMBAY !

" I have seen where the inland seas
Drop in the West like our great Ganges
Into thy Hindostan of wheat,
Where shall arise Calcutta's seat ;

" Send thy son to that infant mart !
Teach him the Parsee's merchant art !
He shall beget one beautiful !
She shall marry the Great Mogul ! "

There they parted but back, anon,
Leiter bending above his son,
Little fingers felt in his hair,
Clutching a ruby tangled there.

" This was meant for our baby's dower;
That dark man was a man of power :
With the jewel the boy shall grow,
Lighted by wisdom to Chicago ! "

Long but sure was the infant's fate ;
He was a merchant where trade was great ;
From his life like a lance's sheen,
Grew a daughter that looked a queen.

She was loved by a statesman wise, —
Mighty India was his prize
Millions held in the famine's sway
Knelt as she landed at Bombay.

Tall and fair from her hair to her feet
She was saluted : " Lady of wheat !
Spirit of bread ! as we die we pray
Be our white lily, Queen of Bombay ! "

But the bride of the Viceroy sees
One, most agèd of the Parsees,
Piping to her like the croon of the wind,
" Lady of Leitersburg ! Ruby of Ind !

" Red as the ruby thy veins they wave
Through the star'd midnight where groped the
     white slave !
Thou and thy country are messaged with light !
Day of the Guebre ! Freedom from Night ! "

JACOB GRUBER

1819

SALLY HOWARD, Sally *Gruber*, dat one nigger left to you
Makes me seem so inconsistent! Lawyers named her — she is *Sue!*
When I glaze and paint de parsonage boys in Fred'rick going past
Yells at me, " Presiding Elder, has you bought a soul at last? "

Well! For de Redeemed de devil sets a woman in his trap
And I loved you, Sally Gruber, with your nigger in your lap.
When I said, " Emancipate her! Set her free and say good-bye,"
Then you and that nigger Susan hugged each other for to cry.

I had said to dem soul drivers what de gospe bade me tell
When at Hogeboom's woods I thundered " Slavery is part of Hell! "
Then dey bound me over, Sally, for de court at Hagerstown
I de venue moved to Fred'rick; was acquitted with renown.

Lawyer Taney spoke two hundred dollars' worth of eloquence,

For I paid de money to him, two years' hire for
    my defence,
Jury, people, Methodism, patted Gruber on de
    back:
Lord amercy! Here in Frederick I must own dat
    gal so black!

If I was agin a blacksmith, people at me would
    not hoot,
Shoeing horses with my nigger, both of us as
    black as soot;
But as Freedom's whitest hero, Susan in my
    servitude,
Nigger-buyers yell behind me: "Gruber by him-
    self is *Sued!*"

Like de richest men in Fred'rick if uncurrent
    bills I shave
Then dey call me "Jacob Greedy dat has married
    Sally's slave."
But de Book Concern expects me for dem books
    at par to pay,
And to get back lawyer's money I can find no
    other way.

When I feed de oats I carry, my necessity to fit,
To my critter at the roadside, sinners call me
    "Hypocrite."
Tavern keepers twit me, saying, "He's converted
    mighty good, —
Preacher owning of a nigger and too stingy to
    buy food!"

I was sharp myself at scooting veils, high bonnets,
    coffee, tea,
Dogs and canes, campmeeting courting: now dey
    throw dem up to me.
Vendues scattered when dey saw me in my drab
    and broad brim come,
Now de asses call me " Balaam," saying " Cuss us
    Slavery some !"

Your blue eyes and pious beauty touched me in a
    tender cord,
And like Abraham in Egypt where King Pharaoh
    was Lord,
I did call you " Sister Sarah," never thinking
    what would be:
Love decoyed me in your image to bow down to
    Slavery.

Could I know de slave's affection Freedom's gift
    would be above
And within de house of bondage Hagar stay for
    Sarah's love ?
Love, excuse our inconsistence ! Love has put us
    all astray.
Call de handmaid in, my Sarah, and we three will
    kneel and pray.

MAGRUDER

MAGRUDER was our foemen's name,
They won my seat and youthful fame
And drove me from the public aim ;
    O how my father, tawny, fierce,

On my swift downfall was a brooder!
　　As lightning doth a black cloud pierce
He flashed "Farewell, my son — Magruder!"

Betwixt our houses, forkèd, sleek,
Spread into bays a salty creek,
And rival neighbors still must speak;
　　My father foxed and rioted,
Took hand and cup with each intruder,
　　But in his laugh was something dead
At greeting each fair-haired Magruder.

Meantime the law I learned to plead
And in a distant place succeed,
I took a wife of different creed
　　And my deep temper like a monk
I strove to alter when I wooed her,
　　Till of the chalice as I drunk
I said "Communion with Magruder!"

My mother fled and sought my side
And sighed unto me as she died
"Dear son! have not thy father's pride!"
　　In holy ground I had her laid,
The Jesuits would not exclude her, —
　　Hard poverty came to my aid
And in my cares I lost — Magruder.

High handed was our Irish race;
I won our old colonial place
By tricking of the populace.
　　In the State Senate, thorough willed,
I led my party like a Tudor

Till came a sound, " Thy father killed
In lust and choler young — Magruder ! "

He slew the boy beside his board,
Into his breast he drove a sword,
Because a child they both adored ;
  Magruder's heart was young and bright,
My sire was gloomier and ruder,
  He fled for hoary shame by night
And on his hearth expired Magruder.

The old man died of black despair
Hard by me in a mountain lair, —
A faithful slave hid with him there
  And in his garden him interred :
No printer to it was alluder ;
  The old plantations only heard
That by our name was slain Magruder.

Magruder's race died of chagrin ;
They got no justice for their kin.
I grew more humble for our sin
  Till came my time when high in station
I leaped, an unknown interluder,
  And wrung the withers of the nation
And trembled for the sound — " Magruder."

I brought a wail from ruined trade
As from the homicidal blade, —
O had Magruder's buried shade
  Told but his tale I had been ended,
My furious race's last concluder !
  To solemn heights I still ascended
And crossed myself to lay Magruder.

The paroxysm left me long,
But party frenzy, deadly strong,
Lured my old age to human wrong;
   I smote the helpless from my height
As in my father's frosty *pudeur :*
   The world cried out in my despite,
But not a raven croaked " Magruder ! "

Five years and forty since the crime
Had left me but a wrinkled mime.
To seal that record old with grime
   I wrote my life, I passed it bland
To one who would still be excluder
   Of that which would my pandect brand
And on my statue write " Magruder."

Then in that Jesuit's guarded spot
Wherein my father's grave was not,
I thought his shade would be forgot
   That I would be beyond the crowd
My secret knowing no obtruder :
   I quit my coffin in my shroud —
The tombstones next me spelled " *Magruder.*"

There do they stand in pallid white.
They see my spectre every night
And balk my purgatorial flight :
   " Justice ! " they cry, " thou, Justice Chief !
Thy fame was won as a deluder !
   Thy neighbor's life took like a thief
Stands in thy court of death, — Magruder ! "

FREDERICK, MD., AUGUST 30, 1898.

ROSCOE CONKLING

THE peevish school exclaims,
  That thy return so gladdens great New York!
These spiteful leaders make us miss the more
  One man of lofty mark;

One young man yet sincere,
  Whose scorn is scorn and his affection sweet,
Whose mind was never humbled to the crowd,
  Nor cowered by defeat;

Who thinks exalted things,
  And typifies the Empire of our State
His brain amidst the atmosphere of kings,
  And strong among the great;

For such New York forgives
  His manly frailties in the love of her,
Her pride contented while a statesman lives
  To be her Senator.

No lobby Warwick made
  This royal nature to be bought and sold,
His honors never were the gains of trade,
  Nor compliments of gold.

He walked to our respect,
  Nor crept and courted like a devious dog;
His forehead bore the sign of one elect,
  Beyond the demagogue.

In his inherent strength
  Of classic mind and national intent,

All schools and parties sought the leader out,
  Within his argument.

There shall he shine a star,
  When baying foes and envious presses cease,
His record gallant in the time of war,
  And gentlest after peace.
  1876.

TO JAMES A. GARFIELD

A PROPHECY

THOU who did'st ride on Chickamauga's day,
All solitary down the fiery line,
And saw the ranks of battle rusty shine,
Where grand old Thomas held them from dismay,
Regret not now, while meaner pageants play
Their brief campaigns against the best of men!
For those spent balls of scandal pass their way,
And thou shalt see the victory again.
Modest and faithful, though these broken lines
Of party reel and thine own honor bleeds,
That mole is blind which Garfield undermines,
That dart falls short which hired malice speeds,
That man will stay whose place the State assigns,
And whose high mind a mighty people needs.
  1874.

R. B. HAYES

THE silent taker of abuse
  Not friendless proves when death, as still,
Takes him into the camp of truce
  And beats the taps on good and ill;

Soldier, who did life's work fulfil,
   However compromised by fame !
The sunny world respects thy end,
   The states united speak thy name,
The soldiery thy grave attend,
   And wives of gentles do the same,
To join thee to the beauteous mold
   Who waits her bridegroom in that wood,
Where but the good denotes the bold,
   And all of beauty is the good.

ANDREW JOHNSON

THEY who in Northern hamlets drew
   The warrior breath of freedom in,
The Southrons' struggle little knew —
That obdurate and sturdy few
   Whose feet were set against their kin,

Who for the Union sought the hills
   And lived like hunted things of prey;
In household feud and civil ills
That put to test their iron wills —
   Those renegadoes held their way.

Tall, bony men of Irish stock,
   And local loves that bound them fast,
The Union only was their rock,
And like the pines they stood the shock
   And grew the tougher for the blast.

The fife and drum they did not hear
   That mustered millions to resist;

The State's command, high and austere,
Reached not their mountain atmosphere;
  The Nation's roar alone they list.

But peace renewed a hundred ties
  The Northern statesmen never feel:
Traditions steadfast as the skies,
That slowly fade among the wise,
  And wounds of pride that slowly heal.

No negro was the mountaineer
  Whose freedom was his fathers' spoil —
What time they mustered with Sevier —
He felt himself the planter's peer,
  And nothing servile for his toil.

Yet rights like his, with blood bequeathed,
  Were now the bondsman's easy prize;
For this his willing sword unsheathed,
The peon's brow with bays had wreathed —
  Himself, his brood the sacrifice.

So Andrew Johnson's neighbors spoke,
  And half their sullenness was his;
He was a man of lowly folk,
And restive under every yoke,
  Except the yoke of prejudice.

He governed men from that estate
  Of humble birth and old neglect
When on his tailor's bench he sate,
And, sewing, mused on man and fate
  And tyranny of caste and sect.

Still in his soul the phrases clung
His wife from ancient charters read;
They grew inspired upon his tongue,
And to the hills his challenge rung,
And unto Fame the echoes led.

One grand invective was his life,
But rounded yet by reverence;
His one superior was his wife,
His route to power only strife,
His egotism ne'er pretence.

The slavery he hated most
Was slavery of the freeborn mind;
The freedom that he made his boast
Was not a sentimental toast,
But freedom for his white mankind;

And honest hands made courage sure,
Thrift grew on blessed penury;
A Congress mighty but impure,
In freedom's plea, could not endure
This lonely man of Tennessee.

The subtler Lincoln suckled still
A poor white Southern mother's breast;
So freedom chose to work her will,
One ruler from the Southern hill,
Another from the prairie West.

And freedom came from such as these,
Who felt the slavery they broke;
Not from scholastic halls of ease,
Not from the dreamy Eastern seas,
But from the hovel and the yoke.
1870.

WILLIAM H. SEWARD

Son of New York! sit thou amongst us daily
          Where all go by,
And Broadway's currents meet and flow most gayly
          In our bright sky!
Reveal that pen whose hidden work was greater
          Than cannon's roar,
And boyish brow, the placid agitator
          Of times of yore!

Sit with thy books, thou man of gentle story!
          There is no heaven
For thee, unless the clangor of its glory
          Shall have their leaven;
Not on the sword, the ermine, or the gavel
          Thy farewell look,
Thou rounded life's adventures with a travel,
          And made a book.

And from thy closest thoughts of power departed,
          Like eagles freed,
And distant foemen saw a lion-hearted
          Hero indeed.
Domestic traitors held thy life abhorrent,
          Thy name a spell,
And still the spring that fed the swelling torrent
          Was but a cell.

Child of the State, whose sceneries imposing
          Are like its acts —
The storm upon its lakes and mountains dozing
          And cataracts —

Thine was the pen that clove the war's disorder
    With our decree,
And wrote on history the Godlike order:
    Let man be free!

Not in a general's dress, a sword and tassels,
    Thou greet'st the age,
Like one who came to free another's vassals
    By might of rage;
But in the simple vesture of thy neighbors,
    With book and pen,
A tired lawyer resting from his labors,
    And citizen.

There where the crowds of every nation haunt thee
    And ne'er desist,
Cosmopolite or pioneer, we plant thee,
    Thou optimist!
Thy mind as various as the race of people
    Thy heart forsaw;
Thy lesson loftier than the Christian steeple —
    A Higher law!

Son of New York! sit thou amongst us daily
    Where all go by,
And Broadway's currents meet and flow most gayly
    In our bright sky;
Reveal that pen whose hidden work was greater
    Than cannon's roar,
And boyish brow, the placid agitator
    Of times of yore!

1875.

"USED UP VAN"

" WE three will make our New Year call
   Upon Van Buren after night,
When lonesome in his palace hall
   Turned out the people and the light!
Seward is master in New York,
   The banks are broke, the wealthy beg;
We'll find the President a stork
   Dozing upon a single leg."

Webster and Clay picked up Calhoun
   To comfort Van in his despair,
The White House bathing in the moon
   Ducked in its brand new *porte cochère.*
The well-known trio passed the door,
   Their echoes chased them in the gloom,
And on the Turkey carpet floor
   They tip-toed to the great East Room.

" He's lost in space, a bumble bee,"
   Growled Webster, " rising less and less ! "
" His Independent Treasury "
   Quoth Clay, " is hollow emptiness."
" He lies in my usurpèd bed
   Beside my bride in damnèd doom,"
Calhoun, the blue-lit Hamlet, said
   And rapped like death upon a tomb.

Light, laugh and shout burst through the door :
   Along the parlor's grand extent

GAPLAND DEN AND LIBRARY, FROM THE SOUTH

Playing at leap-frog on the floor
  They saw the ruined President;
His grown-up sons along the row
  Made him, another playmate, stoop,
And o'er his bald head winged with snow
  They jumped their father with a whoop.

Son Abram's Carolina bride,
  Angelica, just out of school,
Was laughing “fit to split her side”
  To see the great man play the fool.
Martin and John, like heralds stern,
  Kept parent Martin on the run,
And made him leap-frog in his turn
  And saw that he leaped every one.

“ Good friends,” the President exclaimed,
  “ These boys their mother left to me;
I promised not to be ashamed
  Ever to keep their company;
To keep them and myself so young
  And of each other ever fond,
That when our worldly pride was stung
  Our fireside would not have despond.

“ My wife my schoolmate cousin was;
  These youngsters are my cousins, too.
You will not find them frivolous
  When there are harder things to do.
Good-natured Dutch, within our roost
  We keep up holidays with rout,
I play with them as mother used, —
  They will not leave their father out.”

" This is the secret of his court,"
   Said Webster. " Let us learn his joys !
We were too solemn for the sport :
   He practiced leaping with the boys.
Take off your coats, Calhoun and Clay !
   And take a lesson how to leap !
We'll jump Saint Martin yet some day
   Who plays the boy when we're asleep."

WITH GREELEY AT RICHMOND

MAY 18, 1872

At Rocketts' pier the bugles blow,
   The clattering horsemen ride,
And squadrons wheel with naked steel
   By James's peaceful tide,
And up the stones of Richmond town
   The column files at will,
As if a traitor rode to die
   Up Tower or Tyburn hill.

A poor old man, grey-haired and bent,
   Amongst the troopers rides ;
He sees the captured capital
   O'erlooking floods and tides,
Where, in his power, the standards blew,
   Unfurled at his command,
That waved in sight of Washington,
   And dyed the Rio Grande.

Now silently the people peer
   Who used to cheer his name,

As if it were a time of fear,
  And his were all the blame;
They soon forget both fame and power
  Who but disaster win,
And he who ruled, an Empire's chief,
  Must make his jail an inn.

They bring him to the traitor's court,—
  This old and broken man;
And e'en the judge looks down in grudge,
  Like any partisan.
The lawyers wait to tell his crimes,
  The jury hate, forewarned, —
By heaven! it is a fearful thing
  To see a strong man scorned!

Then one stepped out from all the throng,
  And said: " This must not be!
My pen which wrote his cause unjust,
  Shall write his liberty.
On yonder hill the grass is green —
  With pleasant spring's increase,
So green be all the fields of war,
  And all our duty Peace.

" Ye dare not test him lest he 'scape;
  Ye shall not keep him pent;
Each foe stands now a citizen,
  A flock for every tent;
Let kindly law again prevail,
  And victory do no crime,
For hand in hand we twain must walk
  Down all the paths of time!"

They marvelled much who loved him not,
　This quaint old man to see,
Whose name the planters' children knew,
　An ancient enemy;
And though some mocked his loving zeal
　With many a coarse retort,
He made the rebel chieftain feel
　The North had still a heart!

IRVING AT BURR'S TRIAL

1807

My Rip Van Winkle twenty years asleep
I see reversed with Colonel Burr come down,—
Youth, startling these long-haired Virginians.
The Cainish outlaw of New York is here
A Jesus in the temple, routing doctors:
How masterful serene! how lustrous eyed!
Delight of women! linnet of the cage!—
Fresh are the species of America!
I threaded Europe lately with the pang,
"I must return," but this is wonderful.
And yon Chief Justice is Praxiteles
Gazing on Phryne, the stripp'd courtesan,
Whom he means to acquit for loveliness.
I marvel not my brothers were for Burr;
I, mourning Hamilton, compassionate
This beauteous heifer which did gore his life,
Gentle but in her bovine period.
That deer-split hoof, his hand, did fire the shot
Which emptied nature of Minerva's child:
The sons of God were yet like Aaron Burr,

Daughters of men these freakish Jeffersons.
  Men say he ruins women : women never
Have thrown a stone at Burr, their Antony.
His fawns were white.   His sacerdotal touch,
Like Eli's sons, was holy to his dupes, —
Heir of the Eleusinian mysteries.
  Treason or misdemeanor his offenses?
Ridiculous alternatives, i' faith!
Treason is levying War against Us only :
Yon Randolph, Burr's defender, breathed it so,
Gouverneur Morris phrased it thus exact :
Virginia's limitation, New York's words.
Burr is but traitor to Virginia's cockloft
And each one there than he more traitorous :
Madison wrote Secession Resolutions,
Monroe deliverèd our flag to France,
Randolph betrayed us from the cabinet,
This Wilkinson is in the pay of Spain,
And Jefferson plotted the Excise war.
Burr, driven away by their conspiracy,
Drew from the times the filibuster's dream, —
Miranda's, Rogers Clarke's, Eaton's and Lewis's, —
To speed our destiny before its ripeness
In the indefinite Hispanian waste,
His febrile fancy fired by Bonaparte
And the bright recollections of his youth
In martial camps these coistrils never joined.
Long will that West the hunted stag allure.
It is Imagination's substitute
For the fenced Paradise of cherubims
Whose swords on none but their fall'n equals
        flame :

Hark to the British cannon off Virginia! —
Our sailors' shrieks![1] O for one hour of Burr
And Hamilton!
                    Twig now yon other Randolph
Who brought in the indictment! 'Tis high treason
With him to be born anywhere but here:
He looks the snipe with railing faculties
Run lean, — a skeleton in excitation.
John Wickham of Long Island, bred to arms
At Arras, France, o'er-matches William Wirt,
Co-amateur with me in lightsome Letters,
Who has the heavy vividness of armor.
The treatment for this trial is humor:
A cat fight in one's party brought to bar.
Our Constitution makes theology.
That curser is one Jackson, Tennesseean,
Who would not vote respect to Washington
And now damns Madison, — an Almohadè.
What height is in that Scott, the fledgling lawyer!
He's out of Amadis de Gaul; if years
Are sold by inches he'll outlast us all.
Virginia's genius in its women lies,
Their love of pleasure not their men's indulgence:
How lovely were those shoulders at the ball!
And every sylph for Burr but no *man* for him.
  Two lawyers here are drunk by early morning.
There is old Callender, the libeller,
Diogenes in his newspaper tub,
Wherein he wallows, gnashes and snuffs plunder,
And yet I like him better than this Ritchie,
The vaunted genius of his occupation,

[1] Firing on the *Chesapeake* Frigate.

Who like Marat learned medicine to torture
And has a narrow controversial soul.
This city rules by him newspaper-mongers
And he is edited by Jefferson.
'Tis dissipation of *belles lettres* minds
To excel in these midnight exhalations.
The rainbow 'twixt Newspaper and Letters
Is broke in mid air; I'll find the far end;
It may be long or never, but my mind
Shall not be a slave driver's with my quill,
Nor in opinion-fact'ries pewtered out!
   The prosecution is the President,
Who learned his passions in the sects of France,
Wrathful for liberty that in Robespierre,
The smug and incorrupt, destroyed his kind.
Few are not spoiled whom Europe magnifies,
Yet is our politics all European, —
Philology of accusations fetched
To plague plain stay-at-homes like Washington:
Democrat, Monarchist, Aristocrat, —
Words mighty in the foreign tourists' pride.
The name that bless'd me and the Chief whose
      hand
Was raised above me in my nurse's arms
Will stand with Cæsar's when these tribunes fade.
He never would have scoured the coasts for Burr
And dragged him hither through so many States
To try him in the tyrant's local province,
Indicted by his cousin. Not ere long
This slayer did preside upon the trial
Of a high Justice and this grand juror
Did curse the Senate which would not convict:

Now Jeffrey's circuit moves to Richmond town,
But yon loose-jointed Judge has in his orbs
The mighty globe and Richmond is his throne.
Who knows what Revolutions may rise here?
What slavery President like Burr from jail
Be brought to crave his bail and find his Portia?
Then this *Roi Petion*, hunted to the caves,
Saved from the executioner by wolves,
Will be the sign of mercy shining down.

Petion's Madame Roland there I see,
Burr's matron daughter.   Blennerhassett's wife
Was in Queen Theodosia's silver crown
As in her father's sword hilt.   Why had fate
Mismated so?   Burr married with his mother,
Theodosia, her son, and that one with
An idiot.   Burr needed a fine woman
And made her of his child but on illusions
Wasted their substance.   'Tis a gypsy court!
Jefferson's comely daughter I have seen,
Who sought to be a nun in lawless Paris.
All these are finer women than in France
Around the *condottieri* Emperor.
Could faction run its length these ladies might
Go to a guillotine.   Their stay is Burr,
Lex scripta and the plain colonial thought.

In climate Liberty refrigerates;
This summer heat made deadly by strong drink
And carnal by the Slavery around it,
Will soon relinquish to the Northern star
Direction, as the constellations do.
In some day not too far, Literature

Will sit upon the chaos of these presses
And soften partisans to courtesy.
Our area is like the field of stars:
The more they be the light is more diffused,
The wider radiance soothes mankind to peace,
And woman's softness, paramount at night,
Her prejudices drowsy in her realm,
Will draw the soul of strife to love and rest.
Yon golden West will govern in its prime,
With mildness known not to old colonies
Ripped from the civil wars and Bible-cracked.
Then Liberty's haranguers need not scream;
'Twill be the nature of the fertile sea
Of land and woodlands and the snow-warmed lakes;
Men will roam free and sociable as cattle
Which in their increase drive the bisons back.
Faint in that mellow sunset may appear
Among the bars of music one, far down,
Leaning on earth: the Crime of Aaron Burr.

OAK HILL

1893

WHERE through the Hog Back Mountain knots
    the Goose creek's two arms wind
Stands on a knoll a portico with its plain house
    behind,
A portico that faces South in Doric columns lined.

On segment arches this tall porch wide as the
    house expands

And holds a Grecian order up in its columnar
   hands,
With one eye in its pediment winked on the
   templar's lands.

The stiff, square house with chimneys four to
   lowly wings descends
And in the rear it has its door as if for humble
   friends;
In front o'er double drawing-rooms that portico
   portends.

A hall that clips the little wings the two square
   parlors airs
And adds a state solemnity for balls and feasts
   and stairs
But to that rostrum portico the whole house
   gives its cares.

Here, one would think, some rustic man lived
   in his home, snug, slow,
Until he had a public call to come in front and
   show
And then he showed another man in that great
   portico.

Monroe, the last Virginia chief, here spent his
   funds and age,
His Northern wife died in the jowl of this sad
   hermitage,
The portico his former hut took into patronage.

He was a politician's flower, raised from a common
   weed,

Fit for no enterprise in life but following to lead:
To watch the great and imitate, to listen and suc-
    ceed.

Mount Vernon, Monticello and Montpelier tem-
    ples show —
Wide land and Cincinnatian rest, sageness and
    portico,
So all he had into Oak Hill put President Monroe.

Some few weak apprehensive years from public
    pay's release,
He took the only office left, a justice of the peace,
And then the sheriff took his peace and he took
    his surcease.

As in this lofty portico his form plebeian bent
He wound beneath the porticoes of every high event
As the Virginia creeper scales the Doric shaft's
    ascent.

With timid men he passed for brash, with bold
    men for a worm,
He was a soldier on the staff proved by his uni-
    form ;
He set the lines at Bladensburg and braved a
    thunderstorm.

Confederate Congressman, he bored that system
    to its doom ;
Opposed the Constitution since some other State
    might bloom ;
But when his Senator was dead stepped in his
    shoes and room.

There bully for his State's cabal he set domestic
    slur
On Hamilton, above the State the golden minister,
But bared the soldier's pervious place to single-
    combat Burr.

To France he went in room of Burr whom he had
    undermined
And with the bloody Jacobin's our tender streamers
    twined,
Then hurled a book at Washington, for voters in-
    terlined.

The dying chief Virginia stung with " *Governor*
    Monroe,"
His weakling face inspired the slaves such tool to
    overthrow,
Virginia sent him back to France annoyances to
    sow.

He saw upon the river Seine his country's steamer
    ride,
With Livingston's and Fulton's fames he wrote
    his name beside,
Abortive treaties ever made and nowhere did
    abide.

But as the Brahmins may revere the sacerdotal
    cow
Virginians ever kept him place beneath their feed-
    ing mow
And with the heifers of his chief he drave a sub-
    soil plough;

Measured Virginia's mites beside the giants of his
    view, —
The Nelsons, Pitts and Bonapartes the world of
    physics grew, —
And empire-hearted men at home by later knowl-
    edge knew.

The faction feared their sharpened tool, his hardier
    address,
He knew their differential arts and shaken selfish-
    ishness,
And practiced on a wider range an easier success.

He ruled the land by men of stuff in all his
    cabinet,
Enlarged the state and in array its weak defenses
    set,
But plagued himself with cavilling, infirmity and
    fret.

High policies he fought against and called them
    by his name,
Looked ever on where he might lean or, failing,
    next might blame ;
When every opposition ceased, no veneration
    came.

Lamenting powers he did not have when all but
    he so willed,
He saw not slavery's blighting spread while free-
    dom throve and tilled
And Marshall's genius shone abroad to strengthen
    and to build.

Here to Oak Hill old Lafayette with Quincy
       Adams came
On wretched roads in bankrupt times to company
       but tame,
The host was trouble-borrowing and lobbying his
       claim.

Unto John Adams' frosty child Kentucky passed
       the key,
Virginia's nation-hearted son locked out her
       dynasty,
And force with lictors came behind, — the sheik
       of Tennessee.

Perfect the classic portico takes in its hollow ken
The sheeplands where, in warlike times, by night
       rode Mosby's men,
The Bull Run mountains' sapphire blue and Little
       River's glen.

Towàrd Potomac, Goose creek falls through locks
       of old canals,
Telling of public spirit spent for counties and
       cabals ;
The grim old mills at Oatlands grind their drowsy
       madrigals.

Fertile and noble rolls the land and ₁ watered like
       to France,
With kine and horses plentiful and sparse inhabi-
       tants ;
The white pike road beneath the ridge shines like
       a flashing lance.

But naught is here of that old man who reared
    his portico ;
Richmond that made him has his bones where
    James's rapids flow ;
The spirit of his Northern wife the Fortress of
    Monroe.

His western States he never loved, marched o'er
    his mountain's bar,
On roads he vetoed, to his forts made for defensive
    war ;
Free millions flout o'er Africa the faint Monrovian
    star.

New York, Virginia's conqueror, received him,
    debtor-spent ;
Fourth of July, his dying day, scarce felt the
    slight event ;
No man has read his manuscript on balanced gov-
    ernment.

His jockey son-in-law awhile Oak Hill inhabited,
Defaulter in official life to sanctuary fled ;
No ghosts are in the portico ; the tedious are the
    dead.

Contractors city horses breed in Monroe's stables,
    where
He demonstrated country hearts of cities must
    beware ;
Over his mutton modern men his waste of land
    unswear.

The sacrifice he did not try; the means he did not
        prove;
The shiftless motive principle that only seems to
        move;
The office-getting for itself: these bankrupt power
        and love.

He saw the people as they were by mean self-
        measurement,
Rivals his mediocrity preferring for descent,
And wore the nation's patience out to furious
        discontent.

Few pilgrims come to see his shrine, the few who
        come less know;
The whip-poor-will's inquiring cry is answered by
        Echo,
Within the hollow stories of the pillared portico.

Pale order! to neglected lands your Greek ex-
        pression give
Of Academic genius and freedom formative!
So perfect stands the portico its spirit still must
        live.

JOHN QUINCY ADAMS' DIARY

1779–1848,

Lad! I overlap thy life with mine;
Art thou curious, prying and revering?
Lift the lid, — the coffin be not fearing!
Within my Koran book my prophet's bones calcine.

Three score and ten of years I drew bow line
And shot my arrows into friend and foe;
Gather them as the Indian by his bow
And arrows lies! Nothing will I refine!
What for the day seemed true the sun marked so,
And before night's small prayer I wrote not liber-
    tine.
A barbarous age encaged me for its king,
Its captive eagle silenced by its vote,
Each night I pulled a feather from my wing
And dipped it in my cage-chilled blood and wrote.
For thine eye, boy, did I in slavery snatch
Moments of years to trace the dull events:
Judge thou my book when thou shalt read its match
Writ by another of thy Presidents!

TO EDMUND C. STEDMAN

THY pipe clear, cogent, summoning, I heard
Like the long locust's trill, when I was young,
Halting but not dissonant with the bird,
A louder chanson on a thrilling tongue;
Current occurrence poetry became
In thy sweet glottis and thou didst not fear:
I list thy pibroch after years the same
And find thee sweeter as I come more near.
Thy Muse doth balance while thy wants take ramble
On Wall Street's deafening and deadly way,
Like him who walked the wire with many a gambol,
Along the foam line of Niagara.
Thy foot is on Apollo's lyre-strung air;
I know where thou art by a rainbow there.

E. R. T.

APRIL 13, 1897 [1]

BLIND, seeing, dead: good night, Elizabeth!
Thou didst not see and slipped on holy ground.
Thy sight restored thou sawest falsehood's death
And owned thy slip though ever bled thy wound.
Death! Thou art Saviour to all women found
In nature's field! Thou writest in the dust
And draw'st them to thee in repentance sound
When priests and congregations stone their trust!
In that great day when graves give up and must
All shames be owned, matron! Thou wilt be wise
Who faced the world and out by it was thrust
To stand with Magdalen in Paradise;
Aye! and with Mary of supernal fame
Whom Heaven o'ershadowed ere it overcame.

JOSHUA

THE Shemite's roving eye is keen from his tent,
He sees the obvious and speaks sentiment;
His nation a brood under Israel's hem
He knew but one city, Jerusalem.

Enter the Roman with world-wide polity! —
"Believe what ye will but be subject to me!"
As from the rushes had Moses pedigree,
Joshua, the straw-born, thought in poetry:

"Freer this sun the strangers' helmets flash,
Happy Israel whose creeds no longer clash!

[1] Totally blind, recovered her full sight. Died. — *Report.*

Gentiles we hated have stricken off our clogs,
Nobler are mankind than the harsh synagogues!"

That sublimation like a blowing seed
Fell in the furrow that was smoking to breed:
Rome had oped the world with her ploughshare feet,
Joshua went forth and sowed it with bright wheat.

Moralizing without labor is disease.
Catch-cure-workers snare themselves in mysteries.
Agitation agitates sweet sleep away.
Science lay not with the Jew nor Joshua.

The ghost tales creep in the blood of conquerors.
A sure church ever toleration abhors.
Little miracles his followers must see,
And Jove's fatherhood vouch for democracy.

Superstitions strove and his girl head was bowed,
Tears came between him and the simple crowd,
Winds, understood not, whispered from the sky
Imaginations of the old Genii.

Youth is the quickening, age the mummifying,
Youth thinks of loving and age thinks of dying:
Joshua, distempered, counted life a loss,
The beauty of the lilies droops at his cross.

When we know nothing of our own planet's plan,
Fancy must prophesy and priest dream for man,
Joshua who loved the Earth, his one pet bird,
Never to his singing mate has since said word.

Stubborn idolatry mistakes all it can.
Jew-named Christians burnt alive their fellow-man.

Science with miracles to shame sorcery
Bent to the Roman priest the pagan-freed knee.

Japhet in the West took Physics for his mate
And she nursed him like the wolf the twins of state,
Walled her Europe with the towers that suns descry,
Felt her hemispheres of breasts the globe's augury.

Arsenalled her arms with chemistry's retorts,
Made old Rome her polity, chivalry her forts;
States gave stability to tribes' disarray:
Europe for poetry set up Joshua;

Fought for his grave and his peasantry set high,
Put his brethren in its shields of victory;
Joshua's living type they banished and slew:
Europe took the Jewish and enslaved the Jew.

Wider than Joshua, Spinoza loved Space,
In his matter-loving thought all worlds had grace;
Socialistic Joshuas a new earth drew
But the church of Joshua rejected Jew.

We have with us Joshua perfectly new
In the juvenescence of each sanguine Jew,
In his friendly vehemence, Shemite to brim,
But the doors of Japhet's race are shut to him.

He, in Joshua's delight, hails the events,
His disbanded nationhood to all presents,
Drives his golden wedge into Japhet's schism
Profiting honestly by his optimism.

Joshuas arrogate anarchistic powers,
Build themselves no sepulchre but lie in ours;

Joshua, pastoral, preaches and roams,
Turning mobs against the genius of homes;

Rails at society that taketh providence
As the roving Arabs hate Yemen's defense,
Hates the riches that refine and in us dwell
For the riches that o'erburden Ishmael.

Joshua pushes hard as if earth were slow,
And he *imperium in imperio;*
Unto him as Cæsar's coin we render odds,
But refuse to his assault the things of Gods.

Joshua never sought Kepler's wonder laws:
Sentimental, sensuous, effect and cause
Unto him were platitudes: genius wild,
He is reigning and will reign, the little child.

RALSTON

HE who attempts too much success
　　And frets his destiny,
Shall like Napoleon find an isle
　　Or Ralston find a sea.

Yet in the loss of so much power
　　The generous world must weep,
As when some battlemented tower
　　Falls down a lofty steep.

Roll ocean on the golden gate
　　With thrice thy usual sound!
There's nothing left of mortal state
　　Like him that thou hast drowned.

1875.

MEMMINGER'S LIFE

(SECRETARY OF CONFEDERATE TREASURY)

1875

FLYING from Napoleon,
  Flying to Calhoun,
Little Wurtemburger!
  'T was Cæsar to Mahoun.
To one you were a conscript,
  Cipher in t'other's eye ;
One would unify you,
  One would nullify.

O, had Carolina
  Heads like thine, not hot,
She had weighed the iron
  Ere she fired the shot!
All her waste of fury
  No hero left to her
But the man of Jewry,
  Memminger.

1893.

PALOS

I WAKE at Huelva ; sunrise shines
  On Palos, name I know so well
Where Rio Tinto from its mines
  Comes on to join the Odiel.

I seek the quay and hire my boat
  Among the many vessels there
And down the tawny river float
  In that same raw Columbus air,

GAPLAND HALL, FROM THE EAST

In this four hundredth happy spring,
  Since in this port his sail he furled
Who, like yon coots on fluttering wing
  Low flying, dipped them down the world.

Amidst his scenes I sit in awe
  Hushed by my country's cradle story
And watch the hump of Rabida
  Draw nearer on its promontory.

The scaffolds round the shaft just raising
  To him, I think one more depiction
By painters, after time amazing,
  Of Jesus raised for crucifixion,

And as I climb the Prior's height
  Where Christus paused in this far region
His globe soul half eclipsed in night
  I feel a natural religion.

Yon only window well I mark
  Above the postern where his hand
Fray Perez waved, as from the ark,
  To take the dove in bringing land.

And where the travellers entered twain
  I leave behind all harsh complaints,
One gentle priest then lived in Spain
  Whom Science ranks among her saints.

The cool *patios* they're restoring,
  The vaults uptorn, the monks' small cells,
The Saviour nailed for his adoring,
  The convent jail, the Moorish wells,

The stable like the inn's for Mary,
   The *loggia* that o'erhangs the sea,
I thread as in some cave of faery,
   Up to the Prior's library,

Where books of dread by pagans written
   But lamplight threw on that dark sea
And through the windows redly litten
   The sandalled monks spied sorcery.

But Palos tars, accused of robbing,
   Tested that stranger's serious worth,
Her doctor felt a twin world throbbing
   And helped the young idea forth.

Off to the court the country pastor
   Made the first voyage, tonsure-curled,
And on a donkey, like his master,
   Rode into town to save a world.

They thank him for the invitation
   And send their Notary right about
And fine poor Palos from the nation,
   To take the expedition out.

For that, O Palos! I am risking
   (No saddle and no stirrup mine)
This ride and were my mare a-frisking
   I might leave thee my broken chine.

The houseless road with flowers is sprinkled,
   The pinegroves moan, low flaps a stork,
I see old ocean's head unwrinkled
   Beyond the sea strand's trees of cork.

And soldiers guard lest thieves assail us
  The ancient road on Tarshish strand:
There is more danger still by Palos
  Than in the wide Columbian land.

This is not Palos, these wine caverns
  Backed into hillocks with low walls !
Where be the port, the sailors' taverns,
  The smell of tar, the boatswains' calls?

This is some farmers' *hameau* stranded
  High up the land; the old church tower
In a high gravel pit upstanded
  Just peeping o'er this many an hour,

As when the Norman pirates entered
  The Moorish peace of Cadiz bay
And in this mosque the learnèd centred
  Round Almegist and Algebra.

The distant age of printing-paper
  Found Ismail's star o'er Spain senescent,
They might have crossed the sea by vapor
  And on the Indies put the crescent.

Some Koran ever there to read is
  Whose gibberish Geber's lore may throttle;
Mahomet bullies Archimedes
  And Torquemada, Aristotle.

With me the problem now is bitter,
  How to get off this Rozinante
And not to make all Palos titter,
  Which crowds to see this Yankee "ante."

And like Columbus' standing eggs,
    To save my shell requires address ;
They bring a chair ; I bless its legs :
    Something in Palos I must bless.

I disapprove those eyes of her
    Who from one trellised yard grimaces
And on my country puts the slur,
    That of one blood are all man-races :

Was she not here, ancient of species,
    When up the streets like sharks with fins on
The sailors all had Beatriches,
    And Peter's cock crowed thrice at Pinzon ?

Let realisms not displease us !
    Old Niebla jail : *memento mori !*
One thief went in to heaven with Jesus,
    And fifty thieves to Salvadore !

Diogenes and cynics bicker
    On honest men alone to settle,
The wise man asks, whose blood is thicker,
    " Is this my tool, a tool of mettle ? "

The Palos people cease to chatter :
    All gravity they hear me say,
" America was found by matter !
    And matter was America."

With this I scatter silver shekels
    (And while they scramble get me gone)
To various admirals in freckles, —
    And, no doubt, of Columbian spawn.

"Palos, the Marshy" one stone lane
  Drops to its port; the main street forks
To Moguer where they sell their grain
  And olive oil and fungus corks.

There in the forks his farmhouse stands,
  Good Pinzon's, with arched gate and walls;
He left a substance for dreamlands,
  Nor parleyed for Viceregal halls.

I like his life because 'tis short,
  He gives to Palos fame its own,
He made Columbus no retort
  Nor troubled history with a moan.

And later, stout Iberian men,
  From Pinzon's spirit did absorb,
Nuñez who gazed from Darien,
  Magellan, circler of the orb.

Palos was naught but situation
  Beyond the straits, a nook unfriended
Where no adjacent spying nation
  Might hear its wail of doom, world-ended.

That wail I hear in Palos church:
  "Mary! O Mother! Slay this devil!
This crow who on our cross does perch
  And picks our eyes out for his revel,

"Picks son and husband, lover, brother,
  And sails to ports that never were:
Thou art our friend, God's virgin mother!
  O Venus! have us in thy care!"

Prayer volatile as bird or bee is
   And man more oft than Gods hath bended,—
Could wooden women halt ideas
   Columbus in this church had ended.

So prayed that day afflicted creatures,
   Against the good luck to them blown,
They clawed their wooden virgin's features,
   And seldom since has she been shown;

To me they fetch her from a closet,
   A human bowsprit full of scars,
With once blue eyes and cheeks of roset,
   Like Irish wives of Palos tars.

So in Phœnicia's golden crisis,
   When Hiram's ships would counter truly,
The Tyrian woman plead to Isis
   And stopped his galleons short of Thulé.

The men of Thulé were not craven,
   They wintered on the western shore,
But unreturning as the raven,
   Vineland, Red Eric saw no more.

The plain white church with chapels cool
   And floor of tile and altar fret
That day became an urchins' school
   To teach the Pope his alphabet.

And in its pulpit as I stand,
   The same as in that day's suspense,
I feel the strength of Ferdinand
   And government's beneficence.

My country is like Spain *anon*,
  In chivalry's reunion sure,
Castile is one with Aragon
  And in Granada still the Moor.

Not hard far-off adventures be,
  But hard it is not to oppress:
Drive not the Moors to Barbary
  And have barbarian happiness!

And hark! ye priests, for signs who search
  And pulpits close to week day rule:
Think how Columbus of this church
  Made heaven's earthy vestibule!

Loquacious Jews whose God began it,
  Whose victim died for his deep wit,
Did your Messiah to our planet
  Know that he trod but half of it?

That this, the only world he treasured,
  For it dissolved his Trinity —
Was like the smallest orange measured
  In the Arcana's orangery? —

Was less in night's cerulean bosk,
  Than one low arch amid the grove
Of arch on arch in that vast mosque
  The Dryads at Cordova love?

A preacher's blood I feel in me,
  In Palos pulpit where I stand,
To pound its iron tracery,
  Like Goetz, who wore the iron hand.

And as that lone Italian drave,
  Into the Palos mind of murk
The flash light of the western wave,
  I am Columbus' handiwork.

Ocean its revelations clear
  Made not to Arab, Jew or Greek, —
The drifting things from some near sphere
  That of a human neighbor speak.

One notchèd chip, one rotten apple,
  That in earth's faithful currents swum,
Did more the brother worlds to grapple
  Than all the prayers of Christendom.

Long as he took the wheel to plan, —
  Eternal surface smooth and clear,—
Came to the rutted mind of man
  The comprehension of the sphere;

Slowly it passed from Greek to Goth
  And to the wisest seemed a fact;
A sailor groped in ocean's froth
  And shaped the problem to an act.

For no new world Columbus sought;
  Embargoed Ind he hoped to clutch;
His aptness grasped the spheroid thought
  And knew extremes did somewhere touch.

There is a mean amidst extremes,
  There is a half-way happiness;
Between the continents he dreams
  The lost Atlantis lay to bless.

As in a tube a hyacinth,
　　Flowered knowledge in the steel-clad camp:
Religion was a labyrinth
　　But science was a kindling lamp.

Man's bony frame of shadows sick
　　Beat starved against his prison bars,
The owl-bright eye of Copernik
　　Was out by night to catch the stars.

In the Italian schools the Moor,
　　Though beat by these new monarchies,
Hung on the lance of Avenzoar
　　The lamp of old Maimonides.

And in the minds of gentlemen
　　There came a crisis and a jar,
As in the mines of Almaden
　　Quicksilver moves in cinnabar.

His iron casque had pinched the Don:
　　Eight hundred years he fought the Moor.
The bastard line of Aragon
　　Taught Barcelona literature.

From those Sicilian vesper bells,
　　That Popes and poetry enticed,
Down where Amalfi's infidels
　　The loadstone compass left to Christ,

Letters made merchants of the Jews,
　　And sharpened the Italian scent,
But Letters only, that refuse
　　Bright Physics' light, are sentiment.

Physics and martial music came
　To Europe in the Turkman's hand:
Constantinople's dying flame
　Lighted the birth of Ferdinand

And hushed the soft Petrarchian pipes
　And broke the Minnesinger's trance
And Printing flew her beacon types
　Along the walled towns of the Hanse.

Physics her apparatus played
　As in some school for grown-up boys
And in the Nuremberger's trade
　The Globe appeared among his toys.

Thus geometric as the Moor,
　Perforce, his propositions lined,
Learning descended to the poor
　And taught her objects to the blind.

'Twas thus the Genoese was taught,
　On some small isle by Exile's sea;
A new Herodotus was wrought
　To Poetry's audacity.

Upon King Joao's smirk he waits
　Who would with halfpence fame attain,—
Small are the souls of little States!
　He turned him to United Spain.

And Salamanca's monks did snub
　The noblest issue ever seen,
He was no member of a club
　Nor author in a magazine;

Not frittered into piecemeal things
  Are minds of comprehensive ends,
He ranked his genius with kings
  And found them in his simple friends.

He had a clean, transparent mind
  One wick of truth could all illume,
That lighted friendship in his kind
  And scented it with his perfume.

They thought him wholesome more than right;
  He had the good in Adam's fall;
He knew one thing with all his might
  And gods forbid he knew it all!

Ye Palos gentles! in the land
  That by your help Columbus found,
Although his love was contraband
  His *mind's* descendants there abound:

Men who at Pavia learned not long
  Nor wranglers were in smug debates
But in the realm of physics strong
  Columbian blessings left on States.

Palos! as friends of old acquaint,
  Ne'er may your Spain in her eclipse
Match Compostello's burly saint
  Against Columbia's battleships!

Or ye may find your saint's cuirass
  Fade like the Ottoman's lone moon
And Archimedes' burning glass
  Be yonder sun of afternoon!

Columbus turned the missal's page:
  But love of shrines shall I condemn
Who make to Palos pilgrimage
  As he would see Jerusalem?

From superstition half he woked
  Who gazed on Physics' grand *demesne*
As through the church tower I am poked
  To see Algarvè's vision scene.

Beyond her tile roofs' wrinkled net,
  Skin of her shrivelled usufructs,
On Huelva, Palos' look is set
  Flashing her Roman aqueducts, —

Huelva! Whose villas sparkle white
  Above her port of copper mesh
Like the pomegranate's seeds of light
  Dotting its lush and purple flesh.

There friar Bacon's fire retort
  Melts wealth from ore and Spanish dross
With British ships crowds Huelva's port:
  Palos has nothing but the cross.

Nature here noble, man ungrown,
  The tawny rivers at the flood
O'erflow and like the Amazon
  Their lambent boundary stain with mud.

The sailor men of Palos hire
  Like Indians in the copper mines;
Her strand is nought but empty mire
  Where like one shell my shallop shines.

But reverent I look upon
  The sailor-scrivener's index page,
As piously a preacher's son
  Visits his youth's old parsonage

And thinks how by Gennesaret
  All night disciples nothing waft
While on this farther side their net
  Was cast and drew the mighty draught.

The port's lane echoes to my tread
  Like sounds from ocean's chambered shells:
Towns live their period like the dead,
  And never wake by miracles.

Palos! I leave thee with a sigh
  Gravely and sweet thou treated me;
Across the drownèd marsh I fly
  As o'er the Saragossa sea.

I feel that space has worlds to find
  Unknown on Matter's universe,
No waterspouts are in the mind
  No tyrants chain discoverers.

One prayer will be never misspoken,
  It needs no tinkling holy bell,
It is the Public Spirit's token
  To wish all things constructive well.

Skyward our Argonautic prow
  Turns like the thunder-slayer's Kite;
The human Mind is Palos now,
  Its expeditions infinite.

As 'twixt the stars lost monads scatter,
  And pollen floats from sphere to sphere,
We shall see God, pervasive Matter,
  That hath in motion just career.

IN GROTE'S GREECE

From folks insipid and unfeeling
Came one who needed no annealing,
Love childless kept him from congealing.

He lived beside his money-lending,
Learning his concubine and vending
All day, he read at night's descending.

His favorite work was Say on Barter,
He was Republican, no martyr,
And varicosely spurned a garter.

A Benthamite, old ills he flouted
Till came the chance and then he doubted;
He hated slavery till 'twas routed.

He would the ballot give the many
Until too many, then not any,
And in the pound stuck at the penny.

But o'er this money groat's existence
The purple Greece shone in from distance
And gave his vagaries consistence.

Like old Mortality a tintster,
Among the marbles in the Minster
They put away this withered spinster.

JEFFERSON

Why does this politician keep
  The power a century to stir?
In war so weak, in peace so deep
  And feminine in character?
Suspicious of his fellow-chiefs,
  Insinuating and apart
And dropping his posthumous leafs
  The foliage of a withered heart?
Is it because, when Virtue feared
  Science would be Religion's wraith,
He took the prophets by the beard
  And cheered the ever-living faith?
And in his century's slave kiosk,
  Forced for the Moors himself to brand,
Stood like Averroes by the mosque
  With Aristotle in his hand?

GOVERNOR WILLIAM FRANKLIN
1784

My father's policy is wide,
  He manages the selfish town,
Vindictive, placid is his pride,
  He has the pride of pulling down;
My dull Lords Penn, King George, the clouds,—
  I've seen him draw them from their height;
His gainful wisdom tickles crowds,
  His lever is his paper kite.

I know my mother's humble place;
  A vassal ship she came upon,

The pilgrim mother of his race;
　I am his German leman's son,
To him, to her, I owe the span
　Of life's delightful ecstacy,
Yet when he talks the Rights of Man
　I feel a bastard's injury.

Docile to him in filial fear,
　Born to his foot, like Mercury's wing,
Obedience gave me a career,
　I rose above him with his king;
His conscience pricked him at my height,
　My subjects might his virtue mock:
As when a boy I flew his kite
　And down the cord he felt the shock.

England than Franklin more humane
　Raised me to honor's pedigree,
A lady by my rank was lain
　And took my spurious son with me;
His grandsire's tact my offspring won —
　I kept my oath and wrecked my house —
The Revolution took my son,
　I wail a broken-hearted spouse!

Isaac beneath his father's knife
　Was not more still than I obey,
Honoring him who gave me life
　And all that bless'd it lured away:
My native land for which I fought,
　The love domestic that endears.
God spare me thy rewarding thought,
　I must live long as father's years![1]

[1] Their united ages were 168 years.

AT AYR

THERE are no towers like Melrose
  About the land of Ayr,
But all the morning gates unclose
  To who goes pilgrim there;
No Abbotsford demands *largess*,
  Nor money-warders prance,
To show the poet of success
  And banker in romance.

But as the little towns of Burns
  Their names familiar say,
The stranger to the native turns
  And smiles between them play;
A social glee like Bobby's rhymes
  In eye and heart prevails,
As when in Canterbury times
  Sly Chaucer told his tales;

Till Ayr its flat, wide street begins
  And midst his haunts we stand
Who made its humble brigs and inns
  Like scenes in Holy land
And he who water turned to wine,
  And lived not half his span,
Lies in the Scottish Palestine
  The glorious Son of Man.

We drink his tankard full of ale
  And toast him prodigal
As if it were the Holy Grail
  Ourself Knight Parsafal

For that wherever life was sad
    Or self-oppression ruled
He made the hovel-hearted glad
    The dying firelog Yuled.

His spirit was the gale that blows
    Across the Irish sea,
With independence to oppose
    And voice of liberty,
The cattle feel it in their hair
    It cools the ploughman's noon
And blooms the thistle and the tare
    Along the banks of Doon.

Doon's crystal slide on pebbly floor
    In many a stream we find
But not the poet peeping o'er
    With his swift, minnowy mind:
The mind that poises, flashes, falls,
    With instant instincts rife,
And prisoned in by river walls
    Reflects and loses life.

They tire like Gods who would create,
    They sublimate their hour,
Life's quickening to illustrate
    Drains every vital power;
In zenith like the laboring bee
    By beauty's regent charmed,
They from a moment's jubilee
    Drop to the earth deformed.

Gorged on green leaves the silkworm weaves
    His nature earthy, fine;

Beauty and health are poet's leaves,
  He needs good meat and wine;
Grudge not his sweets who drink them up!
  Thy nectar was his soul;
His Highland Mary one day's cup,
  And Jean Armour his bowl.

His butts they were the stiff and smirk,
  His sinners sham and cant,
He railed like Jesus at the Kirk
  And flogged the Covenant;
John Knox so plied on faith his thong,
  Burns went to Luther's school, —
Who loved not woman, wine and song
  Was all his life a fool.

Wide as our British race his wand
  To conjure formalism;
The young world charm from false despond
  And flout the catechism;
Kirk Alloway's a ruin dull,
  Its windows gaping niches,
Except when Tam o' Shanter's full
  And sees it full of witches.

Great babe! who haled thy Scottish sect
  And put its saints thy debtors,
And made thy wayside dialect
  A language of *belles lettres!*
I do not kneel but bow thy due,
  Ent'ring thy hut's low portal:
The unsevere see Nature through,
  The joyous troll immortal.

TRAVELERS' REST

(HOUSE OF GEN. HORATIO GATES)

1781

MRS. GATES: Well! Here, in one county, are
   four of ye of mark,
   Retired for public reasons: Gates, Stephens,
      Lee and Darke;
   While poor Dan Morgan, teamster, and Battle-
      town's bully,
   Will get the county's ballot before the best of
      ye.
GEN. GATES: A natural soldier, Mrs. Gates, his
   rank well won,
   As great in valor as in caution, Washington.
MRS. GATES: Pity your caution hadn't seen to
   this day's work,
   When you and Congress fought him so, close
      by at York!
   He's put Cornwallis in a coop at Yorktown
      three.
GEN. GATES: I hope we'll hear this night, my
   dear, of a great victory!
MRS. GATES: Then you've come down, to wish
   that much for Washington —
GEN. GATES: I see all things more humbly since
   we lost our son.
MRS. GATES: Now, father, sit thee down! take
   my wine-cellar key!
   I said I wouldn't open it, but will, *for thee.*
   Hark! there's the pack of General Lee: that
      key give back!

GEN. GATES: Darling, his sword is broken, too.
    Give him some sack!
MRS. GATES: Your worst adviser, General Gates,
    since that Conway
And drunken Wilkinson who made you such
    repay.
GEN. GATES: Mary, he is my oldest friend since
    Indian frays:
He has no Mary Valence in his dark'ning days.
MRS. GATES: I'll give him no Madeira. A julep
    will do —

(*Gen. Charles Lee enters: pack of hounds bays.*)

GEN. LEE: There's nothing like a julep, Madame,
    made by you!
Well, drink Horatio! to the French. The deed
    is done.
GEN. GATES: Let's toast Virginians first, old
    friend! To *Washington!*
GEN. LEE: Ne'er to that mediocrity I'll bend my
    knee!
MRS. GATES: 'Tis all the greater done by Medi-
    ocrity!
Is Yorktown taken?
GEN. LEE: That's the news to Charlestown come.
The men are drunk, the women dance, the boys
    they drum.
I rode from Cherry tavern here to tell you first,
Though Mistress Dun, at *Prato Rio*, cooled my
    thirst.
MRS. GATES: Madeira it shall be for our country
    is free.

Ye victors in the past! huzza this victory!
When you, Gates, took Burgoyne there was lost
    Brandywine,
But Washington sent cheer to the New Eng-
    land line:
'Tis turn and turn about —
GEN. LEE: I'll see him damned before —
MRS. GATES: Peter, bring back the key of the
    wine-cellar door!
GEN. LEE: Halt! Here's to us Commanders!
    let us all drink hard!
    Washington, and Lee, and Gates, and old Arte-
        mas Ward!
MRS. GATES: Now add your engineer, my gallant
    Polish beau,
    Who drew the lines around your foes, Kosciusko!
    He lay in Travelers' Rest, which the wounded
        enjoy, —
    They all could live but him, my dear, my only
        boy!
GEN. LEE: Lady Gates, your charity to the
    Continental line
    Will make you and your son the Family Divine.
    I have no wife nor child and I live with my
        dogs —
MRS. GATES: With dogs, in tubs or ruins, lived
    all demagogues!
GEN. LEE: And Jezebel also! Your Madeira may
    be good
    But you let it stand so long it tastes bitterwood.
GEN. GATES: Mary, let's make a night! we
    beaten men and thee:

'Tis our duty to get tipsy: give me the key!
There! stingy puss. Treat, the last time, the
  Gates *cabal!*
Come, bring the lantern, Lee! and smell of
  Portugal!

(*Exit Gates and Lee.*)

Mrs. Gates: They love each other, dear, poor
  men of Braddock's fight!
Girls! light the banquet fire and set them out
  a bite!
I think Horatio looks pale: he loved his son.
Now in his grief I'll have him write to
  Washington.
Husband lived lonely once as Lee till I came
  West
And tried to make him happy in his Travelers'
  Rest.
How he did farm! Poor officers of England's
  line!
They do their best. But Lee is such a libertine!
Till he came here my husband was aye *com-
  plaisant,*
And General Washington chose him for Ad-
  jutant:
Gates left alone *is* Washington: Lee comes
  between.
He thinks so many things and husband's so
  serene.
Perhaps we're punished for our Saratoga pride.
The laurels turned to willows and our dear
  boy died.

He loves this country and his soldiers Gates
    respect:
If not the first commander, be the first subject!

    (Reënter Gates and Lee with bottles.)

GEN. LEE: '*Subject?*' Shame, Madame! And
    shall we so re-gorge
That after George the Third we want another
    George?

MRS. GATES: At least four kings *you*'ve had:
    two Georges, Stanislow,
Don Joseph, *debauchee*, but you like not kings
    now.
At Poniatowski's table volunteer you sat:
He gave you no command: but our Congress
    did that!

GEN. LEE: Madame as Tragedy is Queen of
    every feast.

MRS. GATES. You had been a better man if
    married by some priest.

GEN. GATES: Now, wife and friend, be merry!
    We conquer in age:
Think of your friend Burgoyne, and of my
    friend, Gage!
We both are seniors, neighbor, of Washington:
He is only forty-nine, though the war is done.
To-day his name is royal and we cannot pluck
The *baton* from his glory by calling it luck.

MRS. GATES: Eat a bit. The pheasant's cold;
    the mutton's better.

    (They sit. "Yelp! yelp!" from the cellar.)

You careless men the pork-house door have left—

GEN. LEE: My setter!

(Dog with meat rushes through hall.)

She'll drive me out with my pack!

GEN. GATES: I thought of old Nace
  Who robbed that cellar and was hanged.   I see
    his face.
  He earned all he stole; his price they paid to
    me
  I shall give with interest to the slaves I free.

(Mrs. Gates returns.)

GEN. LEE: Chicken heart!

MRS. GATES: Must we live with your dogs and
    your strife?

GEN. LEE: Sweetheart, take my dogs and you
    take my only wife.
  I sent some quail to you and my dog stole but
    one.
  I always think of Mary Gates when I do gun.

GEN. GATES: For this wine Mary's father paid
    thirty pounds cool
  Out of dock ere he died, solid man of Liverpool.

GEN. LEE: How delicious! King Jozay had no
    such wine
  Though his nobles' wines and wives he made
    concubine.
  One more glass and I will sing you what I sang
    Jozay!

(Mrs. Gates retires.)

GEN. GATES: Sing it softly! her bereavement
    Mary takes away.

GEN. LEE (*sings*) :

    Drink to the lass that lingers in the glass!
    Oft as she may pass she's a peri;
    O what a body she,
    And an eye of yellow glee !
    And she makes you bend the knee, —
        Miss Madeira !

    Her breath's boukay, excels the new-mown hay,
    And she holds her age for an era;
    Like honey are the drips
    From her glue-gold kissing lips,
    And she gurgles while one sips
        Miss Madeira.

GEN. GATES: Hark! 'tis a hymn for victory.
        Our German choirs
  Have come from Mecklenburg to sing to their
      esquires.
  MRS. GATES (*entering*): Get them our pear
      cider worked in whiskey barrels!
  Set it out upon the lawn! I love those carols!

GERMAN CHOIR:

    King Fritz he gave his sword
    To the blessèd of the Lord,
    And he only waits the word
      From Washington to die:
    Send him up! Ye Luther's choir!
    In a chariot of fire! —
    He has seen his heart's desire:
      Washington has the Victory !

Cornwallis through our gates
Burst over our estates:
Behind York's fortress grates
  With his army does he lie,
And in spite of all his boasts
He is drowned upon our coasts —
Shout to the Lord of Hosts:
  Washington has the victory!

O God! to us most kind,
Give us one united mind!
And our States united bind
  While our tyrant we defy!
We have passed the Red seas o'er
And are on the farther shore:
Sing! thy people evermore! —
  Washington has the victory!

GEN. GATES: The voice of a nation I surely hear
  at last!

GEN. LEE: You are on the army list but I am out-
  cast.

MRS. GATES: Come among our neighbors and
  with their joys entwine!

GEN. LEE: They won't stand like the French.
  I'll stay here and drink wine.

(Exit General and Mrs. Gates.)

Now if they come not back the whole bottle is
  mine;

That's why I like a dog: he cannot drink my
  wine,

And all I say he wags his tail at, backing me up.

(Dog scratches at back door.)

Come in, Cracow! Hide there! I'll talk to thee
    and sup.
Gates and his wife with his small parentage
    concur:
His father was the butler, mother housekeeper
To the Duke of Leeds; that's why they like
    Virginia,
Where land and money do not need insignia.
I was a General's son, sent to school in Swissland,
And, bred in barracks, made Indian in this land,
Named *Boiling Water* by Mohawks at Johnson
    Hall,
I crossed these States on foot and fought at
    Montreal,
Commanded a division of the Portuguese,
Was Major General for the Poles, the same for
    these
Damned rebels, whose rump Congress treats us
    worse than Draco:
Its test of Generalship is how to hoe tobacco.

(Cheers outside.)

Hear how the Anabaptists and Reformed cheer
    Gates!
The greedy Dutch for once eat victuals out of
    plates!
Gates has one greatness: he likes *me*, a lady's
    son.
I hoped to make and rule him as my Wash-
    ington;
Indulgent rustic squire and hero on the staff

As Governor Jefferson's cock he lost his gaff
At Camden; Jefferson from Tarlton ran away
But like all writing men will fight some other day.
These politicians of Virginia see their fate
If Union be resolved and Washington be great;
Young Monroe is far-sighted: he says Madame
    Gates
More ready income has than any in these States,
'Twill work upon the populace by printing
    presses.
Against a King and Kingdom we'll foment
    addresses.

(Enter Gen. and Mrs. Gates.)

MRS. GATES: Bless me! I smell a dog. General,
    I suppose it's you,
Who live with dogs so much you're dogg'd and
    doggy too.
More wine? Well, those poor folks to General
    Gates were sweet:
Horatio! go get what you will to drink and eat!

*(Mrs. Gates gives the key: Gen. Gates is
followed down by Gen. Lee's dog.)*

GEN. LEE: Lady! Virginia's queen! To you all
    will defer.
Hast heard Gates takes Tom Nelson's place as
    governor?
He drafted and conscripted and he must resign;
His house at Yorktown he has shelled till it's a
    mine.
MRS. GATES: That's honor: to destroy your home
    where foes be guest;

I'd fire a cannon heartily on Travelers' Rest,
If round its humble limestone fort our foemen put
Circumvallations; I would burn it like some hut.
GEN. LEE: This is no home for General Gates: 'tis
  too submiss.
MRS. GATES: The Tower of London's governor
  was Cornwallis.
  These stiff grey walls and chimneyed ends to
    me are dear:
  My son's life bubbled like our springs and
    ended here.
  I see his image everywhere o'er these slate lands.
  He loved the sheep they pastured, the sheep
    dog, his hands;
  Blue mountain tops above our wolds my spirits
    enjoy:
  I think they're heaven where father and I shall
    find our boy.
  Ambition did us harm: I want Horatio good;
  He needs excel in nothing else: we have no
    brood.
  No more than General Washington or you,
    Charles Lee,
  Washington was for the cause, the public family.
  That's why his character stands out, the best
    of you,
  As from North Mountain chain out there abuts
    Fairview.

(Enter Gen. Gates.)

GEN. GATES: Eight thousand foot and sailors
  fifteen hundred were

Taken at York — the prisoners come to Win-
    chester —
Charles Washington sends me a post. of him
    'tis kind!
Lord Fairfax heard the news and he has lost his
    mind.
MRS. GATES: Poor man! He has seen in his life
    William and Mary.
  The Huguenots suppressed in France. — all
    things contrary;
  Cross'd love drove him into his wilds, our Lord
    Lieutenant;
  Child Washington with Indians carried his pen-
    nant,
  Surveying his Culpepper realm.
GEN. LEE: He now knows why
  The devil showed him so much land worship-
    fully!
MRS. GATES: You haven't done so badly, sir:
    Congress paid you
For every acre you possess ere you wore blue!
GEN. GATES: Lincoln received Cornwallis' sword
    who once took his
  And neighbor Otho Williams made a General
    is.
  That young West Indian, Hamilton, stormed a
    redoubt —
GEN. LEE: And if he lives you planter men will
    find him out —
Bastard to Adam Smith, accountant and blade.
MRS. LEE: Father, the Martinsburgers come to
    serenade

And, don't you think! their music is the Hessian band
You took at Saratoga, paroled in Maryland!
I've venison for them! They shall drink all the
  stout!

(*Dog below howls at the Hessian music and bursts
  into the room and is seized by Mrs. Gates.*)

GEN. LEE: Don't beat my dog!
MRS. GATES: He's got a paper I'll make out!

(*Exit General and Mrs. Gates with dog.*)

THE HESSIAN BAND:

I.

Our Landgrave did not right
When he sent us here to fight
Good German brothers white
That we thought were savage red
And our Duke has us misled:
Our drums now they say,
    "We have light!
      Ye have right!"
Hear us Peace's music play!
"We shall be of one band!
This shall be our motherland!
  Hail! great America!"

II.

Rash Britain is undone
By our Gates and Washington.
Our liberty is won

And the long war finishèd!
To the living and the dead
Our drums now they say,
   "To the right!
    Is the might!"
Hear the march that we will play!
"We shall bring by our Band
Thousands from our German land —
  Hail! great America!"

III.

For this Columbus sailed
And the Saxon race prevailed;
Independence exhaled
From the mountains of the West,
Where the eagle builds his nest.
Our drums now they say,
   "O how bright!
    After Night!"
And the loud Assembly play! —
"We shall enter, hand in hand,
To the beauty of your land!
  Hail! great America!"

GEN. LEE (*solus*): The wine makes me friendly;
   I wish I were like others!
They are drinking and kissing like sweethearts
   and brothers.
I sit with my last friend in Europe or o'er here:
Stand by me, my Bottle! my last brave gren-
   adier!
I could not be second; I was second and fell;

The last time I was principal I fell as well;
Mixing ink with my whiskey I wrote with my
    fist
And Congress countersigned it, " Charles Lee is
    dismissed."
When my fingers were shot off why left he my
    hand?
I have duel'd with career and scorned repri-
    mand.
No fighter should write till his history is done!
From me to a star is less than to Washington.

    (He bows his head beside the bottle.)
       (Enter General Gates.)

GEN. GATES: Sad? I have you now. 'Tis the mood
    will do you good:
After Camden all my pride like a son I subdued;
I said: " To my father I will arise and go!"
My father was a servant and his son fall'n low.
I went to General Washington and claimed his
    hand,
He took me to his heart and I felt he was grand.
GEN. LEE: I, Lee of Villa Veltra's fight? —
GEN. GATES: What's that renown?
Europe stands tiptoe gazing on him of York-
    town.
I would not have you stand in shadows from
    that light,
'Twill search us all.
GEN. LEE: Good Dunker! Be not too contrite!
Clinton has an army left: he knows a cam-
    paign —

(Enter Mrs. Gates.)

MRS. GATES: I reckon it is *this* one, out of
    Charles Lee's brain,
  Marked "Copy of the plan left with Howe in
    New York:"
  The dog you taught to steal thought it had the
    smell of pork
  And he slipped it through his collar —

  (She hands the plan to General Gates.)

GEN. GATES: Why, General Lee?
  What's this? *"A plan to break the public
    enemy —*
  Garrisons on tide-water — cut Virginia off
  *And raid the Dutch farmers in the mountain
    trough;*
  *Burn their barns and mills; they are greedy and
    will pause*
  *And cry out for peace though they love the rebel
    cause."*
MRS. LEE: This explains why Arnold and Corn-
    wallis further down
  Raided far up the country into Charlotte town.
  Lee pointed out his neighbors' wealth in these
    designs —
  To save himself, deserter from the English lines!
GEN. LEE: 'Twas versatility when prisoner, —
    time slack.
MRS. GATES: You didn't fight at Monmouth
    when ordered to attack.
GEN. GATES: I cannot take the view that this is
    matter light,

> You were fresh from our lines and showed Howe
>   where to smite.

Mrs. Gates: Showed him our plantation to
  burn, where you are drinking!

Gen. Lee: I did not think —

Gen. Gates: One cannot draft a plan unthinking.
  This plan *we* had discussed; it was all in reason.
  I am in commission: great God! is this treason?

Gen. Lee: Why, I overflow with such military fun!

Mrs. Gates: I am no Margaret Arnold though
  I have no son.

Gen. Lee: Madame, you seek to drive me out
  from Travelers' Rest.

Mrs. Gates: This is Major General Gates; you
  are a dangerous guest!

  O Lee! had you pure-hearted been, outside your
    lines

  You never had been captured by your concubines.

  While Washington to save your neck played all
    the man,

  You sold your talents to our foes and drew this
    plan!

Gen. Lee: I'll never come here more while
  that female is nigh.

Gen. Gates: Madame Gates is my wife —

Mrs. Gates: Here to live and to die!

Gen. Lee: I shall quit Virginia: farewell!

Gen. Gates: I fear 'tis best.

Gen. Lee: Woman and serpent! guard ye well
  your Travelers' Rest.

(*General Gates weeps.   His wife lights General
    Lee to the door.   The dogs bay.*)

WASHINGTON

RARE the chance to be the hero and the pioneer!
Washington has squared the circle and has cubed
    the sphere.
While he lived fame lagged behind him, when he
    died went on
Like the loadstone in his compass and the stars
    at dawn.
They who mock him as the children mocked
    Elisha's cloak,
Meet the she-bears of the forest and the towns
    in smoke;
Shallow skeptic, simple rustic, in his faith unite,
And his portrait like the sunburst fills the world
    with light.

CÆSAR

(FROUDE)

CÆSAR how far thy arrowy name
Pierces the future with its flame!
The greatest name that Jesus knew,
The mightiest man that Shakespere drew,
Plutarch survives but for thy tale,
Peter and Paul by thee prevail,
Namesakes from thee Popes, Kaisers, Tsars,
And every land's Imperators!

As when thy mother called thee nigh
We lisp thy name in warm July,
And to thy calendars go back,
The Gospels and the Almanac.

The German learned his name by thee,
No Gaul was there till thou did'st see,
And British men in every age
Begin their story with thy page;
Spain, Greece, the Moor, the Parthian horde,
Arab, Egyptian, felt thy sword;
Rome's village standard thou unfurled,
The narrow town became the world,
Its Senate let Barbarians in
And all the races made akin.
Then on the fields, all smoothed to sow,
The seeds of Jesus silent blow.
Jesus, thy friend was priest to Jove,
And Jesus, Cæsar, Jove, are Love!

J. B. STILLSON

DECEMBER 26, 1880

DEAD courier that from battle came so fleetly
  Thy bugle full of music for the land,
Thou fall'st at last so weary and so sweetly
  The bells of Christmas tremble where they stand,
And draw the tuneful trumpet from thy hand.
  What beauty in thine eyes and locks of raven
When youth and emulation loosed thy rein!
  What tender welcome on thy lips engraven
That friendship never shall behold again!
  What honor guided aye thy pen so skilful
That mercenary art can never know!
  What indignations womanly and wilful
Bent every golden tendon in thy bow
Till broke thy string and winter laid thee low!

POLITICIANS' CHRISTMAS

A. D. 1

" THERE is no room for you in the inn," said the
　　landlord to the pair.
" The travel this month is lively, and the house
　　filled everywhere;
The Emperor taxes the world he rules, and all
　　Judeans must go
Up to the city of Bethlehem, whether they will or
　　no."

" 'Tis not for me," the traveler said, a carpenter
　　tough and tried,
" I crave a bed but for the maid who has ridden
　　all day at my side."
" The maid, forsooth," the landlord said, " hath a
　　matronly look to me ! "
And he passed a wink to the hotel clerk, who
　　snickered chivalrously.

The guests about the hotel clerk, they did look on
　　askant —
The Pharisee, and the Sadducee and the Greek of
　　the Levant,
To mark this comely, drooping girl, awhile aside
　　they drew
From the themes of taxes and of tolls and internal
　　revenue.

" There is a stall within the barn no camel yet
　　hath ta'en;
'Twill rest the young girl pleasantly, unless per-
　　chance it rain : "

It was a groom who whispered thus; a husband he
　　had been,
And cheerfully his lodge he gave to this poor
　　Nazarene.

Ye fathers nursing on your knee the first-born of
　　your dears,
The priceless for *their* sufferings, the costlier for
　　their fears,
Think over in these winter nights this Virgin's
　　lonely moan,
And Joseph's loving tenderness for offspring not
　　his own !

All night the politicians talked about the Roman
　　yoke ;
The inn blazed up with moving lights, and roared
　　with many a joke :
They all agreed the Jewish state somehow must
　　be made free,
But ever about the " patronage " were sure to dis-
　　agree.

The dromedaries in the stalls also did ruminate ;
The asses and the saddle-nags chewed o'er the
　　themes of state ;
None saw a little new-born star out of the heavens
　　fall,
And with a holy glory kiss the stranger in the
　　stall.

None heard the mystic choirs that sang across the
　　glimmering moors ;

None saw the reverend sages ride up to the hostel
    doors;
And when the earliest Christmas morn o'er crowded
    Bethlehem crept,
The statesmen in the manger knelt, the politicians
    slept.

Still taxed, still taxing, o'er the world the wise and
    noisy spin,
They get the tavern clerk's best cheer, the best
    rooms in the inn.
Thank God! whose stars of choice, scarce seen,
    upon the lowly fall! —
The mother fainting by the way, the baby in the
    stall!
    1870.

COMMANDER LINCOLN

(ADDRESS BEFORE THE ARMY OF THE POTOMAC SOCIETY,
1883)

CIVIL soldiers! reassembled by the river of your
    fame,
Ye who saved the virgin city bathed in Washing-
    ton's clear name!
Which of all your past commanders doth this day
    your memory haunt? —
Scott, McDowell, Burnside, Hooker, Meade, Mc-
    Clellan, Halleck, Grant?

There is one too little mentioned when your proud
    reunions come,
And the thoughtful love of country dies upon the
    sounding drum;

Let me call him in your muster, let me wake him
    in your grief!
Captain by the Constitution, Abram Lincoln was
    your chief!

Ever nearest to his person ye were his defence and
    shield.
He alone of your commanders died upon the battle-
    field.
All your generals were his children, leaning on him,
    childish-willed,
And they all were filial mourners round the
    mighty tomb he filled.

Tender as the harp of David, his soft answers now
    become,
When amid the care of kingdoms rose and fell
    some Absalom;
And his humor gilds his memory like a light
    within a tent,
Or the sunken sun that lingers on the lofty mon-
    ument.

Like the slave who saw the sunrise with his face
    toward the West,
As it flashed, while yet unrisen, on a slender
    steeple's crest;
So while victory turned her from him ere the
    dawn in welcome came,
On his pen Emancipation glittered like an altar
    flame.

Feeling for the doomed deserter, feeling for the
    drafted sire,

For the empty Northern hearthstone and the
    Southern home afire,
Mercy kept him grim as Moloch, all the future
    babes to free,
And eternal peace to garner for the millions yet to
    be.

Not a soldier of the classics, he could see through
    learned pretence —
Master of the greatest science, military common-
    sense.
As he watched your marches, comrades ! hither,
    thither, wayward years,
On his map the roads you followed you can trace
    them by his tears.

In the rear the people clamored, in the front the
    generals missed,
In his inner councils harbored critic and an-
    tagonist,
But he ruled them by an instinct, like the queen's
    among the bees,
With a health of soul that honeyed Publicans and
    Pharisees.

Faint of faith, we looked behind us for a chief of
    higher tone,
While the voice that drowned the trumpets was
    the echo of our own ;
Ever thus, my old companions, Genius has us by
    the hand,
Walking on the tempest with us, every crisis
    to command !

Like the bugle blown at evening by some home-
    sick son of art,
Lincoln's words unearthly quiver in the universal
    heart;
Not an echo left of malice, scarce of triumph in the
    strain,
As when summer thunder murmurs in pathetic
    showers of rain.

Years forever consecrated, here he lived, where
    duties be,
Never railing on the climate, nor the toil's
    monotony;
Here his darling boy he buried and the night in
    vigil wept,
Like the Lord within the garden when the tired
    disciples slept.

How his call for men went ringing round the
    world, a mighty bell,
And the races of creation came the proud revolt
    to quell.
Standing in the last reaction, on the rock of human
    rights,
Worn and mournful grew his features in the flash
    of battle lights.

Once, like Moses from the mountain, looked he on
    the land he won.
When the slaves in burning Richmond knelt and
    thought him Washington,
Then an envious bravo snatched him from the
    theatre of things,

To become a saint of nature in the pantheon of
    kings.

Faded are the golden chevrons, vanished is the
    pride of war,
Mild in heaven his moral glory lingers like the
    morning star,
And the freeman's zone of cotton his white spirit
    seems to be,
And the insects in the harvest beat his army's
    reveille.

All around him spoiled or greedy, women vain and
    honor spent,
Still his faith in human nature lived without dis-
    couragement;
For his country which could raise him, barefoot,
    to the monarch's height,
Could he mock her? or his mother — though *her*
    name she could not write?

Deep the wells of humble childhood, cool the
    springs beside the hut,
Millions more as poor as Lincoln see the door he
    has not shut.
Not till wealth has made its canker every poor
    white's cabin through,
Shall the great republic wither, or the infidel
    subdue!

Stand around your great commander, lay aside
    your little fears!
Every Lincoln carries freedom's car along a
    hundred years.

And when next the call for soldiers rolls along
　　　the golden belt,
Look to see a mightier column rise, and march,
　　　prevail and melt !

NOTHING FALLS SO FAR

Every falling star
　　To its fate is lit.
Nothing falls so far
　　As we pity it.
Woman like the dove
　　From her blasted tree,
Finds some fallen love,
　　Some fierce sympathy.

Out into the night
　　Is not wholly dark ;
On the billows' might
　　Rides the human bark.
What can break the womb
　　Dies not in the pit ;
Hell's a better home
　　Than we pity it.

Nothing falls as deep
　　As we pity it :
By your side may sleep
　　Crime's long hypocrite,
While the bold, frank wolf
　　Acts that dreamer's part,
Taking to his gulf
　　No such sneaking heart.

All the felon's lusts
　　Are the good man's joys.
Age its millions trusts
　　To the convict boys;
In the ranks enrolled,
　　Colors never furled,
Firm the guilty bold
　　Guard the coward world.

Human nature's chief
　　From the gibbet tree
Took the dying thief,
　　Not the Pharisee,
To his heavenhood,
　　Fellow judge of his:
Nothing is so good
　　As we think it is.

Every heavenly orb
　　Has the rust of ours,
All that breathe absorb
　　Errors with their powers;
Habits, virtues are,
　　Stars erode by grit;
Nothing falls so far
　　As we pity it.

Death is not as hard
　　As we pity it:
It is life's reward,
　　Age's sweet acquit;
No more pain than birth,
　　No worse end than rust.

Thou indulgent earth!
Take thy loan of dust!

HENRY M. STANLEY

AT THE LOTOS CLUB, NOVEMBER 27, 1886

AH! little did I ever think,
    Aladdin's lamp, that op'd the dark,
One plain reporter's skull outshone —
To light a dark world with his wink:
    That at my side was Mungo Park,
Who would discover Prester John!

Yet he who wrote the mighty strife
    Where Ethiop's freedom was the gage,
Well-lived to beat Da Gama's cruise,
And strike at slavery's fountain life, —
    Marched overland through Pluto's age,
And was the Orpheus of the News.

Old correspondent of our war!
    You gild our humble craft with gold
That from the Afric sands you bring;
You ride the night like Bethlehem's star;
    And magi follow to behold
That in *our* stall was born the king.

You go where Shakespere's fancy ceased —
    Beyond the Roman and the Nile;
Decatur stopped where you began;
And drooped the missionary priest,
    Lost to his gospel and his isle,
And all but one brave fellow man.

Then, darker lands of envious doubt
    You found returning to your own —
  The shrug, the sneer, the pedant's scorn,
The lazy printer's rival pout:
    Which met Columbus at the throne,
  And were the Saviour's crown of thorn.

Though courts and kings may now avail
    For wealth or glory, of your use,
  And in your name think lineage be,
I only see in Stanley's mail
    The youthful herald of the News,
  And courier of Democracy.

LOCAL GREATNESS

THE wide land has a million streams
  That babble as they flow,
And sweet the plaint of local themes
  The thousand valleys know;
They tell their tales just as they were,
  Not as they ought to be,
And in humanity lay bare
  Our truer history.

In every place a lady fair
  Had lovers thrilled by her,
Love's pastoral was tender there
  And rare with character;
Some Helen, Menelaus wed
  And Paris stole upon,
And in their small republics bred
  The wars of Ilion.

Out steps a man in public strife —
  Twenty as good remain ;
The weakling drew the famous life,
  Homes drew the men of brain ;
They give his nursing starhood sup,
  They fix his astrolabe,
And local kindness holds him up
  As if he were their babe.

Up to their priest the hearers look ;
  So purely shaved and friared,
They hear him read his holy book
  And think he is inspired ;
Heaven's love he macerates at length,
  But while his pleadings roll,
The congregation is his strength,
  Some lady there, his soul.

The suave historian portrays
  As he would have it seem,
And straightens out a nation's maze
  Like Joseph, Pharaoh's dream :
Not miracles can make us see
  Beyond convincing sense,
Their local probability
  Supports the Testaments.

The criminal of an era starts
  Beside some loved hearthstone,
And tramples over kindred hearts
  To infamy alone ;
But neither in the hell below
  Nor in the heavens above

Can they the million outlaws know,
　　Saved by the fireside love.

The silent boy has memories strong,
　　Though he seems not to look,
He wins the cup inscribed erelong:
　　"For Loving of a Book."
And all his life the local things
　　Men marvel where he found;
His genius drank the haunted springs
　　Wherein Narcissus drowned.

Yon miser note, who guards less well
　　His lady than his hoard!
She is not true; a silent yell
　　Goes from his broken board.
On other lands at his decease
　　Great wealth he showers free,
The flower of local injuries,
　　Some World's philanthropy.

The terror of the village goes
　　To its long, glad relief,
And from some savage border grows
　　To be the Nation's chief;
No clue to his high soul they find
　　In his extraction rude;
His isolation was his mind,
　　His virtue Fortitude.

A life that failure has pursued
　　Till but its honest grit
To some volcano's altitude

In splendor carries it,
The Magi of the East go round,
  Their touchstones to employ,
And nothing but a nugget found, —
  His father's country boy.

A millionaire some goddess fair
  To his protection draws,
And thinks she fell into his snare, —
  Himself the great first cause;
But all his joys, the vagrant boys,
  Her idle townsmen had;
From huts they stray their wanton way,
  Who make the monarchs glad.

Not palaces these sweets enclose
  That every hamlet keeps —
The perfume of the wild, wild rose,
  The laborer who sleeps,
The young heart that its mate has caught,
  The tears poor mothers shed,
The Self in only second thought,
  The baby and the dead.

GARLAND HALL, FROM THE WEST

LIBRARY
OF THE
UNIVERSITY

MARYLAND POEMS

NEEDWOOD

UNDER the blue South Mountain, Needwood, the
    home of the Lees,
Stands in the flowing springs and among the
    exotic trees;
An old gray house, mysterious, like a Zurbaran
    monk,
Cowling his face in the shadows that into his soul
    have sunk.

Once 'twas a school of learning, drawing the
    planters' youth
To the classical keeping of Reverend Bartholo-
    mew Booth:
He, a recusant rector, hewed him a school of logs
Out in this western exile, ancient of pedagogues;

Washington's nephew, Bushrod, under his Latin
    was drudge,
Here on the lawn of Needwood starting to be a
    judge;
Often in court he nodded, dreaming his brain was
    cooled
By the long verdurous mountain over his copy-
    book ruled.

Thomas Sim Lee came sleighing over the fences
    and rigs,

From Prince George, with his lady, Mary of Mel-
    wood-Digges,
He was a second son's second, landless except in
    wife,
Almost as tall as a giant and born for the era of
    strife.

Soft as a glove are the Lees and corded in neck
    like the bull;
Wide were the lands of Needwood rolling and
    beautiful,
Let down between the mountains like an apron of
    flowers,
And the blue distance castled with Nature's bat-
    tlement towers.

Thomas's kith in Virginia headed the war for a
    nation,
Thomas's lands and stature singled him out for a
    station;
He was domestic and settled but of such is the
    mastiff and ready one,
Maryland made him her governor after the war
    was a steady one.

He had a work to do after the South was invaded
And all the Chesapeake rivers British blockaded;
Shifted the base of the war to the Maryland moun-
    tains,
Flour and whiskey and beeves to be fed from their
    fountains;

Wagons and vessels to press with a tact and up-
    rightness,
Noblesse of France to amuse and entreat with
    politeness ;
Down at Annapolis day was all straining anxiety,
Night was all dancing and loveliness, state and
    society.

Thus, Cornwallis was taken and Needwood was
    home again ;
Lee from his lands and his dear ones hoped never
    to roam again,
But to watch harvests' and winters' annúal re-
    volving,
And her blue floodgates of mountains Potomac
    dissolving.

But the old drums continental rolled his reëlection.
Out in the West had the whiskey folks made
    insurrection ;
Soldiery streamed through the State like the gold
    in a pennant,
Under his cousin, Hal Lee, the Commander's
    lieutenant.

Carroll of Carrollton, Hanson and Harper, his
    cronies,
Visited Needwood in coaches or canvassed on
    ponies ;
Singly the Maryland Fed'ralists had to be baited,
Like the lone wild cats that lasted till exter-
    minated.

Beat, then, the *reveillé* over his lifetime of action,
Triumphed o'er Washington's friends the Virginia
　　　　faction;
Of Madison's cabinet craven, the governor read
　　　　would,
Chased from their burning metropolis, almost to
　　　　Needwood.

But on his age and Tom Johnson's, his governor-
　　　　neighbor,
Fell the sweet notes of the human birds piping to
　　　　labor,
Building the road to the West and the Armorers
　　　　merry,
Tinkering muskets and sabres close by, at the
　　　　Ferry.

Far waved his wheat like his panther rugs yel-
　　　　lowed by fire;
Stacked like the arms of his armies, his corn rows
　　　　retire;
Dropped in his dozing the tinkle of church bells
　　　　ancestral, —
Plenty and Liberty sang him their anthem or-
　　　　chestral.

Farms he divided from Needwood to daughters
　　　　and sons;
Pure in their paths were his seed as their kinsfolk,
　　　　the nuns;
So he passed out of the vista of life like a bird,
That in the deep vault grows lesser and, last, is
　　　　not heard.

Cannon of civil war belching and squadrons like
    bees
(When on the South mountain passes the last of
    the Lees
Fought for he knew not what) wakened him
    never:
Thomas Sim Lee had passed over the blue bar
    forever!

Needwood, old manse! long neglected, thy
    shadows of trees,
Hug round thee of moonlight and mingle their
    ghosts in the breeze;
Thy form, antiquated, pieced out and partitioned
    and shrunk,
Seems the cells of a soul's transmigration, but ever
    a monk.

PACKHORSE FORD

(NEAR SHEPHERDSTOWN, VA.)

THE Stone Age man learned first the ford, by
    hammer stones his footing taught;
The bison next, which dammed the flood and with
    his dusty nostril, thought;
The Indian from his moccasins their deer foot
    crossing instinct caught.

The wild goose had it in his blood and squawked
    the trail the panther dyed,
The wild crane stalked the ford for pike and
    stood a guide post, man to guide,

The river in more shallow tones expressed the
    shallows it might hide.

So, when the hunted outlaw came, he saw the
    trodden ramparts slant,
The trail go down and reappear like ends of rain-
    bows consonant;
He told the peltry hunter where to guide the
    woods-lost emigrant.

From Rhenish plains where feudal fields minions
    of barons taxed upon,
And Baltic coasts and Holland swamps, some
    wilderness in right to own,
A living river found the ford while planets
    brooded Washington.

The Golden Horseshoe picnic knights from one
    blue Gap had looked afar,
Then, sank in tideland like the orb that is both
    morn and evening star,
Before the Germans flanked the sun, slow as their
    Georgian calendar.

Behind the mountain lines they slid along the
    crystal drains of snows,
And found the Tuscarora's gaps he ambushed
    for Catawba foes,
And passed the ford at dusk's red hour while
    sunset's vizor masks and glows.

Potomac's flowing cools their lives and in the
    ripples cattle bend;

The packhorse feels his burden fall, the smith's
    fire smokes the kit to mend;
Their white knees laving, as they pray, the songs
    of pilgrim maids ascend:

Stout Luther's hymns and Baptist staves from
    John of Leyden's choral tongue,
And Simon Menmo's madrigals, the Dunker
    lovers tuned 'among;
They stood upon Virginia's rim and every hope
    was virgin young.

The katydids the hollow night with their re-
    sounding snoring fill,
The Switzer whistler calls to him the country-
    wondering whippoorwill,
Leaps in the moonbeam gleaming trout and into
    Echo sounds distil.

Yost Hite and Jan Van Meter led the Teutons to
    their grants of space;
Above the ford New Mecklenburg glassed in the
    river lake its face,—
Lord Fairfax measured all within his patent tied
    with royal lace.

At Greenway court his banished life in As You
    Like It joys were sinned,
Young Washington invaded there for Liberty, his
    Rosalind,
And stretched Virginia's sandal foot far as the
    Ganges of our Ind.

The men of Morgan crossed the ford nor stopped
    till Boston's siege they swelled,
They drowned the fame of Gates and Lee who
    past the Packhorse crossing dwelled,
And greeting them, his old chainmen, the great
    Surveyor's eyes o'er welled.

To Rumsey's steamboat screamed reply the fierce
    bald eagle o'er the ford,
As the experimental trip the Cincinnati's chiefs
    record:
A thousand years are but a day to Evolution and
    the Lord.

The bridges o'er Potomac span, and still the old
    ford had its loves;
Josephs and Maries came this way, untaxed amidst
    the thirsty droves
That panted down the cool ravines and lapped the
    pools by willow coves.

Then, closed the vine its vestibules and river
    travelers knew it not;
The Packhorse Ford in slumber lay like some old
    ferry right forgot
Till on its bank. Armies appeared, roused by an
    angry nation's shot.

The natural route of savage times the savage
    issues had restored
And like the loadstone to its star, Northward
    revolved the gleaming sword;
Redder than sunsets was the blood that swelled
    the moan o'er Packhorse Ford.

As, hereabout, the ridges cease, in countermarches
    parallel,
South Mountain in the Short Hills lost, the Blue
    Ridge in Elk Mountain's swell,
Reverberated on the ford the Northern cheer, the
    Southern yell.

Antietam, Gettysburg respond to Strasburg's roar
    and Winchesters;
The armies, like the bisons, dam the waters that
    the guns immerse;
Then, swiftly, peace grew like the corn and Free-
    men's was the universe.

The armies paused as, on the Rhine, the German
    host and German France
Held truce in times of Charlemagne and perished
    every dissonance,
Except the finished German tongue and the soft
    parley of Romance.

A blended race one destiny swelled like Potomac's
    current down,
Each old ingredient making rhyme in the Ameri-
    can renown;
The old ford still its beauty held, like lovely girls
    of Shepherdstown.

The raccoon ogled with the doves that cooed
    above in sycamores,
The fisher cast his fly for bass, wading upon the
    pebbled floors,
And grounded on the hidden path the skiff with
    its suspended oars.

How lovely everything appears, as if composed
    it ever stood!
We do not see the prints of time beneath the
    riffles and the flood.
The ford that our forefathers crossed is in the
    river of our blood.

FREDDIE'S CLOCK

"Nothing to eat; neither pork nor crock,—
We must sell the old tall Clock!"
Dandy Grimes with a tear in his eye
Kissed wife Freddie a smug good-bye.

She was used to being alone;
Only the Clock she could call her own:
Its two cherubs, the Sun and Moon,
Her sole babies, would leave her soon.

'Twixt them, upside, rode a ship;
'Twixt them, downside, a house did slip;
Human-faced were the Moon and Sun:
Save these babies, Freddie had none.

Everything had been sold to live:
Dandy was shiftless and fugitive.
Now he had gone away in the snow:
How the wind on the cape did blow!

Middletown valley the snowdrifts block
From the creek to the high White Rock;
Midst the mountains the old frame house
Was going down, like her ruined spouse.

Orphan child, she had married him, —
So parental, important, prim, —
Cradle he gave her but nothing to rock,
Only the twins in the old tall Clock.

Now he was old and she was young;
Over a Poor House fate she hung:
Faithful, filial, never at times
Saw she a life beyond Dandy Grimes.

Close to the old tall Clock she stood,
In its coffin of cherry wood,
Varnished, respectable and plumb;
Staid as she to her pendulum.

Round its fading dial of white,
Gold and colors remained as bright
As the face of Freddie in tears,
Midst her dial of golden years.

Tall as the minute hand her stand:
Dandy was shrunk like the hour hand.
Merry as Dandy, full of his swig,
Clicked the second hand's thingumagig.

But the Moon with its hairless brow
Wondered, black-eyed, at Freddie now;
Red its cheek as an apple's blush,
Ticking to hear from her: " Baby, *hush!*

" O, how lonely I will be,
Children, dear, when ye go from me !
Time I will know by the farmers' bells
When my little ones Dandy sells.

"Down in the Poor House of Montévue
Frederick's bells. I will think, are you, —
By-o-babies!" was Freddie's cry —
Sobs were choking her lullaby.

Fire went out and Freddie, wrapped
In her last thin coverlets, napped, —
Feeling the old house tremble and rock,
Hearing the notes of the old house Clock.

Dreaming of officers fetched from far,
Friends of her father in the great War,—
Some she nursed, in her child's short frock :
" Tick ! tick ! tick !" said the old tall Clock.

There was one, who had called her "Wife";
Saying her beauty would scent his life;
Saying her youth was his hollyhock :
" Tick ! tick ! tick !" said the old tall Clock.

"Where is Dandy? I hungry grow :
He is feeble and deep the snow !
Dandy has neither a glove nor a sock."
" Tick ! tick ! tick !" said the old tall Clock.

Sudden, sleigh bells trembled a-cold :
Stood in the doorway a stranger bold,
Saying, " Pardon me not to knock !"
" Tick ! tick ! tick !" said the old tall Clock.

" Are they dead like the old man here,
I have fetched in my sleigh, his bier?
Frozen woman ! no fire ! no sock !"
" Tick ! tick ! tick !" said the old tall Clock.

Making a fire of the farmer's fence,
Chafing her body without pretence, —
Fair as a child in her frozen smock,
("Tick! tick! tick!" said the old tall Clock.)

The good stranger performed his task,
Warmed her throat from his brandy flask,
Called her "Freddie, his hollyhock" —
"Tick! tick! tick!" said the old tall Clock.

She arose in a fine man's arms,
Bare as the house were her tingled charms:
"Dandy is frozen!" she cried with a shock:
"Tick! tick! tick!" said the old tall Clock.

"Child! who nursed me out of my death!
Take back from me the warmth and breath
I remembered from thy limbs' lock!
("Tick! tick! tick!" said the old tall Clock.)

"Not thy face, though it is as sweet:
I remember thy beautiful feet,
Straight as the corn ere the battle's shock:
("Tick! tick! tick!" said the old tall Clock.)

"Far have I come, in a widower's glow,
To thy bloom, in the pure, white snow;
Round thy poverty snowbirds flock.
("Tick! tick! tick!" said the old tall Clock.)

"I have the blessing men call wealth;
Thou hast the riches of beauty and health:
Take my name and adorn my gold!"
Freddie clasped him, it was so cold:

"Do not sell my Clock from me!—
Its dear babies will honor thee.
They are the last of Dandy's stock:"
"Tick! tick! tick!" said the old tall Clock.

YERTES' SPRING

(NEAR GAPLAND)

"THE fairy spring wells up from sands,
Beneath the mountain's heavy hands,
And from its pebbly basin's bath
A brook's white feet have worn a path,
While circling round, old beech trees dream,
Like eunuchs guarding an hareme;
So close beneath the mountain bowed
It seems a lakelet in a cloud."

Lionel said so, bending him
Over the percolating brim
Whose many sources flash and cease
With effervescing, silent peace:

"Could I some elf-appointment make,
At midnight, by this spring-starred lake,
Imaginations might arise
Like to these twinkling, fluvial eyes
Within my fluent cells of brain
That fill with thoughts like springs of rain!"

A pheasant boomed his thought away,
A crow called downward "stay! stay! stay!"

Lionel bathed him in the pool
And, lying down, with life blood cool,
Fell into sleep, till midnight drew
Between the peaks her baldric blue.

Lionel woke.   The fairy lin
Spirits effulgent held within;
From every vortex whirled a sprite,
A quivering lily, chemised white,
A lady toiletted for night.
He thought the Dunker maids, baptized,
Had lingered here etherealized,
From the near settlement sedate
On Love feast night to recreate;
But as he sidled round the rim
Their white arms flashed to signal him,
Their voices like the cascade sing:
" Thou hast desired us at the spring."

Lionel old drew near to list:
The first young maid he ever kissed
Dandled upon a silver jet —
He breathed the osculation yet;
She said, " My love, our love was brief,
As in my eddy spins a leaf!"
Another nymph Lionel sprayed,
A different and a country maid:
Sighing " beneath a bridge at dark
You were my daring city spark!"
Another Naiad's voice liquate
Flowed, " Love came to us through a gate!"
A fourth with rhythm like a rune,

" Lionel, once in my ripe June
I lower'd my eyes that flashed a dart
Into thy uncourageous heart!"
" We never touched," said one, " our lips,
Only our trembling finger tips,
But they remembered it till dead!"
Another, " Love, we rioted,
Like these swoll'n sources after storm:
Long have I banqueted the worm!"
" Widow am I, than thou more old, —
Thou would'st have wed me when boy-bold!"
" Lionel, I am one, whose grief,
At my cold hearthstone, for relief,
Fled to thee like a maniac:
Thou wert a friend and led me back!"
" I, one illiterate, in a mart
Who read thy exile with her heart!"
" I am the Nun whose holiday
Thy touch made everlasting May!"
" I, twinkling from this spiral sill,
Am she whose action was thy Will!"
" And I, thou called Rose beauteous
And would have twisted from her pride,
For womanhood lived duteous
And scenting Virtue for thee, died!"

Thus, from the mountain syphon rise
To Amoroso's faded eyes,
His nymphs, who in life's sources moved,
Exhilarated, bubbled, loved;
Returned in hydrostatic power —
They were a hundred in an hour, —

Flowing from Lionel's brain cells
And from the menstruum of the wells ;
Earth's drip from out her cavern chasm
And waste of parent protoplasm, —
The saturation of life's plant
And spill of Pluto's adamant.
   Upon the sand-baked mountain's lymph
Glides each liquescent, fluent nymph ;
And each one, had it vorticed well,
Might have been dame to Lionel !
Each had combined with his some part,
'Livened some recess of his heart,
To its pain's ache her balsam lent
And purled away its sediment.

The constellations over pass
And in the Spring a period glass,
Each shattered in the short embrace
By life's resurging in its face.

Life's active Spring, pneumatic strong,
Retains no orb's impression long,
No dalliance can make it glow,
Like energy of birth below.

The pressure of the life to be,
On everything lies equally ;
And like the bubbles, which escape,
One or another takes our shape.
For momentary is love's touch,
The hungry one his food must clutch,
The pair that float adown the stream
Give and receive the instant's gleam !

Lionel felt that all was good,
And man's refreshment, womanhood ;
Love's every passing chemistry
Had left some immortality.
The scent of its capricious hours,
Was still like banks of graveyard flowers ;
She who in myrtle's streamlets lies
And sends up tendrils of blue bell,
Entwined our instant's destinies
And kissed our heart up from a well.

The camps of stars put out their lights ;
Day breakfasted upon the heights
And sowed with gold the furrowland ;
Lionel's hand was in some hand :
" What were they, husband ? " said his wife.
" *Bubbles, once beautiful, of life !* "

BALTIMORE

HANGING from the bay bough's azure heights —
    Affluent bough like matron's flowing breast —
Baltimore in black and golden lights
    Flashes like the oriole from its nest ;
Round the red warehouses on their slips,
    Through the old commercial city's maze,
Stands a phantom fleet of yarded ships,
    Rumbles the long serenade of drays.

First of Western cities in our land,
    Last born sailor-city of the East,
Inland reached its pike-roads like a hand,

Oceanward, like Venice, it increased.
Washington beheld it as a weed,
  Ere he died its splendor looked upon,
Growing with the genius and speed
  Of its one compeer, Napoleon.

He, the Doge of Europe, reaching o'er,
  Adriatic Chesapeake to wed,
Dropped a wedding ring in Baltimore,
  Left his last successor in its bed;
Still its beauteous women like the noon
  With their dusky eyelids' sweeping wings,
Give the strangers' heart a summer swoon;
  Whom they love are happier than Kings.

Fleeing Congress sought it a retreat;
  Base of vict'ry gathered at Yorktown;
Samson grinding in its mills of wheat,
  All the bayports fell to its renown.
Iron, marble, bitumen and brick
  Grew as shellfish near its deep'ning piers;
Landsmen landed in its *mécanique;*
  All its water-men were privateers.

Athens might old tyrants fawn upon;
  Spartan Baltimore, our young recourse,
Formed her phalanx around Madison —
  Taught America another force.
When our flag the smoke o'er Henry clomb,
  Key's bright anthem, in spontaneous flow,
Arched it like the streaming of the bomb —
  Arch that rounded in the pool of Poe.

As the blue streams flow toward the bay
  And the golden wheat toward the mills,
To the milling city take their way
  Blue and flaxen Germans from the hills.
Like the twilights on the Chesapeake,
  Which through crystal bars their purple pour,
Latin, Creole, Moorish contrasts streak
  British, Celtic, Baltic Baltimore.

Stepping down the spires to the ships,
  Like the cascades from their woodland wells,—
Like the melodies of lovers' lips, —
  Chime the foundry city's tender bells,
And the pungy fleet from Eastern Shore
  Skimming like the wild fowl on the dawn,
Brings the pearly sweets to Baltimore,
  Riding in the basin like its swan.

First in War, his column calm upon,
  Stands the great Virginian, looking o'er,
Where the victor ranks of Wellington
  Broke before the boys of Baltimore ;
And the last survivor, left alone
  Of the Magna Charta's daring theme,
Laid the nave's cathedral corner-stone
  O'er the young nativity of Steam.

As the tree its annual growth compiles,
  Binding silently the circle's marks,
Grew the beech tree Annual of Niles,
  Budded evergreen the staff of Sparks.
O, ye merchants ! on your commonweal

Sits the raven, saying "Nevermore"
To the native palette of your Peale;
  Wirt and Kennedy were Baltimore.

Forum of the Capital, herein
  Met the Tribunes in Convention first,
Making Presidents amidst the din,
  Where the local factions fretted worst;
Jackson broke Virginia's cabal,
  Pierce, Van Buren passed the chariot score,
Lincoln crowned upon the Lupercal
  Faced his martyrdom from Baltimore.

As for Helen's beauty, all the Greeks
  Troy besieged, the valiant armies tore
All thy ports and plateaus, Chesapeake!
  For thy bloom's possession, Baltimore!
In thy heart two spouses did contend
  And to each one thou had'st given thy hand,
But the ring thou cherished to the end
  Was thy mother's blessing, Maryland!

Gliding in the current like the boat,
  That in times colonial was their chaise,
Dove-pure, in the hurly-burly float
  Faces of the old tidewater days;
Matrons of the Marylander peace,
  Daughters of the old housekeeping life;
In their arms is "Multiply! Increase!"
  In their souls, religion of The Wife.

As the white mists go up from the bay
  To the marble heights that oversee,

All the life colonial clears away
  To the city's higher destiny.
On the railways of the mainland shore,
  Midst the Cinque Ports' warden cities strung,
Shines the jewel light of Baltimore,
  Like a star, Orion's Belt among.

SIR JOHN ST. CLAIR

BUILDER OF THE FIRST ROAD ACROSS THE MOUNTAINS

His name is lost save in a brook of water
  That darkly plunges down a forest glen,
Like that lean army pioneered to slaughter
  Through lonely shades to horrible Duquesne;
  But in the road he hewed across the mountains,
Where Braddock sleeps beneath his wagon wheels,
  A living brook goes on from Eastern fountains,
No wars arrest, no killing frost congeals.

His was the skiff that hardily descended
  The wild Potomac to the roaring falls,
His were the floats the soldiery befriended
  To pass the torrent, under mountain walls;
  His were the bridges over the Opequan
And the Antietam in the morn of time,
  Crossed by a multitude no man can reckon
To sceneries and destinies sublime.

Behind his axes formed the van of movement,
  His picks and shovels were the conquering
    swords;

And in the rift of light he ope'd, Improvement
  Went single file, through hidden savage hordes,
  Until the pack mules with their bells were merry
Where rolling drums in vain inspired the fight,
  And sheep and shepherds tarried by the ferry
That drowned a host amidst the battle's fright.

High-mettled Scot! thine is no glory hollow:
  Shall we forget thee in our Westward Ho?—
When thy canoe the laden barges follow
  And up thy path the steaming engines blow?
  No! while the sky the Alleghany arches,
The good road builder's name shall be revealed:
  Sir John St Clair's victorious army marches
Above the army lost on Braddock's field.
    1874.

SOUTH MOUNTAIN

A BROWN STUDY

Bill! my black horse, end your pawing!
  We must have our Sunday canter
On the sky line of South Mountain:
  Take it easy, Billy! Saunter!
Till, above the Gap, five hundred
  Feet you rise and find the level,
Then, warmed up, your eye and nostril
  Take the beauty of the devil
And you show me kingdoms many,
  Fertile valleys bounding free,
But your horse sense never mentioned

" Take them all and worship me! "
Nature's worship is the freest from idolatry.

Like Bellerophon's high saddle,
  Ramps the gap of Solomon,
Where the Blue Ridge swerves Potomac:
  Drooping low, its course is done.
Like its colts, low mountains gambol
  Round its neck, in woodlands bended;
To McClellan's height they ramble
  And Antietam's vale extended
Far as Kittatinny's wand, —
Nation-vale of Cumberland.

Southward, valleys like white arms
Separate from breathing charms
Of pink hillocks; Cupid's locked in
Venus mountains of Catoctin:
Through their embrasures I see
Aurora kiss Monocracy.
Four republics interlock
From the dome of the White Rock;
Penn and Calvert, Smith and Brown,
Circle round me their renown.
Bayward, like an antistrophe,
Tiptoes, tender Sugarloaf.

O! how silent in the air,
Whilst the churchbells low to prayer!
Here, where thunder clouds are riven
And the Christians quail at heaven,
Not a being, scarce a bird,
In the golden light is heard

Of this long cathedral nave,
Where, of yore, the hunted slave
Walked this mountain's bulwark far,
Worshipping the polar star,
Hoping to escape the rod
Of them, downward, praising God !
And the high-souled mountain, free,
Leaped at birth from slavery, —
Without company set forth
For its destiny in the North ;
Striding rivers, till it passed
To New England's rock, at last.[1]

Where the edged-up rock is crusted
Hangs a shelf of green *débris*,
Like a mantel for Penates
In the Greek mythology
And along its cornice groovèd,
Riding o'er the deep abyss,
To be Ovid, I am movèd,
In a metamorphosis.
What is that I see, resolving
From a rock, to be a man ?
By his flat nose and his hoofness,
'Tis the pagan fellow, Pan !

---

[1] The South Mountain of Maryland is the Blue Ridge of
the South, or rather its countermarch, beginning a few miles
south of the Potomac, while the Blue Ridge dies out a few
miles north of the Potomac, near Antietam battlefield. The
"fault" or dislocation is so marked, that the sections of
former Slavery and Freedom appear to be broken by nature,
in these oppositely-proceeding ridges.

" Buy my rattler's rattles, Mister?
I hoodooed the snake with words:
Me and him was brother and sister—
Hissed and kissed like a couple of birds!"

" Pan, thou rascal! Well I know thee!—
Son of Dryops, Hermés by:
Woods and mountain were thy parents,
Tangled in the tingling sky!"

" Hi yi! Mister, you're on to me
And your Greek I understand;
When they Christianized old Hellas
I moved into Maryland.
Every preacher has a sect yer
And United Brethren split,—
Sunday mornings, how they lecture,
When the old zinc churchbells quit!
Nymphs and swains I make afraid;
My South Mountain thunder storms
Beat all preachers in the trade,
And I sell all the Reforms.
Breeches hide my fetlocks hairy,
I go courting like a younker,
And trail up the mountain fairy
With my long beard, like a Dunker."

" Pan, I like thee; come with me!
Let us worship Poetry!"

" My splithoof is no soft sock:
I will race you to Black Rock!

There I have a noble fountain,
Wrist-thick, plunging from the mountain,—
Nectar hidden in a spring,
Jove's own cuckoo bird, to sing:
Give your snaffle-bit release:
Follow me to Gods and Greece!"

Scarce my horse could keep in sight
Pan, who skipped from Gap to height;
All the battle crest he passed,
Now and then a smirk to cast
Back to me, to beckon on,
When the folks to church had gone;
In his head I seemed to trace
Satyr Lincoln's kindly face,
Who his armies thence did see,
And made all the sorry, free.
When his pipe friend Pan inhales
Fancy may free all the vales,
Move the stones of ignorance
And make stocks and reptiles dance!

Worship hushed their hector tune,
As we lost the bells of Boon,
And betwixt two mountains strode,
Up a ravine-smothered road.
Then unto the ridge we cling,
Till we, three, bend to a spring,
And we hear a chorus rise
From the woodlands to the skies.

"Hist!" said Pan, and horn-piped free:
"Hear Grandfather's family!"

THE IMMORTALS

Father! 'twas thy power
Sired us life's fond hour! —
Thy delight bequeathed
When thy strong love breathed:
Bless thy wilful rove!
We are thine by Love.

Mother! 'twas thy charm
Made thy lover warm!
And the mingled blood
Cannot but be good:
Bless the nuptial grove!
Thou art ours by Love.

JOVE, JUNO, LETO, THEMIS, DIONE

Children! Human fruit!
Evil to impute
To the hands that pull
Ye, life beautiful,
Is life to reprove!
Ye are ours by Love.

PAN AND THE BIRDS

The mountain is so slim,
There is only room for him
I bring this Sunday prim,
To know the Gods of old —
Cheery jug hoo-e, pu twit chee!
He loves them for themselves,
The woods and fauns and elves;

His repartee is bold,
And he dropped at once on me:
Jug jug cheery, ha tu pu tsee!

Than from the black firs nigh,
As startled vultures fly,
There came a fluttering, —
Great shadows shook a-wing, —
And Pan to me exclaimed:
"Push on or be heaven-shamed!"

He stooped upon his haunches
And bent aloft the branches.
I followed on the ledge
Out to the mountain's edge,
And such a landscape burst
Upon my sense, that first
I gave not Gods their duty,
In our own Planet's beauty.

The whole world seemed my own,
And I its lover lone,
The great Black Rock my throne.
Its broken pulpits swing
Dizzily staggering
Up from the *débris* scorched,
Where furry forests, torched,
Blackened the acres strown
Of mountain overthrown,
Then grew again in stone:
Pluto's wide blasted mines,
Encompassed by green pines,
That like concentric waves

Moaned in the mountain caves,
And, farther, yet away,
The lands like ocean lay, —
Towns, woods in fainter tone
Fading into a zone,
Till nothing was defined,
But magic, on the mind
And Love, that thrilling is,
Like fear before the kiss.

"O! blue Ægean waves
Of land, that Hellas laves,
Among the isles of arts, —
Along the Lydian marts,
And Thessalonian caves!
Can no Minerva sway
Thy dull inertia?
No Graces oversee
Thy Christianity?
No Muses come to teach
The dervishes who preach?
Nor wake the moral Three
Who sleep eternally?
Xerxes is overthrown
But Pallas is unknown.
Venus is Vulcan's love
But where is golden Jove?
Olympian genius, rise!
And charm our destinies!"

The sound of sledges, breaking
    Of gravestones, for a larking,

And ba-a-ing lambs a-quaking,
  And cut-throat dogs a-barking,
Came to me, echoing up,
  Like Tantalus's cup.

"Welcome, thou friend of Pan!"
A hidden voice began.

Around me, on the rocks,
In store clothes and in frocks,
A gypsy party lay,
In silent holiday, —
A strolling minstrel band.

All rose and shook my hand.

Behind the life that plods,
I recognized the Gods.

As one, high Jove, I deemed,
An eagle rose and screamed.

I said unto him, then,
"Father of Gods and Men!"

He looked a wise man-reader
And sapient woman pleader
And, all around, safe leader.

"Stopped is the world," said Jove,
"When Gods do never move:
We move, where most we love,
With men, our Goddish boys.
As urchins love their toys

And think them real things,
We are infantile kings.
Our origin was wrack
But never look we back,
No more than suns lament
Nebulous sediment:
Onward and formative
We join or would not live.
Conversions we despise, —
Sect-makers so entice.
A natural man art thou?
So are thy Gods, I trow!
　Strong policy and span
Rule all the breathing mass.
　I love thee, for the Man,
That is my looking-glass!"

CHORUS OF HOURS

Man! for whom Sabbaths were made!
　Walk in the cornfield and pluck!
Hunger, the God thou obeyed;
　Ere thou couldst see, thou hadst suck:
Tottering ere thou couldst talk,
　Laughing before thou didst teethe,
Why shouldst thou crawl, who can walk?
　Why shouldst thou mope, who can breathe?

THE GRACES

Woman! for love thou wert born, —
　Hast thou no goddess of Love?
Fade, in the amorous morn,
　All thy sky sisters above:

Venus the star of the Even,
   Jupiter star of the Morn,
Moon, the soft mistress of heaven.
   Loveless thy life is forlorn.

THE MUSES

Mind! in a barren infinity,
   Lost are thy glorious parts!
Dwarfed in a mystical trinity
   Tranced are the beautiful arts:
Fancy, asleep, that enthuses,
   Thought that is stagnant in creeds;
Greed has degraded thy Muses,
   Form has enslaved thee with needs.

—————

Here, Neptune upon Billy springs:
The horse immediately had wings
And bore him off to crystal wells,
Proud as of winter's sleighing bells.

Mercury, with his pinions loosed,
(Pan's father) Juno introduced,
A stalwart dame, who said to me,
" They libel me with jealousy ;
Seldom with Jove am I at odds ;
True Gods are never jealous Gods.
He is not of that passive lymph
Jocund to be with one poor nymph,
He sometimes plays a prank with me,
To test my femininity :
I stamp my foot and make him beg."
(She had a straight, celestial leg.)

" Of all the mothers e'er I saw,
I would take you for mother-in-law ! "

" Here, Hébé, daughter ! Lemonade !
Heaven only keeps one servant maid,
And, more than one, makes earth's distress,
Among the servant-scourged *richesse*."

The red bird dyed not the bough-tryst
Bright as the cup on Hébé's wrist :

" I would that Hébé made a slip —
Many — betwixt her cup and lip ! "

She made me tender Iris know
And said, " Here is my only bow ! "

Mars, in an old blue soldier cloak —
Frog in his throat, — next to me spoke :
" This is my friend, Venus the fiighty,
The wife of Vulcan, — Aphrodité ! "

A trim brunette raised her grey eyes,
She was of loving, precious size,
Her features Greek and regular,
The soft soul of the evening star.
She had a vestal, hearthside look,
Its twilight glow my being shook ;
Her bosom, perfect as the dove,
Breathed coolest innocence of love.
Something of trust her quiet shed,
As on my heart to lay her head.

" O thou for man not always best !
Whence bringest thou that soul of rest ? "

" Man's mightiest needs I rule," said she,
" Mother of Immortality."

The glorious landscape faded quite,
Love was a world more infinite;
No stranger was this lady now:
Once I had kissed her low, white brow
And trembled at my daring feint;
She was my neighbor and a saint.

" Hark! sir, my husband is mending
Bicycles, for our descending! "

VULCAN
(Sings.)

The mountain forges throb no more;
  They lost their iron soul
When failed the ore banks of the ore,
  The woodlands of charcoal:
Far West the fuel and the vein
  Into each other flow, —
But Vulcan's hammer wakes again
  Echó! Echó! Echó!

(Echoes repeat.)

The mountain streams know not the mill,
  Far West the grain fields sweep;
In ruined mills the whippoorwill
  Lulls, with its plaint, to sleep;
But tender arts still haunt the glen,
  Light winks the dynamo, —
And Vulcan loves the sons of men:
  Echó! Echó! Echó!

Now, Pan set up his pipe to blow,
And all the Gods formed in a row
To trip it to the spring and spout —
Apollo led the happy rout, —
A fine book-agent, starved off here,
And dieted on atmosphere.

He said "all books these good Dutch lack,
But one, ' Hagerstown's Almanac.' "

Pallas-Minerva took my arm:
She had a man-in-woman charm,
Her precious book to me she lent,
" Darwin on Species and Descent."

" Goddess," said I, " from Jove's own head, —
Born never in a mother's bed, —
Why are not more born from the skull? "

" Because all would be beautiful."

" Hast thou not loved, who art so kind? "

" Yes, men love me when they grow blind.
I am, in their descending life,
The evening lamp, the second wife.
No beauty have I to repine, —
Never youth's wedded concubine,
My tongue is mellow as my theme
And leads them to the love Supreme.
Prudence, my mother, swallowèd,
Grew, to her time, in father's head :
He paid of birth the cruel tax,

And was delivered with the ax ;
Let men so suffer Wisdom's birth, —
I shall have sisters round the Earth."

Mercury's turtle shell strung lute
And Minerva's pure toned flute, —
Jove, bandmaster, singing bass, —
After Pan's wildpipe made chase.
To Apollo's harp piano
Swayed the quiver of Diana.
Down the wood's track to the glen
All the troupe went dancing then :
When Gods are social, so are men.

Neptune's trident surely shook
From the mountain slide, the brook
That spills down the cairn and cavern,
Near the short-lived drinking tavern,
By whose stone foundations course
Springlets up without a source,
Cool as evening mists distil ;
Cooler yet where bursts a rill
In the roadlet down the height.
Like a naked beam of light,
Or a mountain bather naked,
Chilled by tourists overtakèd.

As upon a roof's descent
Pigeons cluster confident,
On this mountain pitch to sing
The Olympians drank the spring
And beneath them, deep and long,
Earth heard the Libation song.

JOVE

Mortal! friend! down from my height
  I salute thy gallant worth!
Rain, Alluvial, Dew and Light
  My libations to thee, Earth!
Back to me reciprocal,
  Thou libation sendest up:
Faithful son, thy prodigal
  Father, Jove, drains mutual cup!

JUNO

Nephew! often in thy night
  To thyself thou slumb'rest dull,
I stoop o'er thee with my light
  And I see thee, beautiful.
And I know when I am old
  Welcome in thy home I'll be:
In her chalice flashing gold,
  Hearty Hera drinks to thee!

THE GODS

Cousin! take this pledge from us,
  As through youth thy genius plods:
Steady and industrious
  Thou art pattern to all Gods!
In thy orbit spaced afar
  Bravely all thy lights are set.
Glory to thee! little star!
  Thou may'st sway thy system yet!

"Hist!" spoke Pan. "The Dunkers I smell!
Grandfather! whisker us by thy spell!"
Whiskers were on us in a flash,
All but the shaven, beau moustache.
"Now," cried Pan, "as his special treat
That one Mortal shall wash our feet!
Sunday Love Feasts please these churls,
Washing the feet of the men and girls."

I was girt with a napkin swift:
Juno's foot stretched out from her shift.
She as a convert was slightly chipper —
I thought I had pulled down the Great Dipper.
Iris's foot was a blue-veined bow;
A silver thimble was Hébé's toe;
Diana ne'er had shed but by candle
The deerskin shank of her corded sandal;
Pallas-Athena was flat on the sole;
Venus's foot was sleek as a mole;
All the Muses declaimed together
To be assisted out of leather;
Meek were the Graces for heavenly powers;
Fidgety feet had the three young Hours.
Parian cold, from celestial fountains,
"Beautiful feet upon the mountains!"
I preached in tingled soul, when through:
Apollo's wood dove cooed "Cuckoo!"

Leathern scabbard a lady's boot,
Gleaming sword is her naked foot,
Armorers tempered it express
Duelling blade of her loveliness.
Hand in hand is a soothing sense,

Frank young foot is a confidence.
Women none were there at meat
When they washed Disciples' feet,
Had they brightened that repast
Would the Supper have been the Last?

Dunkers, new to the situation,
Muttered that man was an innovation
The feet of *Schwesters* to dry and cool.
Jove said ours was a later school.
Languid after the foot-bath rites,
Nectar sufficed for our appetites:
Cider of pears it seeemed to me
Or honey and water stung by a bee.
"Give us adwise!" chirped old St. John.
The Dunkers hearing the hymn were gone:

APOLLO TO THE DUNKERS

Not everything is God's!
  Beware the levity
To think Olympus nods
  When trifles trouble thee!
Take to the Gods thy joys!
  Take to thyself thy moan!
When life's fulfilment cloys,
  The failure is thine own.

Some other life had been
  A substitute for thee:
Blessèd art thou of men,
  By love's fortuity;
The bee that finds his queen

High in the golden light,
Dies in that heaven serene
For love's wild appetite.

So grasp life's real span,
Nor cheat thyself with dreams,
Thou planetary man!
What is, is but what seems.
A dead man's helpless hand
Can never heal thy sore.[1]
So live to understand:
Thy children may live more.

The beauteous evening, red and pale,
Moved slowly up the golden dale.
" Come forth, sweet Nymphs!" Pan softly blew;
We saw their fire-fly eyes shine through
The bosky woods, their shoulders gleam
Out of the dripping spring and stream,
In every rock and shaggy tree
Coquettish sensibility.
The charmèd snakes, autocthones ran,
Gliding from serpent forms to man;
Tree crickets, members of his quire,
Resounded to Apollo's lyre;
Diana's silver quiver spilled
Her arrows where the wise owl trilled, —
Minerva's bird; and round us browse
Mercury's herd of mountain cows.
Jove drew me from those twinkling elves —
All priests are gentle by themselves.

[1] Healing by a dead man's hand is one of many mountain
superstitions.

"Now, tell me, Zeus! why do men,
When born of women, fall again?"

"Son, why do rocks melt into sands
Unless to soften fertile lands!
Climbing to fall, the circle's revel,
That once was Nebulous and level.
Vigor ascends, a radiant star,
To slide in pleasure back as far;
No depths, no heights, no fall, no rise,
No female and no destinies.
Heaven is a lazy dream of statics;
The Sibyls' books are mathematics.

" My sect calls me the great First Cause
And proves it, by my breaking laws;
Gods no occasion had to be
Unless to aid society.
What need of Gods for blank and dearth?
Olympian Gods succeeded Earth.
Man was the model made in clay,
We were the statues made to stay:
What made us?   Matter!   Not some Spell!
Spell's Gods are immaterial.
O Ignorance! reversing laws
And calling impotence, the Cause!
Nothing sustains thy faith's far end,
But Something is irreverend!
Was Light made first out of the night?
Thou knowest Matter to be Light;
Matter the whirler and the ball,
And quenchless Matter made us All.

" Why am I, alien from my parts,
  In minds of scholars still a force ?
I supervisèd real arts
  And was the soul of intercourse.
Not when my sway was imbecile,
  Did I all people drown but one,
And millions let go wild until
  I thought to give myself a son ;
My happy reign, my temples grand,
  For Popes the Christian artist paints :
I was the Genius of my Land
  And made my family its saints."

Now, by the old burnt tavern's site
It seemed there was a country fight,
And to my feet, by discord thrown,
There fell an apple like a stone ;
Three ladies, Venus, Juno, Pallas,
Ran after it with pretty malice,
And each one pleaded, " Give it me ! "
Said Jove : " Name thy divinity ! "

The apple could its mistress read,
Attracted toward her by its seed.
Had apples three been on the stem
The ladies three had taken them.
But like to Eve, I had but one,

And One was in my heart alone.
In simple mind, a Paris man,
(Not taking cue from winking Pan),
I said to Venus, without art,
" What's mine is thine, my old sweetheart ! "

"Nature," said Jove, " is always wit:
Venus, he is no hypocrite!"
"Paris I knew," she said, "in France:
Come be my partner in the dance!"

Now, as it chanced, the thickets from,
Were Dunkers playing Peeping Tom,
With mountaineers, whom Jove abhors
To eavesdrop on his visitors;
Their wild beard tufted from their throats,
Jove turned them all to billy-goats;
Then on the turf beside the spring
Jove led off with a Highland Fling.
The Muses and Wood Dryads met
In a decórous minuet.

Venus with buskin like a glove,
In somnolent, mesmeric move,
Grew to me as the woodbines creep
Or dreams glide in the mind asleep.
Drowsy the breath she drank of mine
And hers inspiring as a wine,
Her motion passive but as close
As to the rose stem hangs the rose.
Submission is the female might,
Her yielding coy and recondite:
When in the waltz I turned her round
I seemed to bear her from the ground.
She brimmed my being with her mould
And we were timid more than bold,
Though on my breast her little brain
Lay like a throb of parting pain.

"Thy horse!" the Goddess faintly sighed,
"Give me the night wind! let us ride!
My rivals watch us and their hate
Means something evil in your fate."

Her wish, straightway, unto us brings
Billy, Bellerophoned with wings;
She raised her foot my hand unto
And in my palm she left her shoe.

Out in the air and o'er the knolls
Catoctin's ragged valley bowls,
We sprang so high that o'er both heights
We saw the pulsing, pearly lights,
Amid the plain with hamlets thick,
Of Hagerstown and Frederick.
The earth dropped smaller yet and far,
We entered in a glowing star;
Its scented atmosphere we clove
And rested in the planet, Love.
I felt a chaste, maternal kiss
And sighed 'twixt holiness and bliss.

"Look out!" spoke Venus, "do not fear!
See of thy system every sphere! —
And each does every other draw:
Attraction is eternal law.
So thou selected Venus well;
In equilibrium is her spell,
She is the tender influence
Of centre and circumference.
Be to thine own attraction true,
And to thy friend will fit my shoe!"

I woke next morn at Gapland Hall
And found black Billy in his stall.

But though my story is all true,
I cannot fit that Venus shoe.

WASHINGTON CITY POEMS.

THE SMITHSONIAN

SEE'ST thou the Abbey of warm stone
  On the green island, orient red?
What does it here in States our own,
  When feudal Priors long are dead?

Its Baron like the Norman was
  Unto high dukes of bastard kith,
And gave his fortune's overplus
  Beneath the royal name of Smith,

To us, the land of guardian hope,
  That he a conqueror's rank would score,
And have his Ishmael brethren cope
  With them who Learning's peerage bore;

Whose cold cabal denied him space
  And made him unto dice betake:
The gamesters' nature saves the race,
  And sacred issues play a stake.

In foreign exile plighting troth,
  To powers occult he gave his word

GAPLAND LIBRARY AND DEN, FROM THE NORTH

(A gracious devil took his oath)
  "The voiceless tyros shall be heard!

" My two proud parents, wilful willed,
  Did shame and gold on me entail:
I will to bastard Science build
  An Abbey heaven shall aye assail!"

And first Respect refused the trust
  And Patriarchy did control,
Fire laid the battlements in dust
  And all the fund the People stole.

They built anew the abbey towers
  Around the purpose so grotesque
And into Gothic tracery flowers
  A fortalice of Romanesque.

And Merlin is its resident,
  Aladdin its conspirator,
Its regent aye our President,
  Lord Justice its High Chancellor.

What vested fear would fain repress
  Within came forth like vagrant rats
And cavernous inflúences
  Worked in the Abbey like the bats.

Original ideas found
  A publication never given,
A distribution underground,
  A circumvention over heaven.

New mischiefs to facilitate
  And lead the earth some young turmoil,

The Abbey spirits ruminate
  Around a magnet's serpent coil;

Where humble finders rank their peers
  And Aristotle's laws dispute;
A newsboy pulls the Mufti's ears
  And mocks the Royal Institute.

For, o'er that Abbey devil's jag
  A genii's banner flaunts its creed;
The unheraldic people's flag
  Waves, of the hordes unpedigreed;

Their parents did beget them snug
  And secondary made the rite,
They see not with the sleek and smug
  But with the gift of second sight;

They see refractedly from straight,
  At no precedent Afrite fright'ning,
As into Paradise's gate
  The Peri's zigzag glance of lightning.

They diagnose the pretty fibs
  The old nurse tells her nubile boy,
As in the horse's wooden ribs
  The Greeks the gossip heard in Troy.

This Abbey rests not pilgrim heads
  But sets tall-shafted thoughts a plinth
And lends the clues that wind the threads
  Through Nature's wizard labyrinth.

The pre-historic man it brings,
  Who knew not metals but in stone

Revell'd with implemental Kings
  And thought the golden age his own.

"Ha! ha!" the Prior laughs in glee,
  "Who cares for thunder, bell or ban?
Matter is immortality
  And no one knows the age of man!

"Ay! thou Sesostri, come and see
  The myths these Western mounds declare!
Oasis made society
  And Adam's birth was everywhere.

"If fifty thousand years had gone
  Ere to this skill his hand could school,
How long was it to human dawn
  Before the monkey made a tool?"

Lo! there the Prior's museum
  To mock man's sole decline and fall!
Where forward to perfection come
  His mechanisms, one and all,

From wheels that are not circular
  And scoopèd boats of idiot wit,
To telescopes trailed on a star
  That magnify and mirror it.

See! when the long tree shadows wave
  In the electric lantern's track,
The fallen Prior's lost conclave
  In their Satanic suits of black,

Gather within the Abbey red,
  Around some vampire snail or mole,

As if it were of holy dead
  And they were seeking for its soul!

See'st thou the slitted windows' height
  On which the sunset broke its heart?
Within, they burn the pictured light
  That spoiled the churchly Raphael's art!

And see'st thou the battlements
  From which bright fancy's angels fall
In gravity's incontinence
  And flight unanatomical?

Go not within or say a prayer
  By cerements of Pharaoh's corse!
The skull of wizard Lincoln's there
  And incantation tools of Morse.

So this loose gotten son of dukes
  Himself a dispensation swears,
Stands not with peers in their perukes
  Nor lets Delilahs clip his hairs,

But from the grave's green, grassy withes,
  He burst a Samson, love-betrayed,
And heading the heroic Smiths,
  Among the Titans flings his shade.

I hear the sprinkled church bells ring;
  I see on Freedom's dome her fire:
I will go cite this Abbey's King
  Though he may curse me in his ire:

"Ho, Prior! On thy door I smite!
  This Battle Abbey who begun?"
"*William the Norman I am hight:
  Robert the Devil's bastard son.*"

MARY OF THE CAPITOL

" ONE of our senators, surely?"
  Said the queer old girl to me;
I answered to her demurely
  " Only a Member you see."
" There is something dear about you,"
  She said, with an agèd bloom, —
" Were I young I would never doubt you:
  Is *this* your Committee room?"

" Come in!" I said to the lady, —
  'Twas a Saturday holiday —
" Shut the door! it will be more shady:
  Are you December, or May?
Whichever, a magnetism
  You shed on my widower life.
Your eyes are of crystal chrism, —
  You make me think of my wife."

" O thank you! that sounds so holy!
  To many a wife I have been,
Though ever the wayward, lowly,
  And penitent Magdalene;
But ever my Lord and Master
  I knew from his kingly ken:
'Twas my glory and my disaster,
  To worship the Congress men.

" Some women for sailors tarry,
  Some are *vivandières* in the camps,
Some Virgins are Wise and marry,
  Some are Foolish and trim no lamps:

American or Roman,
  Since this bright world began,
The proper place for woman
  Is where she comforts Man!"

Reluctant admiration
  My cold thoughts melted through:
"I see that you love our Nation?"
  "I love all the men who do!
Great men deserve love younger, —
  More beauteous than men common,
And ardently did I hunger
  To be some patriot's woman.

"I heard a trumpet sounded
  In my quiet countryside,
I followed the note as it bounded —
  He loved me here and he died, —
Died while my youth betrothing;
  Our souls were as pure as flame.
O, could I drop to nothing?
  Or should I be true to Fame?

"Next, an old benevolent gentle
  And a Senator called me his,
He was moral rather than mental
  But he had a grandfatherly kiss;
I found he was somewhat roving
  And it seemed just a little ingrate,
So I paid him off in loving
  A dashing young Delegate.

"His State, it was soon admitted, —
  Not I to the wedded state;

But his frailty I pardoned and pitied,
  And called it political fate.
Then, a Christian statesman named me his spouse,
  His church, and his bride of affairs;
He set me up in a furnished house
  And helped me to say my prayers.

" They came from near and they came from far,
  Bright spirits born to control,
As into a well burns a glorious star
  Their ardor drank up my soul;
None dared, none needed, my love to buy,
  And my beauty lasted well,
I yield to love my aged sigh —
  Love is too sweet for hell.

" Smile not! I bear my testament,
  Though not just the one who should,
That women are queer and different,
  But all of the men are good!
Whenever this poor old life of mine ends,
  I vow by the angels above,
I parted, with one and all, good friends,
  And never did spite to love!

" Thank you! a little wine is good:
  My head it is weak to-day.
Kind friend, say, am I misunderstood?
  See I am so old and grey!
Let all your charity abide,
  And Christ-like may you prove!
Here is a woman poor in pride
  But rich as God in love!"

Her face grew long, her sight was dull,
  Down sank the old grey head.
The old belle of the Capitol
  Within its walls was dead.
Still follow Gods, who most forgive,
  The loving and unclean,
And where the public heroes live
  There loves the Magdalene.

CLOTURE

1893.

THE Senate sloths sit up to-night —
  Dear Kitty come with me!"
The crowded Capitol was bright,
  Dark was our gallery;
They crowded me and Kitty so,
  Her courage to assure
My arm around her waist I throw:
  "The subject is *Cloture.*"

"How mad they get," said Kitty soon,
  "On matters so demure!
They rush upon each other close,
  Is that not like *Cloture?*"
"No, *This* more like that thing occult"—
  She cuddled up demure:
"I hope we'll come to some result
  And early pass *Cloture.*"

Nought did we hear that blessèd night
  Yet sat in perfect bliss;
When noise and wrath were at their height

Cloture concealed a kiss :
" Are you in favor of repeal !
  I think 'tis quite obscure."
" Light up the subject with your lips ! —
  Dear Kitty, press *Cloture !*

" Why do we need so much Reserve ?
  I'm sure we are secure.
I think more faith would give them nerve, —
  And therefore more *Cloture*."
" Kitty, our circulation's high,
  This panic may endure,
And Legal Tender's in my eye
  If you but say *Cloture ?* "

At panic prices we drove back, —
  That Herdic tilted sure ;
Kitty came sliding down the hack
  And all went on cloture :
" I've changed my mind ; 'tis nice to wait, —
  Engagements can endure.
But never let them close debate
  While we can have *Cloture*."

GAPLAND POEMS

GUY LOSEL

GUY LOSEL's heritage in hand,
He had a daring thought to rove,
And pleasure find from land to land
In an inconstancy of love;
He said Farewell to one, his dove,
Round whom his springtime blood had purled, —
Her heart was his did he command;
She was too modest to reprove
His flourish cool, " I'm going round the world ! "

So, unengaged, he did depart,
Handsome and liberal and clever,
Though with some twinges at his heart
From Mary's beauty so to sever;
But frowardness is selfish ever
And Mary's singleness he trusted.
He named Experience and Art
The vagrant quests of his endeavor:
Forbidden fruit, — it was for that he lusted.

He threw himself in British revels,
They had the pall of Mammon's play;
French demoiselles were painted devils,
The Belgic idols broken clay.
Yonder and farther, yet away,
Of flaxen Swedes Guy Losel sated

And pined in Pommeranian levels;
The Viennese were soulless gay.
Spain's lazy loose, they all were pawned or mated.

Europe exhausting, lonely, lost, —
Spite of his wish a Benedict, —
Guy Losel heathen waters crossed,
Himself of pleasure to convict.
He would be loved in candour strict
Where conscience lax allowed of freedom.
Arab, Egyptian, Moor, they tossed
Mocking deceit him to afflict,
And left his heart a wilderness of Edom.

" Is there no land where pleasure reigns
And love halts not its choice to ponder?"
" Not here, for here love has fond pains, —
'Tis in the next land, — yonder! yonder!"
The Persians, Guy was told were fonder;
The Persians pointed Ind to him;
The Hindoo, Java's lapse explains;
Javans at China's frailty wonder,
And China says, "Pleasures in Yedo brim."

" This world is better than its fame.
Each heart seeks one, so I have found it.
I have the only heart to blame
In all the world — I have been round it.
Some broken heart, I may compound it,
Exchanging with it my desire,
But love is never safe with shame.
One heart I left — O did I wound it? —
Dear Mary's heart! There are no hearts for hire."

Guy Losel hasted to his city;
Mary was blooming like the rose,
Blushing and *débonnaire* and witty;
He lost no moment to propose:
Her face grew pale, her lips shut close:
"I am engaged," at last she spoke,
"You wrote me not."　"O God! in pity,
Reclaim thy word! assuage my woes!
If I have not thy heart, my heart is broke!"

Penance he did; back round the earth
In spirit crawled.　The time was long.
Cold was his heart and eke his hearth.
When vows are passed the chain is strong.
But woman loves, though man is wrong:
She could not leave him solitary.
The night of anguish waked to mirth,
His sighing ceased in wedding song.
The land of Houris was the land of Mary.

TANGIER

FARTHEST away in space and time,
I take in this Columbian year
One day its winding lanes to climb —
The ancient city of Tangier.
Old was it in Mahomet's dawn,
Old when the Cæsars ruled these shores;
Since ancient nations have withdrawn
The oldest people are the Moors.

Tarifa's towers our eyes release;
Gibraltar's outlines grow more soft,
The pillars fade of Hercules
And Atlas holds the world aloft;
Atlantic's gales the billows high
The open roadstead dash upon,
Beyond the breakers props the sky
The mountain named for Washington.

He tribute paid to these corsairs,
Wild, nervous men, who know not fear,
And while we Christians mutter prayers
Row to the beach of old Tangier;
Row past her mole, Tangier her dower, —
The sea reflects the shivered beam, —
When English Charles, Braganza's flower
Sultana made of his hareme.

The turbaned Customs men scarce nod,
The saw-toothed walls their gates retain,
We climb the street that Musa trod
When Tarik plucked the cross from Spain;
A thousand years we backward stem —
The sight our modern age dispels —
We are in old Jerusalem
When Jesus told the parables:

The potter shapes, the blind man grieves,
The palsied woman starts to walk,
And yonder marked the Forty Thieves
On Ali Baba's door with chalk;
Aladdin's uncle bawls his lamps,
The barber bleeds them who would shear,

The camel drivers pitch their camps
Outside the walls of old Tangier.

I see the Koran teacher's school,
Where little hairless heads, like eggs
Some pelican would overrule,
Wag to the texts he in them pegs;
And the high caller unto prayers
Does not disturb him who recites
Tinkling his bell, on drowsy airs,
Tales from the soft Arabian Nights.

The squatted Berbers dreamy chant
In a café some desert troll,
Love is their sole intoxicant
And on its kiss no alcohol.
In hidden haunt, less lewd than poor,
With lancing height and bowstring thew,
The antelopèd, hussy Moor,
Dances with filly of the Jew.

In little shops their prices quote
Dealers in arms and stuffs and balms:
" All merchants cheat," Mahomet wrote,
" Therefore do ye requite in alms."
Though in the mosques we may not see,
Their socialism feel we may;
Religion is of Arabs three, —
Moses, Mahomet, Joshua !

His amputated hand in salt,
In the high jail, a festering man
Dies slowly for his desperate fault, —
The robber of the caravan ;

No lawyers here acquit a thief,
Nor wealth ill-gotten can illude
Him at Maroc, the Great Shareef,
Who is of Mahmoud's holy blood.

Plain as the desert round Tangier,
Whose paths the cactus does not shade,
Are the few laws they need them here,
Where are no engines grasping trade ;
One tyrant answers for a brood,
And immemorial is his right,
Marked like the palm's tall solitude
Against the Atlas mountain's height.

Morocco's state leans on the sky,
Its moon and stars the Arab's light,
No Ottoman's fell victory
Here has usurped a caliph's right ;
For Muley Hassan's banner green
He did not get by barbarous force ;
It streams like yonder green marine
That bounds in freedom like his horse.

Can we not blend with Islam's life
Our Christian slavery, so complex ? —
The scullions' rule, the dress-thralled wife,
And houses built to tax and vex ?
Thou desert robber ! my cloak great
Strip off ! it loads me like a chain ;
To pass thy enemy in wait
I'll go with thee, miles, one or twain.

But climate, moisture, living chance,
More than his Gods make man excel :

O had Arabia conquered France
She had made gracious Charles Martel!—
Softened the vandal Christian's clan
That malt and mead had muddled thick,
And knighted into Solyman
The lame, black soul of Genseric.

Beneath my blind she cannot pierce,
A tall, young Berber mother slips,
Her babe she drops in hunger fierce,
She draws a knife, her face she strips,
And cuts some grass around my inn, —
Her clean and stringy lines I've booked:
'Tis by her creed a deadly sin
That on her charms a man has looked!

Such Moors their conqueror Akbah bought
With gold, a thousand pieces each.
To blend their Arab grace with thought,
O, could their like some Soldan teach
Woman's religious hate to cease,
That curses Christians passing through!
At Tafilet to treat a peace
And loose the slaves at Timbuctoo.

With such sweet airs as Westward blow,
From lands where zealots rage in vain,
The States of Barbary might know
A wealth they never had in Spain!
Their beauteous women might be free,
Their shambles might again be homes!
As when the Gods of poetry
Were rich Numidia's and Rome's.

Like desert springs which flood with rain,
These Berber wastes the sects outpoured
That deluged Islam's star in Spain
And withered it like Jonah's gourd;
Preachers like Balaam and his ass
Their sinewy state a sect made be:
They see the ships of Europe pass,—
Wild Ishmaels of theology.

This fragment of a former age
Thrust into Europe's feverish breath,
Is like our childhood's limpid page,
Or unawakening, restful death.
No wheels nor mechanisms here,
We have no adventitious power,
And, like the dead in dead Tangier,
Naked we shall be in that hour!

BOB WHITE

I HEAR in the orchestral morn,
Midst the flute, the jewsharp and the horn,
A bird with a note like a vote,
Straight and sweet from the throat;
Like the voice from the light after night:
    " Bob White."

I know 'tis the Quail calling so,
But his language is English, I know;
How human the bird with that word!
By my heart it is heard—
Like friendship by love done despite,
    " Bob White."

The friend of his youth he would find,
There's no name but his friend's on his mind,
His life is all boyhood and joy, —
What is constant as boy? —
O, my friend of the morn and the light,
    Bob White! —

I roved through the stubble with thee,
Barefooted, to hawbush and tree,
By brook and by vale like the Quail;
Every day without fail
I called at thy gate, early bright,
    Bob White!

You answered, dear partner, my bleat,
Like the mate of the Quail from the wheat,
My heart to your halloo pursuant,
To school or to truant,
You parted from me not till night,
    Bob White.

The orchards, the fields, they were ours,
And the sky and the seed and the flowers,
The farmer, not we, paid the tax;
At the sound of his axe
Low whistled our warning or fright:
    "Bob White!"

Where *are* you, my chum, all these years?
Has the world swallowed you in its fears?
Or, mated, say, have you a flock?
Are you hen now, or cock?
Do I hear you out yonder aright,
    Bob White?

If you, O, the sweet notes again,
Raise them boldly, whom ever thy hen! —
Say, " Madame, that friend was my first,
In the dawn-hour of erst,
And he called me, ere you were my sprite,
    ' Bob White!' "

Then I will forget night and blight —
Do you hear how I whistle, Bob White?
O, lonely are all things in truth,
But the birds have our youth.
Say on. make me boy, set me right,
     Bob White!

QUEEN CHRISTINE

FOUNDER OF DELAWARE STATE
FONTAINEBLEAU, 1657

FATHER, is he dead?   Then I'll confess me:
His period is my pause where Aftertime
Will lay my book down and consider me.
You shall be my posterity and judge!

I had no child but Sweden and foreswore it;
Homeless by choice. I chose a homeless staff
From generosity; the man just slain
Monaldeschi, was nothing but a servant.
Marquis I made him like the Marquis Ancre,
King Louis' father slew.   Italian like
He mixed in my concerns, my lonely state
Unpitying, set his wits to work to spoil
My independence ; forged his comrade's hand

And traded in my livery like a traitor.
His plot he brought me: 'twas assassination;
Thinking a Queen ten years o'er Sweden's council
Could be so shallow. "Let me execute him!"
The jockey swore. The table's turned: he's dead.
His lesson is not lost on Latindom.
Let women twit! Christine was crowned a *King*.

 Defence I scorn, whose court, like old King Lear's,
Is where I visit. Am I yet a nun?
Vasa's resentment certain as his justice
Wakes in his grandson's child. Father and son
I executed, ere I abdicated,
For prodding my resignment ere its time.
 Absolute Queen I pass from throne to Pope,
No subject anywhere, my rent crown lands,
My confidence state secrets; treason, death!
She who of late by armies executed,
Visited kings with thunders, dyeing rivers
Blood red, was gloriously commended;
Heretic then she was, but worth conversion.
This day I sentenced one, — but one, — all shrived,
Who articled with me, and mutinied.

What did my Judas sell? That's perished with him:
I trapped him ere he bit. Was he my lover?
Cowards will say so for two hundred years.
Eve had it said of her, all nature's mother.
Listen, thou priest! 'Twas Knowledge bit us both.
Knowledge has bit thy church. At Westphalia
I forced to peace the Thirty Years of war,
And Toleration was my crown. Therefore
I took the cross in Lenity's crusade,

To minimize the consequence of creeds,
Nor ever have I Sweden asked to follow.
  I went to Rome to help the milder dawn,
When warring sects shall merge their strength
        for earth,
And fill the moats of feudal states with Heaven,—
Sunlight's illusion on the cold-throned Alps,
Mass's illusion in smug churchmen's hearts,
Women's illusion in their sex-sick heads,—
Heaven, not hell, makes earth yawn wide from
        man,
And draws its small portcullises of churches
Upward or down like selfish castellans.

  My filial shame was Christ's triumphant day:
A white-horsed Amazon, the penitent
Rode like Alaric or the Vandal king
Through Rome: Herodias with her father's head.

Then French and Spanish parties played for me,
Like Pilate's Roman dicers. Up I gat
With my small *suite* and sought politest France.
Italians ruled it; Mazarin, step-monarch,
His nieces, queens.   Ladies wore warriors' crowns.
None felt my sarcasm when the magdalen,
Ninon de l'Enclos, mistress of an abbé,
I singled out and wrote around her slime:
" Frondeurs unsinning! sling the first stone here! "

  The woman is a plant, her flower early,
Her reproduction her biography.
My mother pined and died for her Gustavus;
His only child I was, to wear his sword;

His sister had a son who wooed me hard;
I felt the Vasa jealousy of partners
And fed my brain and let my bosom starve.
My mind had no companionships in Sweden:
I sent abroad for scholars.　Soon contempt
Of amorous thought withered my wedding wreath.
Our Lutherans were lusty, women forward;
Magnus, my fancy, wedded Charles's sister;
I promised Charles my crown without my hand
And formed the Order of the Amaranth,
The monks and nuns of Learning; *one* stood fast.
My frame grew steel, my mind became all man:
Monaldeschi trifled with an Amazon.
　　But I have proved the sexes have reversion —
And from Minerva's brain Mars can be born:
The King I chose has rounded Sweden's bounds
And beaten Poland.　Scania is a fief
Of the Roman empire and Christina ends
Semiramis, like Margaret of the North.

　　The Woman left in me was my Conversion:
I tired of sermons but to woo my soul
Was an amour, sweet, timorous, and sighful,
Like the annunciation of the Virgin.
Spain, Portugal, the Pope, sent pursuivants
Who talked in liquid tongues, which I had learned
Without a master, of supernal love.
Long I coquetted with those Jesuits,
Resisted, threw them off, returned and yielded,
And never told the soft solicitation:
One woman kept a secret; it was pure.
To learn our fate we seek the fortune teller

Who promises it all: Rome outbid Luther.
We know not much; on them who swear they know
We lay our doubts: Rome has one Swede; she,
    Rome.
  Rome's civil law and Koster's printed bible,
Fermented in rude states; the age is loosed:
High intellects are readjusting knowledge.
The Northern Schools Kepler and Tycho Brahe
Have graduated to revise the lights
And Earth's circumferential to her Sun.
Rome has reformed; Christine reforms to Rome,
To be Hypatia to the fading Gods.

  The year my father fell in Lutzen fight
Old Galilei did abjure the truth
In Rome. No more will Rome science suppress.
Intolerance will take its stand in France
And from this old château. who knows, but Louis
Will shame his grandsire Henry more than I
Gustave Adolphus? Priest-kings are the worst.
I will against intolerance be Protéstant
In Rome itself. The earth awakes from sleep
By revolution. France may turn too swift.

Who's yonder? Henriette of England comes;
Cromwell supplies the head of her and Charles.
Von Wallenstein took counsel of the stars
But fell like Monaldeschi, Captain-slashed.
The forest here has a Black Huntsman in it,
King Henry's apparition ere he died;
There will I ride alone, who ne'er saw ghost.
How indolently safe to trust one's priest!

Nature! I sighed thee that I had no babe!
There was one, Little Sweden, that I swaddled
In the new world; its mart was named for me.
The Dutch have taken it and changed the name;
In neither Sweden have I left a chick.

Error preserves us often, like misfortune.
The wayward child is still the best beloved.
I took my crown off for sweet Independence.
Fashion I like not; business wore me out.
I will be humble when I live in Rome.
    Meantime these French who bought my father's
        death
Shall keep me for two years at their expense!
I will resume my study, — true devotion;
My books, — the holy graves of saints; myself, —
Portent of learning in the female plant.
As Mazarin collects his books for France,
I will become Rome's vestal bibliophile,
Cumæan sibyl for new oracles.
The riddle of the woman who shall bruise
The serpent's head, bear children and be ruled
By her desire of husband, therein lies,
As in the Sibyl's books Christ was acrostic.

The negative of man is his child-bearer.
The serpent's head is this small female head,
Which coils on man's and has no separate growth;
The quickening contact mounts not to her reason.
Diana's priestesses had each one breast;
One was too many for symmetric art
And Sappho's lyre was lovesick.   Woman grew

Half on, with single breast, and Greece was dam
To the strong brood of woman-minded thoughts,
In the harmonious temples of her head ;
That, draggled through the Arab caliphs' lusts,
Glanced off from Spain and lodged in Italy,
And on the barren rock of Peter grew
The lillied Renaissance.   Still negative
Is woman, led by France and fashion down
Below the stature of her column's head :
Man grows a tree and woman grows a vine
And chokes the tree of Knowledge.   Earth's o'er-
        brooded !

All faiths that are have superstitious ends.
Earth has no end in its continual sphere.
Material truths one day will be a faith,
When woman comprehends and holds the ground
That man has won.   The vast negation waits.

When I was at Nykoping, Oxenstiern, —
A greater mind than Richelieu's, but in Sweden, —
Gave me a dog called *Fidés*, saying " Chris.,
Thou learn'st too much from books; learn from
        this setter ! "
We had an Echo on the water there ;
My dog's bark barked at him and the first night
He barked all night at Echo.   The next night
Fidés kept all awake.   My aunt cried " Kill him ! "
" 'Tis his devotion," said my uncle John,
" He worships at the unaccountable."
    How ghostly seem we to ourselves in mirrors
At dusk, as they reflect our coming shade !

In dusk I ferried *Fidés* tow'rd his Echo.
I spoke myself one name for the last time;
" *Magnus.*"
    Art listening, priest?
        (He is asleep.
The death he has seen done this hour prostrates
  him.)
 The rest I'll tell to Echo, whispering here,
In the long halls where Henry kissed Diana
In Rondelet's fireplace, where kiss quenched flame.
In her Initial, Henry is the cipher.
She subdued him when Dauphin, nineteen years
Her junior. But she married at thirteen;
Widowed at thirty-two: it is my age!
She was re-born and turned a man in love.
Once in an age old woman has her reign.
(Would I had tilted with Montgomery!)
The renaissance at Fontainebleau was Love.

Mary of Scots was here a bride and Philip
Of Spain did wed his murdered son's affianced;
Francis was satyr to his market girls;
Navarre in love-war met his Ravaillac.
Kings get no more than peasants from the sex!
 The furious love scenes painted by Italians
Are just effaced by Anne of Austria,
Lest Mazarin admire them more than her.
In this château, where art was stripped to Isis
A hundred years ago, they stand me off,
Who am an honest monk, a maiden queen.

 When brother Guises in some such château
Were foully stabbed, the Valois line expired!

My traitor wore a corselet like a woman,
His sentence paralyzed his lizard tongue.
I'll whisper to this sleeping priest my secret,—
God's drowsy ear, the old maid's deaf confessor.

'Twas play for Poland, which the Jesuits
Have made another Spain, and smothered knowl-
      edge.
Has been the silent secret of my soul !

Sweden is flanked by Denmark, our oppressor;
Poland and Russia are conjoined with it.
Jagellon's line concluded with a woman
Who wed my father's uncle, John of Vasa;
Sweden and Poland were their son's demesnes, —
Sigismund.   *He* would force the Poles' religion
Upon our Lutherans, who did depose him.
The Dissidents he persecutes in Poland,
Its Huguenots, who do solicit me
To be their Henry of Navarre and join
Against the Russians our united powers,
Else Russia will devour both Swedes and Poles.
I must be Catholic if Queen in Poland!
   I set my cousin Charles upon my throne,
He in my secrets as my ardent lover,
To shatter Denmark and King Sigismund,
And stepped me down, a wondrous Catholic.

Learning had taught me silliness of churches:
Religions are the national costumes,
More silken Southward and more woollen North.
I could afford to humor them I vanquished,
They were not subtle to discern my play.

Like *Fidés*, Echo from the farther side
Returned to this, as I to it went nearer
(The dog did reason it when he was hoarse).
Who shall chase Echoes from opposing shores?
What of Christine is altered by exchanging
The creed of Odin for the creed of Venus?
The toasted babes in Thirty Years of war
Called on the motherhood in my dry milk
To taste the sacrament that I had humbled,
As Jesus dipped with John.   Not by the Cross
But by the Dove was writ the sign of *Conquer!*

Poland, Bohemia, Sweden, Hungary,
Beneath a woman's love, would wall the Tartar
And Bear, out of Midgarden's paradise:
I wished to be the tolerant queen of Poland!
   Lest this might be, the Jesuits mine equerry
Hired, — Monaldeschi, — to snook over me.
I caught him with my letters, trapped him here,
And send his ghost to Rome to give me awe!

Rome will sit squat.   Her morals are Conversion.
Public Opinion, ever absolute,
In midnight tyranny as in the day,
Now has Christine beneath its microscope:
Poland, I fear, is frozen from my love!

   The woman's reign in Eden was not long;
The curse of children was her balance wheel.
Sweden is lost to me; Poland affrighted;
Rome is uneasy with its roving convert:
I have no other home.   Father, awake!
Absolve Rome's daughter from her passing sin!

WASHINGTON'S MONUMENT

LONG UNFINISHED

Sunk in the sands by its own weight, the Sphinx
  Intelligible lies; its nobler part, —
    That sweet, great face — still touching every
      heart,
That 'midst the lonely ruins walks, and thinks
  On perished states, made perfect by such art.
But thou! *our* Sphynx, — lone column, strong and
    white,
  When this our empire totters to decay,
The senile riddle of thy broken height
  And feeble unfulfillment, who shall say?
  "A race unstable and degenerate," they
Who pass may cry, "here sought some shrine to
    lift —
Not such as carved complete yon wondrous disk
In Egypt, but some brood ingrate with thrift,
  And souls unfinished like this obelisk!"

1871.

CLOY

As the Earth is surrounded
  By naked air,
Life's sphere is bounded
  By an azure care;
Only moments of time
  Is the rainbow bended,
And wherever we climb,
  The world is ended.

There's a hopelessness
  In careers succeeding,
More than the distress
  Of the dying and bleeding;
The nature which scaleth
  Cathedral towers,
Hears nearer where waileth
  The tolling hours.

ROCKING CHAIR

'TIS not Diana on her bow
  I seem to see, so straight and spare, —
A lady moving to and fro
  So calmly in a rocking chair.

Like some old clock's slow pendulum,
  Her wavy line, her features fair,
Across my memories go and come, —
  The lady in the rocking chair.

In woman's realm, a little home, —
  Her little arc of life's career, —
I see sweep past her silver comb;
  The lady in the rocking chair.

It makes me weep, it makes me sleep,
  That gentle motion · tell me where
I felt it o'er the ocean deep? —
  Dear mother, in thy rocking chair!

SANCTUMONIOUS

THE Editor and Writer met in Twilight's lonely
    lane,
Bohemian and Sadducee, enforced to meet again:
" When next we walk, successful friend! the dark-
    ness will be deep ";
Said the Bohemian, " Tell me, now, what have
    you done to keep?"

" My self-esteem, my spotless work, my influence
    austere!
I edited the Higher Thought, the economic seer!
Never to error did I stoop and when the State
    must fall,
Let history consult my files: I did predict it all.

" You wrote and lived incontinent; I had to let
    you drop;
And still you are a rolling-stone and I the per-
    fect stop;
The ink-drops from my Draco's pen fall like the
    gibbet's rope
And splash into that stoic blank where but Bo-
    hemians hope."

Finished the sinless Sadducee and the Bohemian
    said,
" The measure of a fellow's length is taken when
    he's dead.
I have had all of life's good things yet never wor-
    shipped me;
You, born with introverted eyes, worshipped your
    cavity.

" You superseded God at school, your country later
        on ;
Plenty of earth you have possessed but none of
        horizon.
My talent I have not improved ; I kept it in my
        hand :
Mine is the faith my fathers had in my dear, native
        land !

" One drop," the old Bohemian said, " within its
        channel strong,
I mingle in the mighty tide and with it move
        along,
I have no other creed than this, no power of my
        own :
Flow, beauteous river ! Not in thee have ever I
        thrown a stone ! "

From Twilight lane they parted last, the years
        were growing dark ;
Neither upon the century left more than finger
        mark ;
" Silentia " was the epitaph upon the scolding
        man,
But all the bands of music play past the Bo-
        hemian.

RESPECTABILITY

PERHAPS I owe to my temerity
Some lost advantages of little force ;
At life's outgoing they will quit my corse,

I shall have seen what I desired to see,
Eye-single, not with Ishmael's remorse,
But by the beam of nature given me.
Some question Shakespere for his way apart,
Because invited little by the great;
He kept his pedigree, a country heart,
And laureated was to illustrate.
Than imitation is no meaner fate,
To be respectable is not to rise;
There is a strength that does not borrow state,
It is to serve the light within thine eyes.

DYING LETTERS

HERE strangled in the West
  See gentle Letters lie!
Where he had hoped the best
  Despair is in his eye.
'Twas Mammon stabbed him first
  And piracy severe,
The gash that bled him worst
  Was dealt him by a sneer.

"Go to!" says worldly wise,
  "What time have we to read?
The past is full of books, —
  Enjoy the present deed!
Down with ideal things!
  Melt down the wizard bell!
Strike off the poet's wings!
  We still can buy and sell."

Yes, for ye all are sold
    To what your souls despise, —
The avarice of gold
    And small anxieties;
To wives who spend and pine
    And scandals base discuss,
To sons who die in wine,
    And daughters frivolous.

Read not or wanton read,
    That wanton dreams may be!
Have authors like your need,
    Serfs of your pleasantry!
Here strangled in the West
    See gentle Letters lie! —
Where he had hoped the best
    Despair is in his eye.

RICHARD, O MY KING

VERSAILLES, OCTOBER 3, 1789

O RICHARD, O my king!
    Beneath thy prison bars
I touch the lute's light string,
    Soft as the light of stars;
They steal into thy sight,
    Unto thy soul I sing:
Awake! O captive knight!
    O Richard, O my king!

(*Chorus, repeat.*)
O Richard, O my king!

O Richard, O my king!
  Not of thine arms I sigh;
The love to thee I bring
  Is of thy Poesy.
Thou king of troubadors!
  List to the night bird's wing,
And twang thy prison bars,
  O Richard, O my king!

O Richard, O my king!
  The air it is thine own,
Made in thy life's young spring
  Before thou had'st a throne;
Then music filled thy heart
  Far more than anything, —
Thy sceptre was my Art,
  O Richard, O my king!

O Richard, O my king!
  Thy voice is singing now;
I hear its deep notes ring
  Like stormwind on the bough.
Song pierced thy stone redoubt,
  'Tis thy recovering:
Thy song has found thee out,
  O Richard, O my king!

(*Chorus, repeat.*)

O Richard, O my king!

MIRROR SONG

FROM *DECATUR*, AN OPERA

THE lily's mirror is the pond,
  The rose's mirror is the dew,
The empress's the diamond,
  And in my mirror I see *you*.
O am I fit for you to cull?
In your eyes am I beautiful?
Your glorious strength shall I consume,
And with my weakness make perfume? —
Our features blend as man and wife
And flower in immortal life?

The star has mirrors in the air,
  The rainbow, mirrors, in the rain,
But thou art mirrored everywhere,
  In all my bliss, in all my pain!
O let me gaze upon the charms,
Worthy to enter in thy arms!
My mind is but a giddy scroll,
My beauty is my only soul, —
Be thine career! the glorious strife!
Take me in thy immortal life!

Thy fame has mirrors in the crowd,
  Thy courage shines in thy cuirass,
The guns reflect thy victories loud:
  My echo is my Looking Glass.
O, till thou drink me in thy kiss,
I no assurance have but this, —
That I am fit to blend with thee,

My face in immortality
With thine, whose eyes reflect thy wife,
In crystal of immortal life!

AMERICAN SLAVES IN TRIPOLI

1805

FAREWELL, our native land!
  Farewell, O freshening sea!
We choose the suffocating sand
  To shame and liberty.
Earth shall not rue that we existed, —
  This is our one reply:
We swore to die when we enlisted,
  Go, show us where to die!

Perhaps our cheerful parts,
  Our hearty work, our songs,
May soften our taskmasters' hearts
  And mitigate our wrongs.
On honest bread we have subsisted,
  We would not terrify,
We swore to die when we enlisted,
  Go, show us where to die!

Where'er we go our name,
  Our land's example wins,
Degraded realms we shall reclaim
  And soften Jacobins!
Unfurl the flag that we assisted!
  Dear country, hear our sigh! —
We swore to die when we enlisted,
  Go show us where to die!

SHAKESPERE'S FRIENDS

FROM TALBOT'S HAWKS. A ROMANCE

BENEATH the roots of these old trees
   That shade the river bends,
There lie the buried images
   That once were Shakespere's friends;
As still as in his theatre,
   Beside their thrilling dames,
They never stir, beneath the fir,
   That lulls the river James.

The vine, whose dye of royal red,
   The locust tree ascends,
Takes splendor from the perishèd
   That once were Shakespere's friends;
His mind luxuriant seems to bloom,
   His ardent nature flames,
And from their charnel sheds perfume
   Along the river James.

Around their rest no hates endure,
   His noble mind forfends —
The holy rites of Literature
   Were said o'er Shakespere's friends;
They talked the lofty style he wrote
   And coursed heroic fames,
And through the Tempest sailed their boat
   Unto the river James.

These saw the bard a man, like them,
   Though so his scope transcends

That we would think his garment's hem
  Was kissed by Shakespere's friends;
But poor disciple fishermen,
  That fancy lifts to fames,
Were no more apostolic, then,
  Than those who fished the James.

If men would of his Scripture learn
  Life's universal ends, —
Bend o'er this old colonial urn,
  That once held Shakespere's friends!
There is for each his own career,
  But dust for all our aims, —
Imagination bounds our sphere;
  Life is the city, James.

Yet far, afar, dissolving forms
  Will find infinite blends,
Like to the moisture in the storms,
  The dew of Shakespere's friends;
The globe, evaporate, goes on,
  Itself the mote reclaims,
And nought is lost when all is gone:
  Bloom on! O city James!

SONGS OF YOUTH

THE songs I wrote when I was young,
  I did not think were good;
I sat me down to write some songs,
  When life was understood.
But, everywhere, the bright and fair,

To my first numbers sprung, —
They did not want my songs of care,
But songs I made when young.

The love I made when I was young,
Was not love *débonnaire;*
I thought love would refine its tongue
When I could love prepare;
But, everywhere, the bright and fair,
I, stranger, seemed among;
They did not want my sober air,
But love I made, when young.

The travels made when I was young,
Were not in wisdom's way.
Again I travelled in those lands
In life's meridian day;
But, everywhere, the bright and fair,
My lonely heartstrings wrung;
My settled thoughts they did not share,
But thoughts I had, when young.

Song, Love, and Travel! ye are young,
And I am almost old.
The golden bell vibrates when rung,
The cracked old bell is tolled.
Ye young and fair! my time beware!
In morn's bright Arc be swung!
Wait not for evening time to pair,
Life's life is but life young.

NEW ENGLAND

(TO JOHN GODFREY MOORE)

NEW ENGLAND'S head is cool,
  Her heart a living spring,
Her hand a tempered tool,
  Her throat was made to sing,
Her genius comprehends,
  Her habits ever steady,
Her means embrace her ends,
  Her spunk is right and ready.

She did conceive our land
  A Continental nation,
She made the mighty stand,
  She forced the Declaration,
She gave us clocks to heed,
  She set the West in motion,
She made our fathers read,
  Her food fields were the ocean.

Wherever went her sons
  The mill wheels churned the waters,
The spin wheel swifter runs
  For her free-jointed daughters,
Her poverty can lend,
  She never is depender,
A teacher or a friend
  New England is the lender.

Who blames her that she strove
  To be the saint-elected?

As from the brain of Jove
  Minerva was projected?
Idealist alone,
  She drew her out of Edom;
A Book is still her throne,
  Her influence is Freedom.

Fatter are others' fields;
  Her dower is some duty.
Her rocky verdure yields
  The most transcendent beauty.
Organic as some realm
  And scented like a blossom,
Her spread is like her elm,
  The Mayflower's in her bosom.

UNSERVED

Our nation leads the age
  But every man is drafted,
The mighty heritage
  Into our sap is grafted;
We somewhat know our wives
  And know our children's faces
And when old age arrives
  We have no resting spaces.

'Tis money makes our friends,
  Its want our disconsoling,
Life's sweet endeavor ends
  When ends our burden-rolling;
The evening hour is dull,

'Tis sleep or dissipation,
For home life beautiful
  We made no preparation.

The poor they know us not;
  Our servants haste to leave us ;
Our wealth has them forgot,
  Their free-born thoughts perceive us ;
Our distance they respect,
  We are our money's sequels,
Deserting us, select,
  They seek their hearty equals.

I think upon a time
  The kitchen was our play-house,
The chimney's whitewashed grime
  'Twixt air and home, half-way house,
Our orphan bounden maid
  The sweetheart that we read to,
And ere compelled to bed,
  Her loving lap we fled to.

Her dishes washed, she walked
  Into the high folks' sitting ;
She and the old cook talked
  With mother round the knitting ;
Our neighbors did not start
  Nor look our " help's " demission, —
It was as if some heart
  Played shuttle through condition.

Little we knew that maid
  Had source so sentimental :

Her mother was betrayed,
   Her father was a gentle.
Wealth does no more allow
   Those tender patronages,
And foreign convicts now
   Eat all our poor folks' wages.

In outskirt huts I note
   The laborer's straight-limbed daughters,
Wild music in their throat,
   And leap of mountain waters ;
They never seek his door, —
   The poor, rich man they border, —
Both poor and rich are poor,
   Without a Servant order.

Helpless our lady hears
   Her kitchen tales' distresses,
With diamonds in her ears
   And only silken dresses,
Untaught with heart to speak,
   In nature's sister spirit,
Unto her sex's meek,
   Who shall her earth inherit.

What patriotic guild,
   Exploiting past condition,
Can match the woman-willed
   In wife's or daughter's mission ? —
Morgiana to set free,
   'Neath Ali Baba's eaves,
Who served the family,
   And boiled the Forty Thieves ?

MORMON'S OLD WIFE

ABED, and failing and old and gray,
On the thirtieth morn of her wedding day, —

First wife in time, but the ninth in number,
Old Betsy Perkins awoke from slumber;

And she heard the bells of Salt Lake shedding
Their melody, over her husband's wedding!

This morn he wedded the tenth young spouse,
In the cloisters of the Endowment House;

One fair enough midst the daughters of men,
To make an old man gallant again;

For he in the church was a reigning star,
One of the Twelve and a Counsellor,

And many missions had made him wise,
And deepened the lights in his handsome eyes,

While she, bedridden, with babes and cares,
Lost the rose from her cheeks and the brown from
     her hairs;

Lost hope and husband, and all but belief
In the church of the Saints and the might of its
     chief.

And the wedding bells were strong and sharp
As arrows shot from the chords of a harp.

Ah ! tenderer bells had pealed for her
That wedding morn in Exeter,

When in the Parish Church she stood,
Upon the threshold of womanhood,

And trustfully, heartily, gave her all
To the strong young blacksmith, frank and tall ; —

His silver watch his thrift confessed ;
A nosegay smartly bloomed on his breast ;

His Cornish accent, deep and queer,
Like Psalmist's melody thrilled on her ear ;

Of reverent mind and serious fashion,
His love had something more than passion ; —

And she felt on his broad breast, anchored fast,
The peace that understanding passed.

Now over her grey, adobè home,
The Wahsatch mountains, dome on dome,

Alone kept sentry ; their snowy spears
Had changed no feature in twenty years —

The rills that babbled about her lot
Talked cold in the orchards of apricot ;

And her sight grew dim in the lonely days,
Like the vale of Deseret lost in the haze.

Alone, neglected, her daughters the prize
Of solemn Bishops and " Seventies " ;

Her sons engrossed in their wives and farms
And her husband sealed in a maiden's arms,

She cried, " Oh! blessed Master above!
This morn of my wedding I perish for love!

" I am chill and blind.   Let me lean once more
On the breast that received me so gladly of yore!

" If ever my heart cried its pain and hunger,
To see him look down in the eyes of one younger,

" Or uttered my crushed love's agony
To hear, oft repeated, the vow made to me,

" When happy in girlhood my bridegroom stood by
        me,
This prayer of my old age, my Saviour! deny me!

" Not all, but a moment of love I entreat,
To hear on my threshold the sound of his feet,

" To hide on his bosom, and die on his kiss —
Oh, Jesus! thou comforter, grant me but this!"

The light on the mountains grew dark as she spake,
And the rills of the cañons that ran to the lake;

As cold as the Jordan in winter, the room,
And like snow on the fire died her hope in the
        gloom.

But a hand like a lover's she felt in her palm
And a voice that was healing, spoke out of the
        calm:

"Oh, weary and laden one, come unto Me!
Your prayer it is answered; your love you shall
  see."

By the bedside, all brightness, One beautiful, stood,
But the prints on His feet and His side were like
  blood.

But like the ideal she had wept to embrace,
The groom of her girlhood He seemed by His face.

And she cried: "O, my lost one, for absence aton-
  ing,
You have suffered like me, you have bled without
  moaning!

"Oh, tarry a day, ere forever we part;
For the bliss of your coming brings death to my
  heart!"

Then it seemed that the cot and the mountains
  sank down,
And the stars thronging round, hid the lights of the
  town;

But her fears were assuaged on the breast of her
  choice,
"And the comfort, unspeakable, borne on His voice:

"Oh, soul-seeking love! to requite for thy loss,
In the sight of my mother, I wedded the cross,

And espoused in my pain, with my arms opened
  wide;
The old and neglected, by men cast aside!"

John Perkins, Apostle, as seldom of late,
Came up to old Betsy's and opened the gate.

He stole through the orchard, passed softly the
    door,
And set his great basket of gifts on the floor;

There lay on the cot, with her face to the South,
The wife of his youth with a smile round her
    mouth;

The smile that she wore in her freshness of charms,
When he woke in the morn and she slept in his
    arms;

Like the light on Twin Peaks, when the day lin-
    gers low,
It lay 'neath her white hair sand tinted their snow:

Recognition of love everlasting it spake,
When father and mother and husband forsake.

"Oh, Gentiles!" cried Perkins, and knelt by place,
"Can your wives die like ours with a smile on
    their face?

"O women! who yield up all heaven for a kiss!
Ye pity our old wives, who slumber like this!"

SALT LAKE, 1871.

HARPER'S FERRY SUNSET

Rosy glow the rugged heights
  Half way up the mountain hole,
As sunset o'er the funnel, lights
  With wine, the grand communion bowl;
'Twixt farther peaks Potomac's sheet
  In pale wide bays extends its floss,
These and the sky seem hands and feet
  When stretched the Saviour on the cross;
Rock bars, the scars of civil wars,
  Like music scales on rift and ridge,
Sing of the Sunday when the cars
  Stopped, like an organ, on the bridge:
His gallows' beams o'ertop the town,
  The mountains, only, hanged John Brown.

Name so lowly, sponsored never,
  Parent of his mighty thought,
Rhapsody was his endeavor,
  Like Prometheus he fought.
Nothing since has here abided
  But the spell of Nature's spasm,
He the scenery divided
  And his spectre fills the chasm.
Armorers and all their din,
  Feudal times, he gathered in;
Him suspended, when he went,
  He suspended government!
As a whirlpool leaves a tragic
  Rift aghast where it sucked down,
In the camera of magic
  Swims thy maelstrom face, old Brown!

HER FIRST GLASSES

" I CANNOT see." my lady writes ;
" Get glasses for my blinded sights ! "
The plaintive cry brings tears to me
That those bright orbs no longer see.

A century's third has o'er us past,
Since childhood's eyes to eyes we cast, —
Her eyes so black, my eyes so grey, —
They looked the love we dared not say.

Those glorious eyes beamed in my soul
And warmed my blood beyond control,
O'er lands, o'er seas, they softly shone,
I fled, I plead, — they were my own.

And all our children bore her eyes ;
Some look down on me from the skies ;
Some watch me in this human wild,
And some in children of our child.

Those radiant lenses, fading some,
Tell years autumnal almost come,
I feel remorse to hear her plea :
" Give me my eyes to look on Thee ! "

The faithful service rises up,
It fills my eyes, it fills my cup,
It puts my small complaints to rest ;
I only feel I have been blest :

One gentle being lived for me,
Looked on me long as she could see,
And will look on me from the skies,
With love eternal in her eyes.

BESSIE

Bless her heart!   I see her shake
All the lawn weeds from her rake,
In her home she seems to take
Such a comfort, such a care,
As if these old mountain fields
Were her precious annual yields,
And her back their warrior shields,
Like the children she did bear.

Now the peach tree boughs she strips,
Now her flower borders clips:
These are the same earnest lips,
Thirty years and three agone,
That to me in beauty came,
Fearing not my fiery flame,
Sinking in my name her name —
That dear lady on the lawn.

Diligence was all her art,
Open as the day her heart,
Nothing subtle, double, smart —
Now I know it, now I weep;
For her hair is growing grey,
And I feel some lonely day,
None will rake the spring-time hay,
Where she lowly lies asleep.

But no rust is in her hair,
In her hands or anywhere;
Like some gold-piece lost by wear,
She has wasted grain by grain.

After her will live her fruit,
May they get her tireless foot!
There can be no dust nor soot
In the orbit of that brain.

MARY WASHINGTON

READ AT HER MONUMENT'S DEDICATION, FREDERICKS-
BURG, VA., MAY 10, 1894

THE Rappahannock ran in the reign of good Queen
    Anne,
All townless from the mountains to the sea,
Old Jamestown was forlorn and King Williams-
    burg scarce born —
'Twas the year of Blenheim's victory,
Whose trumpets died away in far Virginia
    On the cabin of an old tobacco farm,
Where a planter's little wife to a little girl gave
    life
And the fire in the chimney made it warm.

It was little Mary Ball, and she had no fame at all,
    But the world was all the same as if she had;
For she had the right to breathe and to tottle and
    to teethe,
And to love some other cunning little lad:
Though he proved a widower, it was all the same
    to her,
For he gave her many a daughter and a son,
And the family was large and the oldest, little
    George,
Was the hope of little Widow Washington.

That name resounded not in the time we have
    forgot,
  It was nothing more than Smith or Jones or Ball;
And George's big half brothers had the call on
    their stepmother's
Affection, like the babes of her own stall;
They paid the larger taxes and the Ayletts and
    Fairfaxes
  Received them in their families and lands,
While the widow thought upon it, as she rode in
    her sunbonnet,
  Midst her slaves who tilled her gulleys and her
    sands ;

Till they sought to take her George upon the royal
    barge,
  And give him a commission and a crest,
When her heart cried out " O, no ! something says
    he must not go ;
  My first born is a father to the rest."
She could find him little schooling, but he did not
    learn much fooling,
  And he dragged the mountains o'er with chain
    and rod.
The Blue Ridge was his cover and the Indian his
    lover
  And his Duty was his Sovereign and God.

Still her rival in his heart was the Military art,
  And the epaulettes she dreaded still were there.
There are households still where glory is a broken-
    hearted story,

And the drum is a mockery and snare.
From the far-off Barbadoes, from the yell of
    Frenchmen foes,
From the ghosts of Braddock's unavailing strife,
She beheld her boy return and his bridal candles
    burn,
And a widow like herself become his wife.

By Potomac's pleasant tide he was settled with his
    bride,
Overseeing horses, hounds and cocks and wards,
And it seemed but second nature to go to the
    legislature
And play his hand at politics and cards;
Three-score-and-ten had come when the widow
    heard the drum:
"My God!" she cried, "what demon is at
    large?"
'Tis the conflict with the King, 'tis two worlds a
    mustering,
And the call of Duty comes to mother's George.

"O war! To plague me so! Must my first born
    ever go?"
The answer is the bugle and the gun.
The town fills up again with the horse of Mercer's
    men,
And the name they call aloud is "Washington."
In the long, distracting years none may count the
    widow's tears;
She is banished o'er the mountains from her farm;
She is old and lives with strangers, while ride wide
    the King's red rangers,

And the only word is " Arm ! " and " Arm ! "
   and " Arm ! "

" Come home and see your son, the immortal
    Washington !
  He has beat the King and mighty Cornwallis ! "
They crowd her little door and she sees her boy
    once more,
  But there is no glory in him like his kiss.
The Marquises and Dukes, in their orders and
    perukes,
  The Aids-de-camp, the Generals and all,
Stand by to see and listen how her aged eyes will
    glisten
  To hear from him the tale of Yorktown's fall.

Upon that her lips are dumb to the trumpet and
    the drum ;
  All their pageantry is vanity and stuff.
So he leans upon her breast she cares nothing for
    the rest —
  It is *he* and that is victory enough !
In the life that mothers give is their thirst that
    man shall live
  And the species never lose the legacy,
To love again on earth and repeat the wondrous
    birth —
  That is glory — that is immortality.

Unto Fredericksburg at last, when her four-score
    years are past,
  Now gray himself, he rides all night to say :

"Madame — mother — ere I went, to become the
        President,
   I have come to kiss you till another day."
" No, George ; the sight of thee, which I can hardly
        see,
   Is all, for all — good-by ! I can be brave.
Fulfill your great career as I have fulfilled my
        sphere !
   My station can be nothing but the grave."

The mother's love sank down, and its sunset on
        his crown
   Shone like the dying beams of perfect day.
He has none like her to mix in the draught of
        politics
   The balm that softens injury away.
But he was his mother's son till his weary race
        was done ;
   Her gravity, her peace, her golden mean,
Shed on the State the good of her sterling woman-
        hood,
   And like her own was George's closing scene.

WAR CORRESPONDENTS' MEMORIAL

(AT GAPLAND, MD., 1896)

ARCH aërial, view ethereal,
   Sky and stars and moonlit cloud,
Harvest fields of golden cereal,
   Rainbow on the mountains bowed ;
Mountain ridges stepped like bridges,

O'er the rich campagna vale;
Storm which marches with lightning torches
    Firing volleys of bullet hail;
Windstorm boreal, rainstorm oriel,
    Snow pictorial on knob and town —
All are revealed through our Memorial,
    Grim as a cyclop staring down.

Born so rigid, stony and frigid,
    Moor and Roman it must be,
Long erected, a gate dissected
    From some castle's feudality;
Or set in the passes, where saying masses,
    Pilgrims, crusaders, kneeling them,
Gazed and trembled, with undissembled
    Joy, in the sight of Jerusalem.
Vale of Catoctin, like jewels locked in
    An azure casket, flash thy lights!
Like the Escorial, our Memorial
    Guards them all from the mountain heights.

Yawning fortalice, thine the portal is
    Freedom opened with her pen,
When the valley so musically
    Pealed with bugles of armèd men;
Walls of mountain burst with a fountain,
    Smitten from rock by our Moses,
Frowning height arched with the light,
    Bloomed the Bastile into roses.
Prison and light, ruin and right,
    Show in the gap, grim and lean;
Homely, manorial, our Memorial
    Witnesses what it has seen.

War Correspondents' Memorial Arch, from the East

Windows stand triple, each of them typal,
  Each an evangel's page white;
One is Depiction, one is Description,
  One is Photography's light.
These in acclivity, arch on activity,
  Horse-shod the Centaur uprears;
Unicorn-towered, forest embowered,
  Sun dial, sentry of years;
Letters amidst the arms, history o'er the farms,
  Socketing moon and the stars,
High and pictorial, our Memorial
  Tells of the tellers of wars!

NEWS AND LOVE

1862.

THE fight just done, I snatched my notes,
While Jack, my gelding, ate his oats,
And ran my chance without a guard,
And for Pamunkey I rode hard;
What made me want to leave the camps,
  And beat the mail with what I penned?
It was not glory and not "stamps";
  It was my girl at the other end.

I wound the oaks and pines among
And felt so buoyant and so young,
You would not think I had a list
Of dead and wounded in my fist;
What said those sweet birds in the brush?
  Why made that squirrel seem my friend?

What made my nag so gaily push?
  It was my girl at the other end.

Last night our flanks the rebels turned ;
I see the sutlers' wagons burned,
The sunken sloops at Putneys see —
It was JEB. Stuart's cavalry !
What makes me out alone so far ?
  (I may to Libby prison wend !)
You bet your life it is not war !
  It is my girl at the other end.

And now I reach the morning boat,
The large lump passes from my throat,
The crooked river glides so flat,
While I am writing on my hat ;
And when I sign my name below
  I hope to kiss it one will tend ?
Is it the Public ?   Buncombe !   No ;
  It is that girl at the other end.

I change my boat ; I vault ashore
The second morn at Baltimore,
And make such steps, 'twould shame a stork,
To catch the first train for New York ;
Why do I toil and amplify,
  And style and matter so much mend ?
'Tis for the pride in her black eye —
  The one dear girl at the other end !

The " Office " makes for me a stir,
Up to the managing editor ;
They say it was a real " beat,"

And I must rest and clothe and eat;
Though grateful all these praises be,
  Why do I want one gentle friend
To put the crown of love on me? —
  That one dear girl, at the other end!

SNOWFALL AT NIGHT

GAPLAND OR CRAMPTON'S GAP

THE fire of forest wood
  My mountain woodlands grew,
Warms my thin winter's blood
  And boils the tempting brew.
I hear the farmer's sleigh
  Come to my hermit's den;
The sleighbell's roundelay
  Makes my heart young again.

They let the snowdrift in,
  My study's light streams out;
Spirits in raiment thin
  Are whiskering about;
The old wives' cheeks are roses,
  The young wife's eyes are spells,
The farmer's heart jocose is
  And every voice has bells.

Like Santa Claus' party
  They muffle up and go,
Their bells, their good night hearty
  Melt in the falling snow;

And as I read my history
  Of Northern hosts at Rome,
White camps in silent mystery,
  Are pitched around my home.

At morn I look in wonder:
  The argent valleys shine
'Twixt mountains drawn asunder, —
  Potosi's silver mine.
Blue woods, in plumage hoary,
  Descend from peaceful skies,
A seraph host of story
  Set guard on Paradise.

One crow like Satan croaking
  Flaps o'er the saintly plan,
This silver shield no joking
  When he would blacken man;
The rabbit's feet wide springing,
  His burrow would conceal,
That tell-tale snowbirds, singing,
  Unto the dogs reveal.

The roofs are sheets of paper,
  My doves their loving crest;
With lace some subtle draper
  (And bridal wreaths) has dressed
The vines, the weeds, the sedges;
  In filigree so light.
The quail his covey fledges,
  And truly calls " Bob White."

The mountain laurel's stringers
  Are chased in silver net, —
The peach tree's baby fingers
  Wear mits of fairy fret,
Like woodmen's blows with axes,
  The starving crows at morn,
Caw on their withheld taxes,
  Due from the farmer's corn.

Still as the meteor falling
  Across the disc of night,
These few strong sounds are calling
  Adown earth's urn of white;
Like marble statuary
  The noble landscapes stand
In one grand cemetery,
  Above a hero-land.

Of old Antietam's story,
  The sculptor of the snow
Carves out the allegory,
  Like Michael Angelo:
These peaks of alabaster
  Entomb the scene of peace,
Where Pollux fought with Castor,
  And Freedom came to Greece.

DELAWARE POEMS

GEORGETOWN

DELAWARE

BETWEEN the Indian River, that of the ocean tastes,
And springs that seek the Nanticoke through sandy
    forest wastes,
And mill-ponds that in mighty swamps the buried
    timber soak,
And deluge all the cypress lands to gain the Poco-
    moke,
The court-house village cleaves a space and little
    has to spare —
So many miles, by statute, from each and every-
    where.

The houses are of shingle, and gardens hem them
    round,
Lean grow the elms and maples about the court-
    house ground,
And in the public corner, like some old town-
    pump's ghost,
The chicken thief of moonlight observes the whip-
    ping-post, —
He who has clasped it fondly knew not, I fear me,
    then,
It was a peaceful heirloom from gracious William
    Penn.

No house is so forsaken the chickens are not there,
Tax dogs, tax hogs, but mulct ye not the hens of
    Delaware!
They won the mains at Valley Forge, and should
    be quartered now
Upon the ancient arms of State beside the brindled
    cow.
Let mountain people eagles love and on their
    standards plant 'em,
The bird of Sussex fights or fries — it is the azure
    bantam.

Around the stores to empty carts the yokes of oxen
    stand,
Or drag the knees and keels of ships from saw-
    mills close at hand;
The solemn bank is locked at noon to let the
    Crœsus dine,
And grave old county clerks come forth to tipple
    apple wine.
Not unobserved their noses bloom, for at the win-
    dow blinds,
Old ladies sit the whole day long of criticising
    minds.

With sheriffs' sales and country studs the tavern
    walls are filled,
And, save in the election heats, all politics is
    stilled;
Then nature to disorder runs, society to fear,
Lest Jones or Smith might get a place worth ninety
    pounds a year.

So old they grow by quiet lives, the graveyard fills
    but slow,
And only age and infancy upon the tombstones
    show.

Old lawyers to their students speak when evening
    comes apace,
Of many a mighty advocate in many a storied
    case —
How Robert Frame took but a dram to make him-
    self austere,
And John M. Clayton got a fee would keep a man
    a year.
The church bell sounds at twilight, and shadows
    cross the square,
Young couples full of wedlock and widows full of
    prayer.

The peach trees grapple with the pines and drive
    the forest back,
And move to town the teams of fruit o'er many a
    woodland track;
Far cities stretch their hands to take the crimson
    harvest in,
And bribe the negro to release his haul of terrapin.
The perch in all the inlets run, the crabs unslip
    their shells,
And deep in sweet potato vines the heifers clink
    their bells.

Then, when the fodder of the corn is bundled in
    the stack,

And through the turning autumn leaves the mill-
    ponds glisten black,
The hunting dogs grow restive and round their
    masters pant —
They sniff the odor of the quail, the flavor of the
    brant.
And bid adieu by half the town, some one old lady
    starts
By railroad to the city to see the styles and arts.

Now, chuckling low of winter nights beside his
    office fire,
The old Recorder reads the wills of many a family
    sire,
Who made his mark and left a sow to several
    various heirs,
And had the barrow slaughtered to pay for funeral
    prayers.
"Ho! ho!" he quoth, "how some proud heads
    would never bow to me,
If ever they should know I poked about their fam-
    ily tree!"

And level as the sandy land is human life diffused;
To preacher turns the stricken lad a maiden has
    refused;
A little lawsuit with its cares the rival homesteads
    haunts,
And hastens to untimely graves the aged litigants;
So are the years repeated, as tell an ancient few,
Since Lewes lost the court-house, soon after Ninety-
    Two.

So life moves on from year to year, unstirred by
    fears or schisms,
And old men read their Bibles and nurse their
    rheumatisms ;
The moss grows on some older roof, familiar signs
    grow dim,
Or from a venerable tree falls some decrepit limb.
So still it is, I almost hear the cry I raised, that
    morn,
When here, past thirty years ago, my mother's son
    was born.
    1876.

SWEDE AND INDIAN CANTICO

1638

LITTLE Minqua girl on the Christine kill!
  Go get your sisters five
And stand them here twixt the kill and the hill,
  Till the boatswain pipes alive!
Then, whistle, my Jack! and fiddle, Mynheer!
  Till the Minqua girl so neat,
Can not stand still for the little brown ear
    That tells such tunes to her feet!
      Then whistle, my Jack! and fiddle Mynheer!
        And the brandy wine kag tip more!
      The Minqua maid is my little brown dear, —
      The Swede man's happy ashore!

The Kalmar Nyckel's a right fine ship,
  The Vogel Gripen's fast,
But the Minqua girl has a cherry lip

And a lean like the vessel's mast ;
Then whistle, my Jack! and fiddle, Mynheer!
  Till the Minqua girl so young,
Shall feel no man but the Swede man near,
  And teach him the Minqua tongue !
      Then whistle, my Jack ! and fiddle, Mynheer !
        And the brandywine kag tip more !
      The Minqua maid is my little fawn deer, —
        The Swede man's happy ashore !

I love our queen, the little Christine,
  Nor Stockholm's lassies slur,
But the Minqua girl has the red doe's lean,
  And the sleek of the beaver fur ;
Then whistle, my Jack ! and fiddle, Mynheer !
  Till we fire the Kalmar's gun
And the Minqua girl runs away with fear
  In the woods where is venison !
      Then whistle, my Jack ! and fiddle, Mynheer !
        And the brandywine kag tip more !
      The Minqua maid is my little game deer, —
        The Swede man's happy ashore !

DOVER

DELAWARE

In a bracket mortisèd,
Like a bust with fractured head
Of some lady delicate,
Stands the Delawarean State.

Counties, three, are all her own,
Rising like a triple stone;
Down her profile like her hair
Showers the golden Delaware.

In her lids, retiring shy,
Brown Newcastle is her eye;
In the ocean's ewer thrust
Rosy Lewes tips her bust.

In her throat's slim interval
Dover is her capital.
Like a modest brooch within
Velvet recess of her chin.

From its agate to the bay
Ribbons a soft creek away,
Through the lotos lily ponds
And the marshes' diamonds.

Humid in the groves it stands,
Like some town in Netherlands,
Rising steepled o'er the fen, —
A mirage of Hindlopen.

As within the locket's lid
Him, the lady loved, is hid,
Delaware, her face demure,
Shows in Dover's miniature:

Edmond Andros wigged so grand,
Francis Lovelace granting land,
Royal York and William Penn
And the Calvert gentlemen.

While the Dutchman trapped for furs,
Here were glebe and worshippers
Whilst the separate State began,
In the fresh years of Queen Anne.

And the sheriff set his stocks
In St. Jones's splatterdocks;
When its rent it would not pay
The Assembly drove away.

In his marshes wrote with grace,
By his cornered fire-place,
Dickinson, with eagle wing,
"Farmer's Letters" for the King.

Here the bell, like falchion keen,
Rang the soldiers to the green,
Who, erewhile, to court had come
At the beating of the drum.

Like a trumpet of his Lord's,
Guarded by the gentry's swords,
Preached the schoolhouse steps upon
"Tory" Freeborn Garrettson.

Barratt's chapel was the lists,
Where old Wesley's Methodists
Bishops did themselves create,
In a new Episcopate.

Whatcoat's grave is in the town.
Bassett, convert of renown,
(Landed statesman in the strife,)
Bayard gave his child to wife.

Found by Presbyterian kirks
Are the heroes and their works,
With the Irish and the Scot
And their kindred Huguenot.

Every nook its own equips, —
Jones, McDonough fought their ships
With the country-hearted air
Breathed in sylvan Delaware.

Like the gamecock first to crow,
While imperial states were slow,
Delaware her blessing sent
To a Federal government.

Count de Segur bringing gold,
Peeped on Dover's sleep, and told;
Marshal Grouchy, gunning through,
Shot more than at Waterloo.

Through our borders making tours,
Here came Du Pont de Nemours,
With his sons Lavoisier taught
To make powder full of thought.

Straight as it were almost new,
The cool house of Quaker Chew
Echoes more than war's renown
Round his hall at Germantown;

Not his daughters, royal fine,
Not his old Madeira wine,
But all filial war's surcease:
Clayton's, Bulwer's solemn peace.

Clayton to young Fisher there
Told the lore of Delaware ;
Local-hearted was his breast
As the fishhawk to its nest.

Bayards four, to Senates sent,
From the rented State house went.
Cross the square, unspeaking, three
Rival brothers Saulsbury !

Who shall know a magazine
Crept to print on Dover green?
Or that Smithers, lawyer prim,
Here composed in Latin hymn?

Or that jurist Ridgelys sank
Sterling talents in a bank ?
And, her Blue Hen's chickens canned,
Dover gave the world her brand.

Surgery its native realms
Founded under Dover elms
And, its green retreats within,
Letters gave to medicine.[1]

Delaware's tranquil increase
Comes from times of Prince Maurice,
Fragment of their souls' concern —
Grotius and Oxenstiern.

Down her creek ports from the ways
Glide her sloops, where cattle graze,

---

[1] Doctors James Sykes and Edward Miller, 1799.

Ever fattening, never gone,
On Van Rembrandt's river lawn.

Jurisprudence of its courts
Dignified by its reports;
By its Senators sustained
The equality it gained.

Not the fractious rights of States
Riots in her water gates;
Kirtled in her slender zone,
Daughter of our Union.

Ancient blendings in her type
Give her beauty rare and ripe,
All of Europe's races born
In the orient of her morn.

Wanton cities spoil her not;
Like her peach and apricot,
She, within her little tree,
Has the orchard's luxury.

LAND OF NO ACCOUNT

A TOAST to them the sage contemn,
  As only fit for pelf:
Here's to the State of people great
  That never knew itself!
We never knew our statesmen true,
  Our quorums and our twelves,
Our senators and congressmen —
  They never knew themselves.

The traveled prig whose soul was big —
  That patronizing elf —
The college sprig, saw through his wig
  The State knew not itself.
We humble fools, a million schools
  Made of us reading elves;
We sat on stools, we plied our tools,
  We never knew ourselves.

We had no lords, we wore no swords,
  Not Ghiblin nor yet Guelf,
Our parent fount of no account
  We never knew ourself;
More wooden we in company
  Than our good axes' helves,
We read our fate not to be great
  And never knew ourselves.

Yet still we grew, as simples do,
  And wealth was on our shelf;
From sea to sea all folks were free, —
  Our neighbor was ourself.
"See yonder lout!" He comes not out,
  He dickers and he delves;
Let's smite his hip, blow up his ship!" —
  They never knew ourselves.

To farthest world our shots are hurled —
  Old Spain has dug her delf —
Hapsburgers great! Beware the state
  That never knew itself!
Lest if we quit our humble wit —

The dry goods on our shelves —
All hell may feel our home-made steel
And we may know ourselves!

THE OREGON

I AM coming, Uncle Sam!
And a little sore I am;
Twelve thousand miles of palm,
Through tropics twain, I trode,
From my own golden gate
Down past Magellan's Strait,
And round the Horn with freight,
          Precious load.

Four hundred sons of mine
From the groves of giant pine,
The vineyards of the vine,
The mountain and the dall,
They come along with me
Their Uncle Sam to see;
Oh, next time, let it be
          By canal!

We outsailed Captain Cook
And Sinbad in the book;
Our steel frames never shook,
For our smiths we swore upon;
The Stars and Stripes they blew
Past the Incas of Peru,
And the Patagonian knew
          Oregon.

No cable of our own
Spoke in our uncle's tone;
All voiceless and alone,
Deep laden with our guns,
We slipped the Spaniard's snares
In the Bay of Buenos Ayres
By the good saint in our prayers —
     Washington.

They gave us right good will,
The Republic of Brazil;
Of fuel we took fill,
And out again we wheeled;
The Equator it was hot,
But we never slacked our trot,
To reach that hotter spot —
     Battlefield.

The Amazon's wide mouth,
We crossed its burning drouth,
Left Orinoco south
And all the brood of Spain's;
Till the air it seemed our own,
And the stars were purer sown,
And we felt our native zone
     · In our veins.

They may waylay us yet,
But the world will not forget
What workmanship we set,
That could stand this mighty trip;
It will fear our Arts afar

More than our guns of war,
And the ship shall be our star;
Workmanship.

1898.

THE CIRCUIT PREACHER

His thin wife's cheek grows pinched and pale with
　　anxiousness intense;
He sees the brethren's prayerful eyes o'er all the
　　conference;
He hears the Bishop slowly call the long "Ap-
　　pointment" rolls,
Where in his vineyard God would place these
　　gatherers of souls.

Apart, austere, the knot of grim Presiding Elders
　　sit;
He wonders if some city "Charge" may not for
　　him have writ?
Certes! could they his sermon hear on Paul and
　　Luke awreck,
Then had his talent ne'er been hid on Annomessix
　　Neck!

Poor rugged heart! be still a pause, and you, worn
　　wife be meek!
Two years of banishment they read far down the
　　Chesapeake!
Though Brother Bates, less eloquent, by Wilming-
　　ton is wooed,
The Lord that counts the sparrows fall shall feed
　　his little brood.

CIRCUIT PREACHER AND WIFE: THE AUTHOR'S PARENTS

"Cheer up, my girl! Here Brother Riggs our cir-
    cuit knows 'twill please.
He raised three hundred dollars there, besides the
    marriage fees.
What! tears from us who preached the word these
    thirty years or so?
Two years on barren Chincoteague, and two in
    Tuckahoe?

" The schools are good, the brethren say, and our
    Church holds the wheel;
The Presbyterians lost their house; the Baptists
    lost their zeal.
The parsonage is clean and dry; the town has
    friendly folk, —
Not as Rehoboth half so dull, nor proud like Poco-
    moke.

" Oh! thy just will, our Lord! be done, though
    these eight seasons more,
We see our ague-crippled boys pine on the Eastern
    Shore,
While we, thy steward, journey out our dedicated
    years
Midst foresters of Nanticoke, or heathen of Tan-
    giers!

" Yea! some must serve on God's frontiers, and I
    shall fail, perforce,
To sow upon some better ground my most select
    discourse;
At Sassafras, or Smyrna, preach my argument on
    ' Drink,'
My series on the Pentateuch, at Appoquinimink.

“ Gray am I, brethren, in the work, though tough
      to bear my part ;
It is these drooping little ones that sometimes wring
      my heart,
And cheat me with the vain conceit the cleverness
      is mine
To fill the churches of the Elk, and pass the
      Brandywine.

“ These hairs were brown, when, full of hope,
      ent’ring these holy lists,
Proud of my Order as a knight, — the shouting
      Methodists, —
I made the pine woods ring with hymns, with
      prayer the night-winds shook,
And preached from Assawaman Light far North as
      Bombay Hook.

“ My nag was gray, my gig was new; fast went
      the sandy miles ;
The eldest Trustees gave me praise, the fairest sis-
      ters smiles ;
Still I recall how Elder Smith of Worten Heights
      averred
My Apostolic Parallels the best he ever heard.

“ All winter long I rode the snows, rejoicing on my
      way ;
At midnight our Revival hymns rolled o’er the sob-
      bing bay ;
Three Sabbath sermons, every week, should tire a
      man of brass, —
And still our fervent membership must have their
      extra Class !

"Aggressive with the zeal of youth, in many a
    warm requite
I terrified Immersionists, and scourged the Mil-
    lerite ;
But larger, tenderer charities such vain debates
    supplant.
When the dear wife, saved by my zeal, loved the
    Itinerant.

" No cooing dove of storms afeared, she shared my
    life's distress,
A singing Miriam, alway, in God's poor wilderness ;
The wretched at her footstep smiled, the frivolous
    were still ;
A bright path marked her pilgrimage, from Black-
    bird to Snowhill.

" A new face in the parsonage, at church a double
    pride ! —
Like Joseph's Mary and her babe they filled the
    ' Amen-side ' —
Crouched at my feet in the old gig, my boy, so fair
    and frank,
Naswongo's darkest marshes cheered, or sluices of
    Choptank.

" My cloth drew close ; too fruitful love my fruit-
    less life outran ;
The townfolk marvelled, when we moved, at such
    a caravan !
I wonder not my lads grew wild, when, bright
    without the door
Spread the ripe, luring, wanton world, — and we,
    within, so poor !

“ For, down the silent cypress aisles came shapes
    even me to scout,
Mocking the lean flanks of my mare, my boy’s
    patched roundabout,
And saying: ‘ Have these starveling stocks, thy
    congregation, souls,
That on their dull heads Heaven and thou pour
    forth such living coals?’

“ Then prayer brought hopes, half secular, like
    seers by Endor’s witch:
Beyond our barren Maryland God’s folks were wise
    and rich ;
Where climbing spires and easy pews showed how
    the preacher thrived,
And all old brethren paid their rents, and many
    young ones wived !

“ I saw the ships Henlopen pass with chaplains fat
    and sleek ;
From Bishopshead with fancy’s sails I crossed the
    Chesapeake ;
In velvet pulpits of the North said my best ser-
    mons o’er, —
And that on Paul to Patmos driven, drew tears in
    Baltimore.

“ Well! well! my brethren, it is true we should
    not preach for pelf, —
(I would my sermon on Saint Paul the Bishop
    heard himself !)

But this crushed wife,—these boys,— these hairs!
    they cut me to the core;
Is it not hard, year after year, to ride the Eastern
    Shore?

"Next year? Yes! yes! I thank you much! Then,
    my reward may fall.
(That is a downright fine discourse on Patmos and
    St. Paul!)
So, Brother Riggs, once more my voice shall ring
    in the old lists.
Cheer up, sick heart! who would not die among
    these Methodists?"

    1866.

LITTLE GRISETTE

LITTLE Grisette, you haunt me yet;
   My passion for you was long ago,
   Before my head was heavy with snow,
Or mine eye had lost its lustre of jet.
In the dim old *Quartier Latin* we met;
   We plighted faith one night in June,
   And all our life was honeymoon;
We did not ask if it were sin,
   We did not go to kirk to know,
We only loved and let the world
   Hum on its pelfish way below:
Marked from our castle in the air,
   How pigmy its triumphal cars —
Eight stages from the entry stair,
   But near the stars!

Little Grisette, rich or in debt,
  We were too fond to chide or sigh, —
  Never so poor that I could not buy
A sweet, sweet kiss, from my little Grisette.
If I could nothing gain or get,
  By hook, or crook, or song, or story,
  Along the starving road to glory,
I marvelled how your nimble thimble,
  As to a tune, danced fast and fleeting,
And stopped my pen to catch the music,
  But only heard my heart a-beating;
The quaint old roofs and gables airy
  Flung down the light, for you to wear it,
And made my love a queen in faery,
  To haunt my garret.

Little Grisette, the meals you set
  Were sweeter to me than banquet feast;
  Your face was a blessing fit for a priest;
At your smile the candle went out in a pet.
The wonderful chops, I shall never forget!
  If the wine was a trifle too sharp or rank,
  We kissed each time before we drank.
The old gilt clock, e'er wrong, was swinging;
  The waxèd floor your feet reflected;
And dear Béranger's *chansons* singing,
  You tricked at *picquet* till detected.
You fill my pipe; — is it your eyes
  Whereat I light your cigarette? —
On all but me the darkness lies,
  And my Grisette!

Little Grisette, the soft sunset
  Lingered a long while, that we might stay,
  To mark the Seine from the breezy quay
Around the bridges foam and fret;
How came it that your eyes were wet,
  When I ambitiously would be,
  A man renowned across the sea?
I told you I should come again, —
  It was but half way round the globe, —
To bring you diamonds for your faith,
  And for your gray a silken robe:
You were more wise than lovers are;
  I meant, Sweetheart, to tell you true,
I said a tearful *"Au revoir;"*
  You said: *"Adieu!"*

Little Grisette, we both regret;
  For I am wedded more than wived;
  Those careless days, in thought revived,
But teach me I cannot forget.
Perhaps old age must pay the debt
  Folly contracted long ago, —
  I only know, I only know,
That phantoms haunt me everywhere
  By busy day, in peopled gloam, —
They rise between me and my prayer,
  They chafe the holiness of home!
My wife is proud, my boy is cold,
  I dare not speak of what I fret:
'Tis my heart's rest with thee, I fold,
  Little Grisette!

FLORENCE, 1863.

THE PIGEON GIRL

On the sloping market-place,
  In the city of Compiègne,
Every Saturday her face,
  Like a Sunday, comes again;
Daylight finds her in her seat,
With her panier at her feet,
  Where her pigeons lie in pairs;
Like their plumage gray her gown,
To her sabots drooping down;
And a kerchief, brightly brown,
  Binds her smooth, dark hairs.

All the buyers knew her well,
  And, perforce, her face must see,
As a holy Raphael
  Lures us in a gallery;
Round about the rustics gape,
Drinking in her comely shape,
  And the housewives gently speak,
When into her eyes they look,
As within some holy book,
And the gables high and crook,
  Fling their sunshine on her cheek.

In her hands two milk-white doves,
  Happy in her lap to lie,
Softly murmur of their loves,
  Envied by the passers-by;
One by one their flight they take,
Bought and cherished for her sake,

Leaving so reluctantly;
Till the shadows close approach,
Fades the pageant. foot and coach,
And the giants in the cloche
   Ring the noon for Picardie.

Round the city see her glide,
   With a slender sunbeam's pace!
Mirrored in the Oise's tide,
   The gold-fish hover on her face;
All the soldiers touch their caps;
In the cafés quit their naps
   Garçon. guest, to wish her back;
And the fat old beadles smile
As she kneels along the aisle,
Like Pucelle in other while,
   In the dim church of Saint Jacques.

Now she climbs her dappled ass. —
   He well-pleased such friend to know, —
And right merrily they pass
   The armorial château;
Down the long, straight paths they tread
Till the forest. overhead,
   Whispers low its leafy love;
In the archway's green caress
Rides the wondrous dryadess —
Thrills the grass beneath her press,
   And the blue-eyed sky above.

I have met her, o'er and o'er,
   As I strolled alone apart,
By a lonely carrefour

In the forest's tangled heart,
Safe as any stag that bore
Imprint of the Emperor;
  In the copse that round her grew
Tiptoe the straight saplings stood,
Peeped the wild boar's satyr brood,
Like an arrow clove the wood
  The glad note of the cuckoo.

How I wished myself her friend!
  (So she wished that I were more)
Jogging toward her journey's end
  At Saint Jean au Bois before,
Where her father's acres fall
Just without the abbey wall;
  By the cool well loiteringly
The shaggy Norman horses stray,
In the thatch the pigeons play,
And the forest round alway
  Folds the hamlet, like a sea.

Far forgotten all the feud
  In my New World's childhood haunts,
If my childhood she renewed
  In this pleasant nook of France;
Might she make the bleuze I wear,
Welcome, then, her homely fare
  And her sensuous religion!
To the market we should ride,
In the Mass kneel side by side,
Might I warm, each eventide,
  In my nest, my pretty pigeon!
1864.

THE FIRST HUNGER

THE apples are water, Dearest,
   The dates are only sweet,
There is no flesh in the juice of the grape,
   Nor life in the berry we eat!
In the blood of the kid we have slain
   In our new and terrible greed,
   Lie the gristle and marrow we need, —
In the pitiful yield of the grain:
The barley that beards the wild rain,
   The corn that the crow contests,
   The milk in the white wheat's breasts, —
Behold my red hands as I speak,
And the curse of the sweat on my cheek!

The garden was all before us
   Where reaches to-day a waste,
Its plentiful clusters o'er us,
   Eternity in their taste;
I could lie in your tresses, and reach
   In the roses, the flush of the South;
   Power fell, with the figs, in my mouth,
And youth in the bite of the peach;
I am weary, but still they beseech, —
   These sinews, that hunger and thirst
   In their famine the fiercest and first;
And thine eyes, where love's wishes I read,
Look the eloquence only of — bread.

No more shall the noons be luscious,
   The nights be tender strolls,

Sweet sleep delightful hushes
　In the fond talk of our souls;
Yoked this stature, thou praised, to the clod,
　Farewell to the leisure so dear!
　No more by the streams shall we hear
The intimate thoughts of our God,
But harrow our hearts with the sod, —
　Dismissed our high quests to the winds,
　And the infinite wish of our minds,
And the beautiful dreams that we prize,
Like the birds that forsake Paradise.

I must seek so late thy kisses,
　So soon thy side discard,
And my tenderest caresses
　Bestow with hands so hard.
It is not for my lot that I plead,
　Too proud at my burden to groan,
　Nor yet, O my wife! for thine own,
But the races of men which succeed:
The cannibal children of greed,
　Who fight at the bosom they crave,
　And walk from the cradle to slave,
Till populous hunger shall shed
The blood of its brethren for bread.

The world from the sun slips farther,
　As we far from God's face;
There is war declared eternal
　'Twixt nature and our race.
But it is not the end that we dread;
　Fighting up to God's feet as we toil,

We shall trample this curse from the soil,
And conquer the bondage of bread,
Making Nature our slave in our stead,
    Till the frost shall say truce, and the rain
    Draw near, at the beck of the grain,
And our sons, with the sheaves at their knee,
Reach again of the fruit of the tree.
1865.

DE WITT CLINTON

In thy Dutch veins thy Irish current ran,
A tempest in the phlegm of a canal;
Hibernian spirits made thee partisan,
De Witt milk tranquilized thee cosmical !
Wasted thy youth in faction's offices
Thy lofty mind thy scullions drove afar,
And, looking downward from thy banished star,
Thou saw'st an isthmian labor like to Suez
When Amrou slashed it with his scimeter :
Niagara's dam to Amsterdam to draw,
The Indian oceans through the lunar Nile
And to another Persia give access !
Letters and Physics are the stones of Law :
Thy inspiration makes an empire smile.

POE

Kepler of verse ! who beauty's starry laws
    Didst rescue and her orbits calculate !

Thou hadst no prince, no Tycho, in thy cause,
  No fellow-centre for thy solar mate;
A dark polemic age hollow applause
  Gave to the weird ellipsis of thy fate.
But thou art in the heavens like a pause,
  Like Al Aaraf's swift and unearthly date,
A diadem'd outlaw like Tamerlane.
  Thy heart strings were a lute like Israfel's,
The raven led thy fame to Ulalume;
  Thou art the Psyche unto Sappho's pain.
So sibylline the leaflets from thy plume
  They sigh like Orpheus melting Pluto's spells.

BYRON

FIRST Englishman to hail my country's scions —
  Henry, Boon, Washington, — in courtly rhyme!
"Still one great clime in full and free defiance
  Yet rears her crest unconquered and sublime,"
And hears thy trumpet of *la belle alliance:*
  Tyrtaeus, to whose overture we chime!
Old friends are dearest: as I read agog,
  In youth the rich invective of thy verse,
I stood beside the trophy of thy dog
  At Newstead, as by tender Æsop's hearse,
And felt that man and nature were thy debtors,
  That thou wert noble by thy discontent,
That thou hadst widened heart and thought and letters
  And breathed afar the glorious Occident.

JOHN JAY

AMONG the portraits of thy Federalists,
  In thy old Bedford manse upon the Highlands,
Where, bathed beneath thee in the snow or mists,
  Manhattan's Greece tints its Ægean islands,
I see thee life's full third pass in thy grot
  But in no monkish mummeries enshrined! —
The soul undaunted of the Huguenot
  Built his God's temple in his classic mind.
Washington was thy Henry of Navarre ;
  For him thou held thy state in loyal fief,
His mystic presence to the knightly bar,
  His dove-winged envoy to our kinsman chief.
Thou, Sully ! with thy eagle quill at work,
  Wert Zeus at the birth-throes of New York !

THE SOUL-DRIVER

THE child's awe that I felt of Slavery,
  When from our door they dragged the faithful
    cook,
I did not need to join a sect to see,
  Nor have it preached at me from any book ;
And when the freedmen wail the horrid laws
  And massacre is slavery's aftermath,
I only feel what the volcano was
  From these red lavas of its senile wrath.
He who was absolute must sometimes kill.
  His Berber sons arrest the mails of light.
His nation float his soon forgotten bill,

Its flag and trade be halted for his spite.
When absolution tempts me with its fruit,
I think that Slavery was absolute.

PSYCHÉ

Thou art but child; thy willow limbs
   Have hardly set their mould;
Light of the fawn, thy large eye brims,
   Thy hair is spun of gold;
So perfect is the woman's might
   Within thy tendril's move,
My look meets thine almost in fright:
   Hast thou conjectured love?

Thy sex's power at once begins,
   When it has one day's bloom,
And man's supremest homage wins
   When he draws near his tomb;
Thy youth, for which he hungereth,
   Is all that can contain
His immortality from death:
   By love he lives again.

LINNÆUS

Carl Von Linn fell in the leashes
   Of a female hind:
Nature is a fight for Species,
   Not for morals nor for mind;
"Lo! the lilies," spoke the teacher,
   "Looking not above,
How their clothes outshine the preacher,

Dyed in purpling love!"
Through the air, a blood-drop fallen,
   Speeds the red bird free,
Carrying the golden pollen
   To the female tree;
So the Swede, in passion richest,
   Straight at Nature aims;
He who flushed the Magdalena
   Fetched the flowers, Names.

STOCKHOLM, 1889.

WILLIAM PENN

(HEPWORTH DIXON'S LIFE)

MANLY teller of the tale!
Thou hast made me thrill and pale.
Almost tears have dimmed the page, —
I have felt in Penn's own age.

His the nature one appeal
From a worldly life could wheel, —
Quit the brink of rank and rule
To go live with ridicule;

For his soul decision had,
To part instant with the bad,
And from youth full stature find
For the conscience in his mind;

Not the wiggèd court to gain,
But be noble with the plain.
In his hat he talked to kings
On the plane of kingly things,

Till his father's giant pride
Humbled his strange son's beside,
Seeing that he did not quail
Rotting in the stinking jail.

Treading down the earth's contempt
Dreams high-hearted aye he dreamt,
Grasped across the ocean's health
More than Milton's Commonwealth;

And he touched it with his hand,
And he landed in his land, —
Brought the persecuted in;
Made them of his wish the kin.

Pennsylvania, wholesome grove!
Philadelphia, brother's love!
There the Continental men
Wrote the will of William Penn.

DEFOE

Born a Foe, he sought out foes,
(There are always hosts of those;)
Writing for the grown folks, he
Gained the height of pillory.
Then he sat, Himself before,
Solitary, shipwrecked, poor,
And gave forth his lonely joys
To the fresh hearts of the boys:
Entering there, the world was won, —
All the world knew Robinson!

BROOKLYN BRIDGE TOWERS
(AS UNCONNECTED)

BRONTÉS.

BROTHER! are you waiting
 Faithfully for me?
Stand fast and at last
 I'll reach my hair to thee.
Though of vacant sight,
 Blindly we are feeling
Tow'rd each other, till the light,
 Through our sockets stealing
O'er the stream, in one beam
 Shall meet, and see!

ARGÉS.

Brother! I am listening
 To the words you say,
As they reach me, whistling
 Across the windy bay.
Though my feet are cold,
 And they long divide us,
Here I'll hold till I am old;
 Our echoes shall provide us
On bounding feet a pathway fleet,
 Till we behold!

BRONTÉS.

Like two gates asunder
 Something swings between.

On our heads the thunder
    Strikes.   We stand serene!
Earliest on our brows,
    Still the latest tarry
The rosy clouds; the birds in crowds
    Sail round to see us marry.
We will win, though, my twin,
    Waves intervene!

ARGÈS.

Hark, behind! the churches
    Faintly lift their bells.
And far below come and go
    The city's hollow swells;
Frightened ferry fleets
    Disappear in vapor,
And the camps of twinkling lamps
    Struggle for a taper.
To them all, starry tall,
    We are sentinels!

BRONTÉS.

Aye! I cannot see them,
    Yet I feel them there;
And clambering stars their silver bars
    Wind o'er me like a stair.
Brother, does a pulse
    Start not in thy shoulder,
For a mystic destiny, —
    Something better, bolder —
When the rainbow its skein
    Twineth in air?

ARGÉS.

Yes! A host of spirits
    In procession creep
O'er me silently,
    From darkened deeps of sleep.
Far away I hear
    Wheels imperious driven
Up the heights of the atmosphere,
    By the image of Heaven!
His path we span, and, brother! Man
Is the charioteer!

1875.

BARTHOLDI'S PHAROS

(RECITED AT THE LOTOS CLUB DINNER, NOV. 14, 1884)

MANHATTAN Bay in glory lay
    When Verrazano entered;
His heart was cold, on thoughts of gold
    And ivory concentred:
"Now go about and sail we out!—
    Although this scene entrances;
For we Italians seek rich mines,
    To satisfy King Francis."

The Portugee came in from sea,
    Sir Estevan de Gomez;
"I smell," said he, "no spicery
    Nor gum, such as at home is;
King Charles of Spain, he would raise Cain
    And cuss-words use terrific,

If we clove not this granite main
  To cloves of the Pacific."

The Half-Moon next our harbor vexed —
  The Dutchman made appearance —
The Northwest Passage was his text,
  And Albany his clearance;
The Indian damsels pleased his ways, —
  He was a gay deceiver, —
And nothing met his sordid praise
  But buffalo and beaver.

Next came Lord Howe, guns at his prow,
  His nose and clothes vermilion,
With Hessian bayonets, to plough
  The hills around new Ilion;
Seven years the fleet stayed here to eat, —
  King George he paid the ration, —
Till French and Yankees down the street
  Saw an evacuation.

The artisan American
  Came now — a buoyant schemer —
With fleets of fire-winged birds to span
  The shores with many a steamer.
At Fulton's wand our sparkling pond
  Leaped into life and duty,
But nothing came to correspond
  Unto the sense of Beauty.

The gold we made, the South-Sea trade,
  The peltries and the spices,
And mechanisms, like crystal prisms,

Refracted our devices.
Yet in the heart the spell of Art
  Slept, like the winter throstle,
Or Faith, in old Diana's mart,
  Awaiting an apostle.

The son of France his kindling glance
  Threw o'er this radiant Edom,
And like a Bayard of romance
  Knelt to the strength of Freedom;
He saw arise athwart our skies
  A Goddess ever living,
Illumination in her eyes,
  And flame to darkness giving.

Lift high thy torch and forward march,
  O dame of Revolution! —
All heaven thy triumphal arch,
  All progress the solution;
And from the earth and all its dross
  May man behold the story —
Friendship is pious as the cross,
  And only Art is glory!

PHYSICAL HOMAGE

When in the bath men strip together,
  A perfect man has admiration,
The mould of grace, the thews of leather,
  The noble port of native station;

No more excelleth moral duty,
  The master mind appears a fakir;
But procreant health and manly beauty
  Become the image of their Maker.

When to the life the beauteous creature,
  The woman, walks, behold the wonder!
Divinity in every feature,
  Her worshippers are rent asunder;
Her beauty rules her moral being,
  Like genius is her stately doing,
The regent of the Ever-seeing,
  She bends the heavens to her wooing.

The beauty of the worlds in motion
  Attracts each other in their courses;
Space has its wooings like the ocean,
  And planets feel persuasive forces;
Perfection everything convulses,
  Beauty is moral elevation,
The symmetry that stirs our pulses,
  Is an eternal admiration.

Health and selection, joy determine,
  Their progeny our orb inherit;
"Behold the lilies!" saith the sermon:
  Beauty is the immortal spirit.
What is unlovely shall not witness
  Final survival of the fitting,
And separating foul from fitness,
  Venus to judge the world is sitting.

GAPLAND AND WAR CORRESPONDENTS' MONUMENT

ROWDY SHAH

THERE once was a shah of Persia,
  Common and rowdy and pert,
Who married by hundreds, virgins,
  To strip them and slide them in dirt;
A platform over a mudhole
  He built with precipitous slides,
And called on the court and people
  To see how he muddied his brides.

The fine Events that are blushing —
  The newspapers strip them of pride;
And I think of the Shah and the mud-hole,
  As I see them rushed down the slide.

FROM GAPLAND

How blue the mountain is to-day!
It is not half so far away.
Distinct on it the shadows play;
Above it a long band of light,
Below it a long band of land,
Revealed in shocks of gathered corn,
In village spires, wax-candle white,
And fields like a wide-open hand,
Shining from a reversèd morn
Below those hills so blue to-day.

The clouds those hills, so blue to-day,
Seem to throw upward as they lay,

From that bright landscape's underplay,
Make all that blueness far away.
The clouds our lives project above
Follow so close our long career,'
They paint it with distinctive strength,
They bring it nearer human love,
Tone it like echoes to the ear,
And accent through their graceful length
The heights that are so dark to-day.

MORSE

THE simplest life told well's a treat.
One push makes any life complete;
One grapple with our deadly fears
Carries us to victorious years:
One night in the dark with foes at hand,
A starving year in a foreign land,
To hold a pen and take a stand:
The effort is the fort betaken,
The bolder that your heart is shaken;
And every young accomplishment
Is a lady in the soldier's tent.
When all but avarice is sated,
And thou hast lived with her thou mated,
Tell all thou didst with truthfulness, —
Thy book shall also be success!

“ MAKE ME A LAP”

Back in those days ere I thought of love,
Kissing at games in a picnic grove,
Cried one lass as she made a spring :
“ Make me a Lap! you stingy thing!”
Down in my lap sat the tired madcap
And in a snap she had “ made her a Lap. ’

Lissome, pliant, innocent vine,
Still to my heart I can feel her twine,
Trustfully as my kitten's play,
Light as the birds in that greenwood day ;
Sweet as the sap in the fruit tree’s tap,
Vine-like her wrap as I “ made her a Lap.”

Country heart! there is no mishap, —
Some good husband has “ made thee a Lap”;
In thy lap to thy trust’s behove,
Children spring in the gush of love :
Thou had’st no trap of “ setting thy cap,”
Teaching a chap how to “ make thee a Lap.”

Earth is wide but its infinite map
Is peopled by courage that leaped in a Lap.
Cold, prude hearts that would Love go round
Consolation have partly found.
Boldly they rap who would wake from his nap
The partner whose snap can “ make them a Lap.”

Widow young! whose grief has been true,
But who has brightened to life anew !

There is a lonely man somewhere
Waiting for thee if thou wouldst but dare :
Fill up the gap in his life's mishap!
Set him thy cap! he can " make thee a Lap."

Maid, too long! art thou not exact?
Not far off must thy worth attract.
Do not shrink from the fate to be!
How did thy mother love for thee?
Smooth thy rough nap! for thyself keep no scrap!
So did it hap ere She " made thee a Lap."

Man to man, be not too removed!
Bashful friendship is not oft loved.
Thou must leap in the heart of thy friend,
If he would carry thee out to life's end.
Throw up thy cap!   Say, " Love me, old chap!"
Thou wilt be loved; he will " make thee a Lap."

Father! Son! if there come a space
'Twixt your affectionate embrace,
Let it not grow o'ershadowing home, —
Ye must kiss in the death to come!
Close up the gap; ye have mutual sap:
Sonny and pap! " make each other a Lap!"

FIRST BLACKBIRDS

As I sit at my window bay
　　Just o'er a Gap's abyss,
A sound mysterious comes my way —
　　It sounds so like a kiss!

Who is it, kissing fierce and fast
　　Within my library? —
As I kissed her I caught at last
　　When I was young as she?

No, 'tis not there, though kisses were —
　　They come up from the woods;
Are angels kissing in the air,
　　Or mountain girls, in hoods?
With smacks like those, old satyrs wooed
　　Cold nymphs a stream conceives:
(Such kisses leave babes in the wood
　　Among the trampled leaves.)

It sounds like fright and appetite,
　　Complaint and jubilee,
Like sleighbells coming in the night,
　　And boiling punch, or tea.
So ends this last of mysteries
　　As I my door unlock:
It is the blackbirds in my trees,
　　The first October flock!

I start them from their chilly roost, —
　　They fly like bolts from bows;
Like inky authors, bedlam-loosed,
　　Who murmur and compose.
Still crackles all the morn like frost,
　　That sighing music is;
It says that summer's something lost,
　　And life a farewell kiss.

The earth shall some day cool and we —
　We know not what or for —
Will flock together dismally
　Along the Equatór.
But life will dye the snowflake red,
　As long as it can float,
And from the frozen sun o'erhead
　Will kiss the blackbird's note!

HANGING LAMP

I wish my father had the story known —
　Its interest his sermon would have nerved —
How the cathedral lamp was ever blown
　That Galileo with his pulse observed,
　　And as it swung, he counted his heart's
　　　beating,
　　And planned a miracle in that dull meeting.

Imagination came to me, I wot,
　In those old churches by the piney forest,
But mathematics was not in my thought,
　Not measure in the bawling Christian chorist;
　　Romance, that is theology again,
　　I drank in church and useless am to men.

O, had the dogma with some wise restrainting
　Child-fancy forced on grooves exact to swerve,
As old Mahomet did forbid them painting
　And made them draw the cosine and the curve,
In algebraic strength I had projected
　More than Aladdin's lamp ways did traverse,

And into heaven passed the God-elected
  Among the sure feet of astronomers.

The Popes who Copernik were negativing
  And Galileo silenced but not sieved,
Were not as ignorant as preachers living
  Who know not Copernik has ever lived,
But follow heathens in their horrid fearing
  Of hornèd Gods like Babylonian kings,
While Learning bends the heavens with persevering.
And parting symbols, finds eternal Things, —
  Finds not our human semblance domineering,
But motion as susceptible as strong,
  Worlds without end exquisitely insphering
And praise intuning, tenderer than song.

For us, the heirs of countless predecessors,
  By Time unanxious to our boyhood brought,
We do not enter Nature as transgressors,
  But on our hand the signet ring of Thought;
Death is our mellowing; facts kill its terrors:
  Both Birth and Death like noble brethren go.
The sum of our exaggerated errors
  Is that we romanced, and we did not know.

AS THE CROW FLIES

  THE air paths go unto homes we do not know,
    But we see that the birds fly straight;
  They have errands where the bow
  Gilds the storm and in the glow

That is rosy at the sunset's gate:
        As the dove flies,
        As the crow flies,
At the end of everywhere is a mate.

The soul's paths go to a home they cannot show,
    But not to a home of hate;
As the stag to seek his doe,
As the arrow from the bow,
The errand of the soul is straight:
        As the dove flies,
        As the crow flies,
Darts the soul that is homesick to its mate.

The seed paths go to a home far down below,
    But we know that the sprouts rise straight
To the light that is aglow,
To the air that kindles so,
To the heaven of the recreate:
        As the dove flies,
        As the crow flies,
The errand of the flower is to mate.

The rain paths go to the caves of frost and snow,
    But we see that the springs flow straight
To the fields the farmers mow,
To the cattle lowing low,
        To the rivers that are wide and great:
        As the dove flies,
        As the crow flies,
The spirits in the elements must mate.

The world's paths go upon arcs so calm and slow,
   That we know not we course like fate,
But the stars in groups that go
Sired the planets twinkling low,
And the universes pair in state:
      As the dove flies,
      As the crow flies,
Flash the lights, never meeting, to their mate.

Forever, loving man! drive on thy caravan!
   Thou canst not be selfish and great;
For what is thy little span
To the universal plan,
And the faith of the congregate?
      As the dove flies,
      As the crow flies,
Immortality seek in thy mate.

IRON HILL

(DELAWARE)

Yon blue plateau to all seems low,
Whose minds some mountain fills,
Except us there in Delaware,
Who ne'er saw higher hills;
At Newark's old academy,
It almost shook our will,
To walk so far and scale that bar
The dome of Iron hill.

On holidays we saw the haze
Around its woodlands lie;

To climb those goals, our level souls
Seemed tempting destiny;
The lesser boys they cease their noise
And hold their laughter still,
To come more near those heights of fear,
On shaggy Iron hill.

Beneath its head the iron, red,
Of ancient ore banks stood,
Where goblin Swedes their evil deeds
Revealed in stains of blood;
Their metal arts our country hearts
Uncanny thought and ill, —
From murdered man the oxides ran
That tinctured Iron hill!

The tombs we search at old Welsh church
That guards the cairn's ascent;
In Cymric writ, those stones of grit
Increase our fear's ferment:
Beneath, the dead, above blood, red! —
The lonely wood paths thrill
Our ghost-awed wits; the old ore pits
Seem graves on Iron hill!

We think we see from some tall tree,
The blue-veined landscapes, where
One far-off streak is Chesapeake,
Another Delaware;
Their long white length this knoll has strength
To sunder by its will;
It disarrays those mighty bays —
The wand of Iron hill.

In those small years, upon such fears
My fancy learned to thrill.
An elevation on me lay, —
The swell of Iron hill.
The misty moods of altitudes,
Romance's glow and chill ;
And not more high Mount Sinai
To me, than Iron hill.

BUILDING

THE mountain summit grows apace
  With walls and walks and spires,
The tribute to ancestral place
  By one of waning fires,
Who never loved but haunts of men,
  And earned in cities, bread,
Yet sought the shaggy rock and glen
  To lay, at last, his head.

The thrill of Nature in his craze
  Was like his love of play —
Medicinal for some brief days,
  And, then, to turn away :
To try the mart and measure Art
  With captains of his guild,
Then, in the lonely mountain's heart,
  To dig and plan and build.

His habitation who can know,
  When life is but a breath ?
Or that his bones are safe below
  The cheerless den of death ?

Yet, in their day, all builded well, —
  Like warrior ants their hills, —
And tender beauty haunts the cell
  Taste and Industry wills.

No house stands faster than this earth
  Which no abiding gives,
Yet love and hope and faith and birth
  Build, while the changeling lives.
Our heaven is promised mansions, too,
  Not made with human hod,
As if the angels nothing knew
  Like Building round their God.

So if we leave where nothing stood
  Some structure pure and true,
Succeeding times will count it good
  And others learn to do.
The bookman's art is left behind
  And letters only vex;
Write, then in stone, ye men of mind!
  And live as architects!

BOCCACCIO

RELIGION is of sex, love sacramental,
  So say the physiologists of love.
Then is not Literature testamental
  Born of the soiled and unangelic dove?
Boccacció, gallant of light Maria!
  In thy amour Italian language sprang
More than from Dante's stately Jeremiah

Or Petrarch's lute that had the proper twang;
Thy look upon King Robert's daughter, mated,
  Thy tales blushed into progeny impure,
The tongues of Europe were articulated
  And stolen kisses started Literature.
Out of the ages black and castellated,
  There climbed the lawless and luxuriant vine,
And Christian lore, when love was satiated,
  Told legends of the Heavens concubine.
Monks shrinking from the tender imitation,
  Sang in the chorus of the passion-blest,
And in the hives of Romanesque creation
  Returned the Isis-bee of human rest.
So, Europe's Letters broke the dungeon portal;
  Love's spasms set all tongues to twittering!
Love, only Love, can feed the life immortal!
  When love is rested angels cannot sing.

OLD KENT

I AM back in the court-house village;
  The houses remain as before;
One or two old roofs may have perished,
  But the neighbors have builded no more;
The river creeps under the drawbridge,
  The wharves are a little more rotten,
The streets are as grassy and sandy,
  And the college more lone and forgotten.

It is sad that the faces are stranger
  When the place so familiar appears!

I came with my heart expectant,—
  It is only twenty years;
But the big boys stare at me queerly,
  And the little boys flatter my tailor,
While the old men look suspicious
  From the constable down to the jailer.

Only the innkeeper greets me
  Like the long-expected one,
And makes me believe a little
  In the tale of the prodigal son;
The fatted calf he slaughters,
  The calf that is tough and arid,
Like the townsfolk's beauteous daughters,
  Who have all "gone off and got married."

There is Mary, with seven children,
  And Marion, jilted and wan,
Saffronia gone to the shambles,
  And Emma, gone under the lawn;
Proud Sally, an editor's conquest, —
  What a fate for an exquisite creature!
And Margie, whose husband is richest,
  A note-shaving Methodist preacher.

Not so were the old-time preachers,
  Who rode on this Eastern Shore;
I seek out the grim brick parsonage, —
  Two years 'twas my father's door;
I see blink northward the window,
  In the gable so broad and bulky,
The lot of grass for the old gray mare,
  And the stable for saddle and sulky.

There was his study lattice
  Where often he wrote and prayed;
And there the garden wicket
  Whence he came to promenade;
And bowed to white and to negro, —
  A pastor, no partisan, —
The women said: " He is handsome!"
  And the men said: " A gentleman!"

By starlight on Sunday morning
  He kissed my mother adieu,
And threaded the Necks of the Chesapeake,
  In the snow-storm or the dew;
Old cross-roads chapels grew temples
  While he lit with his radiant face,
The truest and longest sermons
  That ever brought sinners to grace.

No priest of the Roman conclave
  Had tact or *bonhommie* more;
No brigand, armed to the gorget,
  Felt safer the wild woods o'er;
Priest, friend, Franciscan and doctor,
  At length his renown appears, —
A spirit of civilization,
  A statesman on man's frontiers!

And so, I shall quit the village,
  Content my escutcheon to show;
Content that nothing is stirring.
  But the worm that's at work below,
And the soul of the seed, hence wafted,
  Which the Lord of the Harvest must seek,
In the little old-fashioned places,
  That doze by the Chesapeake.

SAINT GEORGE

When I behold the web around us drawn
From infant pulp to ignorance's end,
To forestall knowledge and the mind transcend
With superstitions from the Arab dawn;
When I see woman, whether doe or fawn,
Hold man's mind back and her stag offspring bend,
And her one half of our progression pawn
At Mont de Piété; when I do count
The unproducing host of medicine men,
Who nibble learning on the convent lawn,
To low, like cattle, from their twilight pen,
That what we know not is life's only fount:
I see a task to make my spirit mount,
I feel my strength is as the strength of ten.

OLD FRANK BLAIR

No more that lost old twain to town
    Shall trot in various weather —
The broad-brimmed hat and great coat brown
    And snow-white braids together;
The snug green home at Silver Springs
    One hermit less shall pension,
She waits to hear the warning wings
    And summons of ascension.

Scotch as the pibroch of Argyle,
    Hard as the granite Highland,
Their fire domestic smoked the while,
    Blue as o'er Ellen's island;

And there they nursed the loyal love
  Of old Saint Andrew's story,
And deemed the Lord's high court above
  Stern as his reign of glory.

Not rebel flames around their roof
  New Orleans' guns could silence,
Nor Freedom's statue look reproof,
  Like Jackson's grim surveillance,
Which met the traitors in their mart
  And made their leader tremble,
And never bent the statesman's art
  To palter or dissemble.

Van Buren's long and subtle skill
  And Benton's various knowledge,
And stout Old Hickory's lofty will
  And Kendall's lore of college,
And plastic grace of Silas Wright,
  Their golden era bounded,
While Francis Blair, both squire and knight,
  The Koran's page compounded.

Not for the bondman's smothered sighs,
  Nor labor, low and humble,
He hailed the Northern columns rise,
  The Southron's kingdom crumble;
He only saw the dark Calhoun
  Above the thunderous action,
And Jackson's spirit, not too soon,
  Ride forth to smite the faction!

The long revenge of stubborn years —
    The private vindication —
He heard above the cannoneers,
    When others hailed a Nation.
And scarce had victory struck her tents, —
    The feudal code revising, —
He felt, in hardening heart and sense,
    The old reaction rising.

The grass-grown forts that to his door
    Brought bloody retrospections,
A less irreverent echo bore
    Than Freedom's full elections;
Yet neither back nor forward halt
    The rival waves of passion;
Alack! the times were all at fault —
    The Blairs were out of fashion!

And so, in bootless intrigue pressed
    His clannish boys their mettle;
And one, most gallant, passed to rest,
    The other lived to fettle,
Till darkness fell on Silver Springs —
    Death's oft-deferred intention! —
But one awaits the warning wings
    And summons of ascension.

Rest there, thou loyal advocate
    And undissembled Hector!
Where o'er the sward the dome of State
    Throws its impartial spectre!

Not less than thou we littler pens
   Forget in one devotion,
Time's infinite circumference,
   And history's boundless ocean.
1876.

ULYSSES S. GRANT

MARCH 4, 1869

YONDER the Capitol stands; the people perhaps
   are assembling.
I know the inaugural music by the ground and
   windows trembling;
I tremble a little myself, as, with a Cadet's desire,
On the field of Palo Alto I first went under fire.

My carriage waits at the gate; the manes of my
   span are rippling
Like those of the great wild studs I broke in Ohio,
   a stripling!
But I never owned a cloak as my coachman's half
   so good,
When I reined down the streets of St. Louis on
   my wagon-load of wood.

I know that this is no dream; my fancy was never
   so strong
As to dream a great deal higher than just to get
   along;
And that was enough for an honest dream — as
   Lincoln used to say
That better than building castles was steady "peg-
   ging away."

The four gold stars on my shoulder, the sword
   upon my hip,
I have put away with my salesman's pen and my
   teamster's leather whip,
And perhaps these different keepsakes my children
   would rather choose
For the symbols of their Father than the Politician's
   screws.

Still wise are the politicians, and the fact that is
   most to be prized
In this world of infinite wisdom is, Nothing must
   be despised.
But God, whom I thank, has thus far permitted
   me success
By the soberest endeavor and a simple No or Yes.

I sat up late last evening with the speech I am to
   deliver,
Thinking again of barrack-life out on the Columbia river,
When I used to conceive in the pipe-smoke that
   curled about my tent,
What sort of a strange old chap might be at the
   head of the government:

Whether he ever wondered what we poor Captains
   won,
With our wives and babies camp-bound by the
   mud or by the sun,
Away from civilization without a play or a school,
Save the music of a fifer or the bray of a teamster's
   mule :

Whether he felt our impulse half Mexico to bag,
Or to march upon Vancouver's and lower the
    English flag,
To summon the Indian traders up to a Drum-head
    Court,
Or to court the Indian woman who loitered around
    the fort.

It seemed a lost, lost youth to me, and somewhat
    did I reck
The school to Cerro Gordo, the way to Chapul-
    tepec,
When, by such devious civil paths, the heights of
    empire came,
And Fame was but an accident, and Power lived
    close to Shame.

Now, looking back, the way seems plain, as from
    the mountain crags
At doubtful Chattanooga I read the signal flags;
The frontier post, the tannery, the farm of barren
    land,
Were parts of the line of battle, and Providence
    had command.

I felt the guns of Sumter like old acquaintances
Come back to me in anger and give but one
    redress —
An earthquake split the nation, and when the frag-
    ments blent
Myself was on the pinnacle and millions in the
    rent!

Upon the dizzy height I stood, as yonder, looking
    down,
Stands Freedom, poised upon her sword, above
    the gazing town —
And politicians, creeping up, explain the State to me
Much as the devil described the world to him of
    Galilee.

The drums I hear sound hollower than those which
    beat to arms;
To some they beat to holiday, to me they beat
    alarms —
To battle-drums fell soldiers' feet on sacrifices bent;
These feet leave all the battle to the coming
    President.

Ten thousand office-seekers to their own inaug-
    ural wind;
A million feeble partisans walk thoughtlessly
    behind.
When those be disappointed, then these will be
    malcontent,
And still on his lonely pinnacle must stand the
    President.

Yet by the strong attrition which crumbled Trea-
    son's wrath,
In summer or in winter fighting it out on that
    path,
I shall move on the works civilian till the govern-
    ment adored
Of the people, by the people, for the people be
    restored!

BENJAMIN HARRISON

1888

HAIL to the grandson better
Than the old grandsire's fetter
  Of lands and station!
Hail to dependence done!
Hail to the Harrison
  New as the nation!

Wide lands of Symmes may roll
In suck of Symmes's hole, —
  The pole star winking;
But all the land is his
Whose victory Freedom's is,
  And birthright, Thinking.

The anvils sound the gains
From melted slavery's chains, —
  The Bourbon wonders,
While batteries of the mills
Speak out to all the hills
  The furnace thunders.

By God-forsaken farms
The market city swarms
  And ends dejection,
Free ships the railways bear;
Free Trade is everywhere
  And all's Protection.

Thy grandsire British fought,
Thy father toiled for naught
　And died unnoted;
The music of the mills
Can never pierce the hills
　Where slaves are *voted*.

The late taskmasters arm
And call their hate Reform,
　And us their Neighbor;
None but wage-payers can
Feed the free artisan
　And muster labor!

Roll on, old ball! once more,
My fathers rolled of yore, —
　Roll mightier, wider!
May Henry's cup come back
In Benjamin's corn sack,
　And all have cider!

SALT RIVER [1]

A STATELY river like a silent aisle,
Led through the cliffs of limestone mile on mile,
And far inland a green and cool retreat,
Lay all embowered and hid from human feet.
The laurel grew to arbors for repose,
The long blue grass was dyed by many a rose,

[1] Defeated candidates for the Presidency were long said to
have "gone up Salt River."

The high gray walls with oaks were corniced o'er
And dropped their creepers to the crystal shore;
And there were walks in groves where silence grew
Profounder for the note of the cuckoo,
Where they, the philosophic few, could walk
In high Arcadian fellowship and talk;
Who climbed each step but one of power's ascent,
And, losing that, were doomed to banishment:
A little handful driven from the sun
Of power to a lonelier Pantheon,
Here they discussed the empire they resigned
And nobler empires of the human mind.

One year in four the wafted vessel sped;
A wounded eagle guided it o'erhead.
The beaten hero who had lost a realm
Blew onward without mariner or helm.
Fate filled the wind, nor foe nor friend pursued,
But grander nature gave her solitude.
No more the world its censure or applause
Heaped on his head, his memory, or his cause.
Grave and respectful was his welcome made,
And immemorial in this high arcade
He kept converse with statesmen as they came,
And felt how Time was kinder still than Fame.

Once on the strand they who the sceptre lost,
Waited at four years' close him to accost
Whose boat was due. And oldest of them all
Was one of figure soldierly and tall;
At Bemis Heights an army back he bore
And took the sword their sullen General wore.

For this he sought to pierce the splendid sun
Where steadier fortune set her Washington.
Cast down for such presumption, he abides
The oldest exile on these silent tides.

In stature less, but not in spirit so,
Stand two who once were mortal foe and foe :
One fell before the other's deadly aim,
But all the winds of Heaven blew his fame ;
The other sought in various empires place,
And lived a long and solitary race.
Still, as they meet in this sequestered spot,
Where mind is mind and rivalry is not,
The victim knows, perchance, their fate reversed,
Had made the martyr of the man accursed.
Again in talk old York's redoubt they storm,
And at Quebec the ranks of Arnold form ;
The Senate's head and the Exchequer's source
Twinkle with themes for luminous discourse.
Rivière du Sel ! What Lethe flows in thee
Where such as Burr and Hamilton agree ?

Who comes with this judicial, searching face —
Scotch in his nature, Southern in his grace ?
'Tis he a Congress chose to lead the crowd,
But to the spite of rancorous faction bowed.
Two exiled here and two who might have been
Poured on his head their jealousy and spleen ;
Since then, tumultuous assemblies make
Rulers, or exiles to this lonely lake.
Yet serving well through good or ill report,
None fear in fame with Crawford to consort.

No, nor that trio yonder in the glen,
With heads of gods on bodies like to men;
The one whose eyes like diamonds in a vault
Might lead the mind high heaven to assault,
And prove that God's intention was at fault:
None lost the sceptre with so deep regret,
No mind on power was so divinely set,
None in its fulness was more fit to rule,
None in its loss to play the graver fool.
Still in the wildness of his whitened hair
There lies the pallor of a long despair.
Rejected from his kingdom like a Saul,
He raised a prophet and foreboded all.
Yet all he saw by logic came to pass:
A nervous giant in a house of glass,
Debate and hate, revolt, contention, gore —
The slave a freeman and the master poor.
Though in the mart his wasted ashes lie,
Here in Valhalla walks Calhoun for aye.

Earnest as he, but lighted like a star,
Shines there the visage of an orator:
Ithuriel's stature and a trumpet's tone:
Where'er he walks he leads, and he alone.
Thrice in the lists he rode to take the crown,
Thrice in the dust his princely head went down.
But though defeated, all the world agree
He had the plenitude of chivalry.
Still in his smile this twilight turns to day,
And nature brightens at the name of Clay.

Austere, revered, voluptuous, endowed
With fire and darkness like a thunder cloud,

Roves he whose eyes with tender greatness shine !
Who stood like Moses on the mountain line,
Worthy to take God's tablets of the law
And break them to a multitude in awe ;
But not to pass into the promised state,
To die unmurmuring, even at the gate,
And leave the name of Webster to the land,
One just too human to be wholly grand.

Here stands but one who wore the crown awhile
And lost it with a wrinkle and a smile —
The live Van Buren, greater in defeat
Than blandly minist'ring in Cæsar's seat.
The torch he wielded better than the sword ;
In his revolt reeled down the feudal lord.
He tarried long behind his time and went
To exile like a veteran to his tent.

Yet there is one whom death bequeathed the
        throne,
And sought to win it, living, for his own :
The gracious Fillmore, fashioned best for love,
To play Apollo at the fall of Jove ;
He saw, like Seward, an invader sail
To conquest, though himself had raised the gale,
And both recite in this enshrined retreat
Their country's glory in their own defeat.

So also he who found the mountain path —
Fremont — but not the road that glory hath, —
And martial Scott, whose many cubits bring
The office of the Guardsman, not the King.
Together these the limpid ripples glass :

The subtle Douglas and the timid Cass;
The yearning Chase, with ermine on his breast,
Over a heart sick in a sceptre's quest;
High-mettled Breckinridge by exile bowed;
And young McClellan, Hamlet of the crowd;
With cautious Seymour in the whirlwind spent,
That threw a soldier forward from his tent.
They speak together, hearty and unvexed,
" Who spies the shallop? Who is coming next?"
  1872.

DEATH OF THE SIAMESE TWINS

Chang and Eng were gallant twins
  Discovered in Siam,
And Eng grew up at Sabbath school,
  While Chang he loved a slam;
A gristly rivet joined the twain,
  The which would not unscrew,
So pious Eng was always slain
  When Chang got on a slew.

In politics Eng was a Whig,
  And Chang a Democrat,
And when they held an argument
  It ended in a spat,
And often when the vote was slick,
  And both sides scored a brother,
'Twas thought throughout the bailiwick,
  They must contest each other.

Poor Eng he loved a Quaker maid
  Who would not roost with Changy,
Because he came to bed so drunk
  And said his prayers so slangy;
They compromised, and took a pair,
  And lived in great dejection, —
The brothers wanted a divorce,
  The sisters a dissection.

And Eng he loved to sing a hymn,
  And Chang to fight a chicken;
Whenever Eng exhorted Chang
  He got a martyr's lickin';
If in the church Eng led his class
  'Twould make an angel kick up,
To see the one with unction pray,
  And t'other sleep and hiccup.

They called a hundred surgeons in
  To pass the righteous sentence,
If 'twould be safe to take a knife
  And cut their own acquaintance.
The Doctors of their hyphen felt
  And came to this solution:
'Twas an action 'twixt the Little Belt
  And the navel Constitution.

At last Chang would not sleep at all,
  So much he was a soaker,
And kept his brother sitting up
  To while him at draw poker;
And when he died the wretch remarked:

" The Lord must raise our bodies —
   And I shall have all Eng's reward,
      And likewise all those toddies."

The ladies sold the frail remains
   To serve a human mission;
The Doctors beat Sir Barnum out
   And gave an exhibition;
They found the belt a derrick was,
   Two sacks — one thin, one thicker —
And Eng had had to brace the beam,
   While Chang contained the liquor.
      1874.

THE FIRE GUEST

CARRIERS' ADDRESS, CHICAGO TRIBUNE, 1872

THE fire burns bright on my hearth to-night;
Thanks to God for its warmth and light!
Warming the toes of our laughing boys,
Radiant over their Christmas toys;
Chasing the ghosts around the ceiling,
Filling our hearts with grateful feeling,
Ushering in the visions of rest,—
Welcome forever, thou beautiful guest!

See the fire from the engine gleaming!
See it over the lighthouse streaming!
Faithful and cheery, see it shine,
Down in the tunnel and deep in the mine!
Whence, O servant! didst thou inherit
Thy willing power and mighty spirit?

Forests of giant trees, they say,
Waved once their boughs in the light of day,
And down their gorgeous blossoms hurled
In the profligate life of a young, new world;
But the world rolled back and they crackled and
      bowed,
Like the stars of heaven rolled under a cloud,
And still in their crystal caverns deep,
Blossom, and beauty, and strength they keep;
And the tints of the forest return to invest
The blooming anew of our beautiful guest.

Alas, thou truant!   Thou canst not see
The ache in our hearts for the freak of thee,
When leaping out of thy cage one night,
Across the city thou took'st thy flight,
Knowing no more of the havoc and wrack,
Than the harmless heart of a maniac.
Thou thought'st it merry to imitate
On a grander scale, the glow of thy grate;
And the noise thou mad'st in thy diligence
Drowned the cry we lifted in impotence:
"O God!   O Fire!   Our hearthstones spare!
Oh, best of servants, return, forbear!
Oh, worst of masters, be satisfied
With the rent thou hast made in the mart of our
      pride!"
In vain; we heard in thy wild carouse
The buried forest's thunderous boughs,
And the brilliant blossoms that grew so high,
Again in their splendor climbed the sky.
We fled from the blaze like the prairie quail,

Or birds from their nests at the scream of the gale,
And stood in the night by the ruins' gleam,
Like the highway vagrant aroused from his dream.
Our Altars were gone and our walls overthrown;
Our temples were razed and our monuments prone;
Our boast—God forgive us! thou doest all best—
Chicago had flown like its beautiful guest.

O beautiful fire! returned anew,
To show us the faces courageous and true,
Assembled again around hearthstones low,
But warmed into hope by thy innocent glow!
The paintings were gone that reflected thy ray;
The books that beguiled the close of the day;
The burnished mirror, the carriage and span,
And the trophies of artist and artisan;
But something remained from the embers and
          wreck—
The wife heroic that clung to our neck;
Our sons that are never degenerate;
Our purpose, returned, like the flame in the grate,
To build the beautiful city again,
As a tower unto fate and example to men.
Oh! fire of the household, what carrier doves
Flew into our windows laden with loves,
From human nature—from foreign queen—
From Pharisee and from Magdalene!
Then, never till then, as thou canst attest,
We wept in thy presence, our beautiful guest!

This New Year's time, O kindly fire!
We gather around thee closer and nigher.

Be unto us a scourge no more,
But be that kindlier friend of yore,
Which warmed the cold limbs, sore and wet,
Of river-seeking, good Marquette,
And made the prairie like an inn
To lonely father Hennepin!
Burn brightly, while we keep in peace
Our dream of empire and increase,
As when the white man's vessel started
Our river's ripples long ago,
And calmly slept the lion-hearted
La Salle, beside the camp fire's glow!

Show us, O fire! in thy graceful curling,
The hut of the negro pioneer,
And the flag of Dearborn first unfurling
In the prairie's smoky atmosphere;
The low *pirogues* of the bold post trader
Set under the bank of poplar trees,
And the prowling form of the Indian raider,
Gartered with skunk's skin around the knees!
And hide, O fire! that scene in phlebotomy,
When the garrison filed through the stockade wall,
And Winnebago and Pottowattamie
Kept time to the tune of the dead march in Saul!

Who said that Chicago was perished, but blun-
    dered,
Though the silence of nature returned to the
    moor,
The gray wolf howled where the cannon had thun-
    dered,

And the wild goose piped to the *voyageur :*
To divide up our raiment contended all races, —
The French of St. Louis, the folks of Calumet;
Toledo, Milwaukee, and other small places,
The which to enumerate is to forget.
But the soldiers returned to their station,
Again the artillery spake,
And like a divine exhalation,
Chicago arose by the lake!
It was thee, O thou tyrant! that glowest, —
Unaware of thy freak or our ire, —
'Twas by thee that we conquered, thou knowest, —
Thou builder and spoiler, the fire!
To thy harness return, we forgive thee;
For the traffic thou gav'st, go in quest!
And the city revived shall enshrine thee,
    Its beautiful guest!

Ah, me!   The cold toes this winter,
And the candles burnt out in the socket;
Let us give them that tinder-box, money,
And burn a warm hole in their pocket!
There's a *carrier's* foot!   Who would shun him?
Perhaps his extremities ache;
Let us heap coals of fire upon him,
And burn him alive at our stake!
Then, to-night, be he son or be sire,
As he counts o'er his coins of bequest,
He will smile at that terrible fire,
And call it HIS BEAUTIFUL GUEST!

SPINOZA

Sweet type of Jew! except that thou
Earned with thy hands thy frugal food,
And led not crowds but solitude,
I almost seem to feel thee, now,
The highest proof of Holyrood!
Polishing lenses for the light
That is the Revelation pure,
Thy convex mind infinite sight
Glassed of the wide Infinitude
And graved pellucid Literature:
Nature and Mind one substance were,
The bread and wine religions take;
God-will aboundeth everywhere
And cannot anything forsake.

EVENTS AND CREED

(RANKE'S HISTORY OF THE POPES)

Events rule all: irruptive Rome made Christ;
Irruptive Greece Italian knowledge woke.
The Christian fantasy, by facts advised, —
When classic Art pontificates enticed, —
Erudite monks the see of Cæsars broke:
Wickliffe and Huss, Luther and Bruno spoke
While modelled Angelo and Raphael;
The voice of Letters dealt the void a stroke
As finds its tongue the dumb, sepulchral bell.
So cannot rest the aye resurgent mind;
Wave upon wave resultant movements thresh

The rock of Peter or the caves of hell,
And every human billow that does grind
The dikes of credence, keeps the ocean fresh.

IN RAMA

A LITTLE face there was,
  When all her pains were done,
Beside that face I loved:
  They said it was a son.
A son to me — how strange —
  Who never was a man,
But lived from change to change
  A boy, as I began!

More boyish still the hope
  That leaped within me, then:
That I, matured in him,
  Should found a house of men,
And all my wasted sheaves,
  Bound up in his ripe shock,
Give seed to sterner times
  And name to sterner stock.

He grew to that ideal,
  And blossomed in my sight.
Strange questions filled his day,
  Sweet visions in the night;
Till he could walk with me,
  Companion, hand in hand.
But nothing seemed to be
  Like him, in wonder-land.

For he was leading me
  Beyond the bounds of mind,
Far down eternity,
  And I so far behind.
One day an angel stepped
  Out of the idle sphere;
The man had entered in,
  The boy is weeping here.

My house is founded there,
  In heaven, that he has won.
Shall I be outlawed, then,
  O, Lord! who hast my son?
This grief that makes me old,
  Those tears that make me pure,
They tell me time is time,
  And only heaven mature.
1874

RACHEL

(DELAWARE GUNNER'S WHISTLE)

Down in the marshes of the Christeen creek
Lives a little reed-bird on which I sneak,
She is so fat that she looks right short
But when she flies she is real good sport.
  Rachel! Rachel! why don't you run?
  Don't you know, Rachel, I carry a gun?
  Rachel! Rachel! I love you the most,
  If I could get you how you would toast!

She has a nest on the Christeen creek;
Come to it softly and don't you speak!

Down in the reeds on the flood-tide bog
I have a skiff and a pointer dog.
 Rachel! Rachel! why don't you fly?
 When he sees Rachel the dog points shy.
 Rachel! Rachel! I tremble too,
 Loading my heart in my gun for you!

Soft are the stars in the Christeen creek
When in the evening my bird I seek,
Plump is her breast in her yellow gown
Soft is her plumage as reed-bird down.
 Rachel! Rachel! why don't you tweet?
 When you know, Rachel, I could you eat?
 Rachel! Rachel! for you I gun,
 I have my bag full when you are won!

Like thorn hedges by the Christeen creek
Tinted with red is my reed-bird's cheek,
Trim as the hedge tops her father clips
Are the soft lines to my sweet bird's lips.
 Rachel! Rachel! why don't you come?
 Let me take Rachel to my own home!
 Rachel! Rachel! thou fat marsh chick,
 How for my supper thy plushing would pick!

Fall comes fast on the Christeen creek;
Soon I must migrate unless thou speak :
Dear little Quaker of frost bethink!
I will be gone with the Bob-o-link.
 Rachel! Rachel! why don't you wed?
 Winter, my Rachel! in my marsh bed!
 Rachel! Rachel! the wind blows bleak,
 Fly to my boat on the Christeen creek!

ANGELS IN MASK

As from the throng of moving masks
    I drew a space apart,
Well known to some unknown to me,
    By my imperfect Art,
One, in the habit of a nun,
    Stopped short, as in surprise,
And through her domino I saw
    Two soft, regarding eyes.

Long looked we both, for half I felt
    Her gaze no mischief spoke,
And knew it, when a woman's hand
    Reached to me from the cloak;
A voice I never heard before,
    But most sincere and sweet,
Said, "Ah! my love, do we once more
    Touch hand to hand and meet?"

"Fair domino," I said, "indeed,
    Unmask before you go,
And tell your trouble in my ear,
    Why do you tremble so?"
"I tremble for the virgin years
    When o'er my mind supreme,
You were the hero of my fears,
    The gallant of my dream."

"And did I never know your will,
    When then, perchance, my heart
Like yours, was longing for a shrine,
    A mistress, or an art?"

ARCH OF THE WAR CORRESPONDENTS, GAPLAND, MD.

" No, mine was all the pleasant pain,
  And heaven permits it here,
To say that still, as when a child,
  I follow your career.

" My husband passes — Nay! you must!
  No guilty secret mine."
A strong man's hand came frankly forth,
  I saw his dark eyes shine;
" In honor's way God keep you long!"
  These manly sounds I heard,
" And never may you cease to be
  Our favorite household word."

They vanished in the moving crowd
  And left me wondering quite,
Until I heard my comrade say:
  " Whom have you seen to-night?"
" To guess," I said, " were fruitless task,
  When all this maze I see;
But, if they ever come in mask,
  Two angels spoke to me."

RIDE FROM FIVE FORKS

APRIL 1, 1865

Ho! pony.   Down the lonely road
  Strike now your cheeriest pace!
The woods on fire do not burn higher
  Than burns my anxious face;
Far have you sped, but all this night

Must feel my nervous spur;
If we be late, the world must wait
    The tidings we aver: —
To home and hamlet, town and hearth,
    To thrill child, mother, man,
I carry to the waiting North
    Great news from Sheridan!

The birds are dead among the pines,
    Slain by the battle fright,
Prone in the road the steed reclines
    That never reached the fight:
Yet on we go, — the wreck below
    Of many a tumbled wain, —
By ghastly pools where stranded mules
    Die, drinking of the rain.
With but my list of killed and missed,
    I spur my stumbling nag,
To tell of death at many a tryst,
    But victory to the flag!

"Halt! who comes there? The countersign!" —
    "A friend." — "Advance! The fight, —
How goes it, say?" — "We won the day!" —
    "Huzza! Pass on!" — "Good-night!" —
And parts the darkness on before,
    And down the mire we tramp,
And the black sky is painted o'er
    With many a pulsing camp;
O'er stumps and ruts, by ruined huts,
    Where ghosts look through the gloam, —
Behind my tread I hear the dead
    Follow the news tow'rd home!

The hunted souls I see behind,
  In swamp and in ravine,
Whose cry of mercy thrills the wind
  Till cracks the sure carbine:
The moving lights which scare the dark,
  And show the trampled place
Where, in his blood, some mother's bud
  Turns up his young, dead face;
The captives spent, whose standards rent
  The conqueror parades,
As at the Five Forks roads arrive
  The General's dashing Aides.

O wondrous Youth! through this grand ruth
  Runs my boy's life its thread;
The General's fame, the battle's name,
  The rolls of maimed and dead
I bear, with my thrilled soul astir,
  And lonely thoughts and fears,
And am but History's courier
  To bind the conquering years;
A battle-ray, through ages gray
  To light to deeds sublime,
And flash the lustre of this day
  Down all the aisles of Time!

Ho! pony, — 'tis the signal gun —
  The night-assault decreed;
On Petersburg the thunderbolts
  Crash from the lines of Meade;
Fade the pale, frightened stars o'erhead,
  And shrieks the bursting air;

The forest foliage, tinted red,
　Grows ghastlier in the glare;
Though in Her towers, reached Her last hours,
　Rocks proud Rebellion's crest —
The world may sag, if but my nag
　Get in before the rest!

With bloody flank, and fetlocks dank,
　And goad, and lash, and shout —
Great God! as every hoof-beat falls
　A hundred lives beat out!
As weary as this broken steed
　Reels down the corduroys,
So, weary, fight for morning light
　Our hot and grimy boys;
Through ditches wet, o'er parapet
　And guns barbette, they catch
The last, lost breach; and I, — I reach
　The mail with my despatch!

Sure it shall speed, the land to read,
　As sped the happiest shell!
The shot I send strike the world's end;
　This tells my pony's knell;
His long race run, the long war done,
　My occupation gone, —
Above his bier, prone on the pier,
　The vultures fleck the dawn.
Still, rest his bones where soldiers dwell,
　Till the Long Roll they catch.
He fell the day that Richmond fell,
　And took the first despatch!

LAND OF POCOMOKE

(EASTERN SHORE OF MARYLAND)

ONE day, worn out with head and pen,
And the debate of public men,
  I said aloud, " O ! if there were
Some place to make me young awhile,
  I would go there, I would go there,
And if it were a many a mile ! "
  Then something cried — perhaps my map,
That not in vain I oft invoke —
  " Go seek again your mother's lap,
  The dear old soil that gave you sap,
And see the land of Pocomoke ! "

A sense of shame that never yet
My foot on that old shore was set,
  Though prodigal in wandering,
Arose ; and with a tingled cheek,
  Like some late wild duck on the wing,
I started down the Chesapeake.
  The morning sunlight, silvery calm,
From basking shores of woodland broke,
  And capes and inlets breathing balm,
  And lovely islands clothed in palm,
Closed round the sound of Pocomoke.

The pungy boats at anchor swing,
The long canoes were oystering,
  And moving barges played the seine
Along the beaches of Tangiers ;
  I heard the British drums again

As in their predatory years,
  When Kedge's Straits the Tories swept,
And Ross's camp-fires hid in smoke.
  They plundered all the coasts except
  The camp the Island Parson kept
For praying men of Pocomoke.

And when we thread in quaint intrigue
Onancock Creek and Pungoteague,
  The world and wars behind us stop.
On God's frontiers we seem to be
  As at Rehoboth wharf we drop,
And see the Kirk of Mackemie:
  The first he was to teach the creed
The rugged Scotch will ne'er revoke;
  His slaves he made to work and read,
  Nor powers Episcopal to heed,
That held the glebes on Pocomoke.

But quiet nooks like these unman
The grim predestinarian,
  Whose soul expands to mountain views;
And Wesley's tenets, like a tide,
  These level shores with love suffuse,
Where'er his patient preachers ride.
  The landscape quivered with the swells
And felt the steamer's paddle stroke,
  That tossed the hollow gum-tree shells,
  As if some puffing craft of hell's
The fisher chased in Pocomoke.

Anon the river spreads to coves,
And in the tides grow giant groves.

The water shines like ebony,
And odors resinous ascend
  From many an old balsamic tree,
Whose roots the terrapin befriend;
  The great ball cypress, fringed with beard,
Presides above the water oak,
    As doth its shingles, well revered,
    O'er many a happy home endeared
To thousands far from Pocomoke.

And solemn hemlocks drink the dew,
Like that old Socrates they slew;
  The piny forests moan and moan,
And in the marshy splutter docks,
  As if they grazed on sky alone,
Rove airily the herds of ox.
  Then, like a narrow strait of light,
The banks draw close, the long trees yoke,
    And strong old manses on the height
    Stand overhead, as to invite
To good old cheer on Pocomoke.

And cunning baskets midstream lie
To trap the perch that gambol by;
  In coves of creek the saw-mills sing,
And trim the spar and hew the mast;
  And the gaunt loons dart on the wing,
To see the steamer looming past.
  Now timber shores and massive piles
Repel our hull with friendly stroke,
    And guide us up the long defiles,
    Till, after many fairy miles
We reach the head of Pocomoke.

Is it Snow Hill that greets me back
To this old loamy *cul-de-sac?* —
  Spread on the level river shore,
Beneath the bending willow-trees
  And speckled trunks of sycamore,
All moist with airs of rival seas?
  Are these old men who gravely bow,
As if a stranger all awoke,
  The same who heard my parents vow,
  — Ah well! in simpler days than now —
To love and serve by Pocomoke?

Does Chincoteague, as then, produce
These rugged ponies, lean and spruce?
  Are these the steers of Accomack
That do the negro's drone obey?
  The things of childhood all come back:
The wonder tales of mother day!
  The jail, the inn, the ivy vines
That yon old English churchside cloak,
  Wherein we read the stately lines
  Of Addison, writ in his signs,
Above the dead of Pocomoke.

The world in this old nook may peep,
And think it listless and asleep;
  But I have seen the world enough
To think its grandeur something dull;
  And here were men of sterling stuff,
In their own era wonderful:
  Young Luther Martin's wayward race,
And William Winder's core of oak,

The lion heart of Samuel Chase,
  And great Decatur's royal face,
And Henry Wise of Pocomoke.

When we have raged our little part,
And weary out of strife and art,
  Oh! could we bring to these still shores
The peace they have who harbor here,
  And rest upon our echoing oars,
And float adown this tranquil sphere!
  Then, might yon stars shine down on me,
With all the hope those lovers spoke,
  Who walked these tranquil streets I see,
  And thought God's love nowhere so free,
Nor life so good, as Pocomoke.

OLD ST. MARY'S

(CAPITAL OF COLONIAL MARYLAND)

THIS is the river.   Like Southampton water
It enters broadly in the woody lands,
As if to break a continent asunder,
And sudden ceasing, lo! the city stands:
St. Mary's — stretching forth its yellow hands
Of beach, beneath the bluff where it commands
In vision only; for the fields are green
Above the pilgrims.   Pleasant is the place;
No ruin mars its immemorial face.
As young as in virginity renewed,
Its widow's sorrows gone without a trace,
And tempting man to woo its solitude.

The river loves it, and embraces still
Its comely form with two small arms of bay,
Whereon, of old, the Calverts' pinnace lay,
The Dove — dear bird ! — the olive in its bill,
That to the Ark returned from every gale
And found a haven by this sheltering hill.

Lo ! all composed, the soft horizons lie
Afloat upon the blueness of the coves,
And sometimes in the mirage does the sky
Seem to continue the dependent groves,
And draw in the canoe that careless roves
Among the stars repeated round the bow.
Far off the larger sails go down the world,
For nothing worldly sees St. Mary's now ;
The ancient windmills all their sails have furled,
The standards of the Lords of Baltimore,
And they, the Lords, have passed to their repose ;
And nothing sounds upon the pebbly shore
Except thy hidden bell, Saint Inigo's !

There, in a wood, the Jesuits' chapel stands
Amongst the gravestones, in secluded calm.
But, Sabbath days, the censer's healing balm,
The Crucified with His extended hands,
And music of the masses, draw the fold
Back to His worship as in days of old.

Upon a cape the priest's house northward blinks,
To see St. Mary's Seminary guard
The dead that sleep within the parish yard,
In English faith — the parish church that links
The present with the perish'd, for its walls

Are of the clay that was the capital's,
When halberdiers and musketeers kept ward,
And armor sounded in the oaken halls.

A fruity smell is in the school-house lane,
The clover bees are sick with evening heats,
A few old houses from the window pane
Fling back the flame of sunset, and there beats
The throb of oars from basking oyster fleets,
And clangorous music of the oyster tongs,
Plunged down in deep bivalvulous retreats,
And sound of seine drawn home with negro songs.

Night falls as heavily in such a clime
As tired childhood after all day's play,
Waiting for mother who has passed away,
And some old nurse, with iterated rhyme
Of hymns or topics of the olden time,
Lulls wonder with her tenderness to rest:
So, old St. Mary's! at the close of day,
Sing thou to me, a truant, on thy breast!

HERMAN OF BOHEMIA MANOR

I. — THE MANOR

"My corn is gathered in the bins,"
  The Lord Augustin Herman said;
"My wild swine romp in chincapins;
Dried are the deer and beaver skins;
  And on Elk Mountain's languid head
  The autumn woods are red.

" So in my heart an autumn falls ;
  I stand a lonely tree unleaved ;
And to my hermit manor walls
The wild-goose from the water calls,
    As if to mock a man bereaved :
    My years are nearly sheaved.

" Go saddle me the Flemish steed
  My brother Verlett gave to me,
What time his sister did concede
Her dainty hand to hear me plead !
    Poor soul ! she's mouldering by the sea
    And I with misery."

The slave man brought the wild-maned horse —
  All wilder that with stags he grazed —
Bred from the seed the knightly Norse
Rode from Araby.   Like remorse
    The eyes in his gray forehead blazed,
    As on his lord he gazed.

" Now guard ye well my lands and stock ;
  Slack not the seine, ply well the axe !
The eagle circles o'er the flock ;
The Indian at my gates may knock ;
    The firelock prime for his attacks !
    I ride the sunrise tracks."

Swift as a wizard on a broom,
  The strong gray horse and rider ran,
Adown the forest stripped of bloom.
By stump and bough that scarce gave room
    To pass the woodman's caravan,
    Rode the Bohemian.

"Lord Herman, stay." the brewer cried.
  " And Huddy's friendly flagon clink ! "
And martial Hinoyóssa spied
The horseman, moving with the tide
    That ebbed from Appoquinimink,
    Nor stopped to rest or drink.

" Where rides old Herman ? " Beekman mused ;
  " That railing wife has turned his head."
" He keeps the saddle as he used,
In younger days, when he infused
    Three provinces," Pierre Alricks said,
    " And mapped their landscapes spread."

Broad rose Zuydt River as the sail
    Above his periauger flew ;
Loud neighed the steed to snuff the gale ;
But Herman saw not, swift and pale,
    Two carrier pigeons, winging true
    Northeast, across the blue.

They quit the cage of Stuyvesant's spy,
    And lurking Willems' message bore:
(" This morn rode Herman rapid by,
Tow'rd Amsterdam, to satisfy
    Yet wider titles than he tore
    From shallow Baltimore ! ")

II. — REPLEVIN

The second sunset at his back
    From Navesink Highlands threw the shade
Of horse and Herman, long and black,

Across the golden ripples' track,
  Where with the Kills the ocean played
  A measured serenade;

There, where to sea a river ran,
  Between tall hills of brown and sand,
A mountain island rose to span
The outlet of the Raritan,
  And made a world on either hand
  Soft as a poet planned:

Fair marshes pierced with brimming creeks,
  Where wild-fowl dived to oyster caves;
And shores that swung to wooded peaks,
Where many a falling water seeks
  The cascade's plunge to reach the waves,
  And greenest farmland laves;

Deep tide to every roadstead slips,
  And many capes confuse the shore,
Yet none do with their forms eclipse
Yon ocean, made for royal ships,
  Whose swells on silver beaches roar
  And rock forevermore.

Old Herman gazed through lengthening shades
  Far up the inland, where the spires,
Defined on rocky palisades,
Flung sunset from their burnished blades,
  And with their bells in evening choirs
  Breathed homesick men's desires:

"New Amsterdam! 'tis thine or mine —
  The foreground of this stately plan!

To me the Indian did assign —
Totem on totem, line on line —
  Both Staten and the groves that ran
  Far up the Raritan.

" By spiteful Stuyvesant long restrained,
  Now, while the English break his power,
Be Achter Kill again regained
And Herman's title entertained! —
  Here float my banner from my tower!
  Here is my right, my hour!"

III. — THE SQUATTERS

He scarce had finished, when a rush,
  Like partridge through the stubble, broke,
And armèd men trod down the brush;
A harsh voice, trembling in the hush,
  As it must either stab or choke,
  Imperiously spoke :

" Ye conquered men of Achter Kill,
  Whose farms by loyal toil ye got,
True Dutchmen! give this traitor will —
And he is yours to loose or kill —
  All that ye have he will allot
  Anew — field, cradle, cot.

" Years past, beyond our Southern bounds,
  On States' commission sent by me,
He mapped the English papists' grounds,
And like a Judas, o'er our wounds,
  Our raiment parted openly :
  This is the man ye see!

" Yet, followed by my sleepless age,
Fast as he rode my pigeons sped —
Straight as the ravens from their cage,
Straight as the arrows of my rage,
Straight as the meteor overhead
That strikes a traitor dead."

They bound Lord Herman fast as hate,
And bore him o'er to Staten Isle ;
Behind him closed the postern gate,
And round him pitiless as fate,
Closed moat and palisade and pile :
" Thou diest at morn," they smile.

IV. — STUYVESANT

Morn broke on lofty Staten's height,
O'er low Amboy and Arthur Kill ;
And ocean dallying with the light,
Between the beaches leprous white,
And silent hook and headland hill,
And Stuyvesant had his will ;

One-legged he stood, his sharp mustache
Stiff as the sword he slashed in ire ;
His bald crown, like a calabash,
Fringed round with ringlets white as ash,
And features scorched with inner fire ;
Age wore him like a briar.

"Bring the Bohemian forth!" he cried ;
"Old man, thy moments are but few."
"So much the better, Dutchman! bide

Thy little time of aged pride,
  Thy poor revenges to pursue! —
  Thy date is hastening, too.

" No crime is mine, save that I sought
  A refuge past thy jealous ken,
And peaceful arts to strangers taught,
And mine own title hither brought,
  Before the laws of Englishmen,
  A banished denizen.

" Yet that thy churlish soul may plead
  A favor to a dying foe,
I'll ask thee, Stuyvesant, ere I bleed,
Let me once more on my gray steed
  Thrice round the timbered *enceinte* go:
  Fire, when I tell thee so! "

" What freak is this? " quoth Stuyvesant grim.
  Quoth Herman, " 'Twas a charger brave —
Like my first bride in eye and limb —
A wedding-gift; indulge the whim!
  And from his back to plunge, I crave,
  A bridegroom, in her grave."

Then, muttered the uneasy guard:
  " We rob an old man of his lands,
And slay him. Sure his fate is hard,
His dying plea to disregard! "
  " Ride then to death! " Stuyvesant commands;
  " Unbind his horse, his hands! "

V. — THE LEAP

The old steed darted in the fort,
  And neighed and shook his long gray mane;
Then, seeing soldiery, his port
Grew savage.   With a charger's snort,
  Upright he reared, as young again
  And scenting a campaign.

Hard on his nostrils Herman laid
  An iron hand and drew him down,
Then, mounting in the esplanade,
The rude Dutch rustics stared afraid:
  "By Santa Claus! he needs no crown,
  To look more proud renown!"

Lame Stuyvesant, also, envious saw
  How straight he sat in courteous power,
Like boldness sanctified by law,
And age gave magisterial awe;
  Though in his last and bitter hour,
  Of knightliness the flower.

His gray hairs o'er his cassock blew,
  And in his peak'd hat waved a plume;
A horn swung loose and shining through
High boots of buckskin, as he drew
  The rein, a jewel burst to bloom:
  The signet ring of doom.

"Thrice round the fort! Then as I raise
  This hand, aim all and murder well!"
His head bends low; the steed's eyes blaze,

But not less bright do Herman's gaze,
  As circling round the citadel,
  He peers for hope in hell.

Fast were the gates; no crevice showed.
  The ramparts, spiked with palisades,
Grew higher as once round he rode;
The arquebusiers prime the load
  And drop to aim from ambuscades;
  No latch, no loophole aids.

But one small hut its chimney thrust
  Between the timbers, close as they;
Twice round and with a desperate trust
Lord Herman muttered: "Die I must:
  There, CHARGE!" and spurred through beam
      and clay —
"By heaven! he is away!"

VI. — THE KILLS

In clouds of dust the muskets fire,
  And volleying oaths old Stuyvesant from:
"Turn out! In yonder Kills he'll mire
Or drown, unless the fiends conspire.
  "Mount! Follow! Still he must succumb —
  That tide was never swum."

Through hut and chimney, down the ditch
  And up the bank, plunge horse and man;
And down the hills of bramble pitch,
Oft stumbling, those old gray knees which,
  Hunting the raccoon, led the van;
  Now, limp yet game he ran.

But cool and supple, Herman sat,
　　His mind at work, his frame the horse's,
And knew with each pulsation, that
Past foe and fen, past crag, and flat,
　　And marsh, the steed he nearer forces
　　To the broad sea's recourses.

" Old friend," he thought, " thou art too weak
　　To try the Kills and drown, or falter,
The while from shore their marksmen seek
My heart.　(Once o'er the Chesapeake
　　I paddled oarless.)　Lest the halter
　　Be mine, I must not palter —

" Thou diest, though my marriage-gift :
　　I still can swim.　Poor Joost, adieu ! "
Ere ceased the heartfelt sigh he lift,
The prospect widened ; all adrift,
　　The salty sluice burst into view,
　　Where grappling tides fought through

And sucked to doom the venturous bear,
　　And from his ferry swept the rower —
How wide, how terrible, how fair !
Yet how inspiriting the air —
　　How tempts the long salt grass the mower !
　　How treacherous the shore !

Far up the right spread Newark Bay,
　　To lone Secaucus wooded rock ;
Nor could the Kill von Kull convey
Passaic's mountain flood away :
　　In Arthur Kill the surges choke,
　　The wild tides interlock.

O'er Arthur Kill the Holland farms
  Their gambril roofs, red painted, show;
Beyond, the newer Yankee swarms —
His cider-presses spread their arms.
    Before, the squatter; back, the foe:
    And the dark waters flow.

As that salt air the stallion felt,
  He whimpers gayly, as if still is
Upon his sight his native Scheldt,
Or Skagger Rack, or Little Belt, —
    Their waving grass and silver lilies,
    Where browsed the amorous fillies.

And o'er the tide some lady nags
  Blew back his challenge. Scarce could Herman
Hold in his seat.   "By John of Prague's
True faith!" he thought, "thy spirit lags
    Not, Joost! Thy course thyself determine!"
    And plunges like a merman.

Leander's spirit in the steed
  Inspired his stroke, not Herman's fear;
And fast the island shores recede,
Fast rise the rider's spirits freed,
    The golden mainland draws more near —
    "O gallant horse! 'tis here!"

VII. — ELUSION

Across the Kills the muskets crack —
    "Ha! ha!" Lord Herman waves his beaver:
"Die of thy spleen ere I come back,

Old Stuyvesant!" With a noise of wrack
   The fort blew up of his aggriever!—
   But not without retriever;

For from the smoke two pigeons fly,
   One south, one westward, separating,
And straight as arrows crossed the sky,
With silent orders (" *He must die*
   Who comes hereafter.   Lie in waiting!")
   Their snowy pinions freighting.

They warn the men of Minisink;
   They warn the Dutchmen of Zuydt River.
Now speed to Jersey's farther brink,
Old horse, old master, ere ye shrink!—
   Or ambushed fall ere moonrise quiver
   On paths where ye shall shiver.

On went the twain till past the ford
   That red-walled Raritan led over,
And lonely woodland shades explored.
Unarmed with firelock or with sword,
   Free-hearted rode the forest rover,
   Of all wild kind the drover:

Fled deer and bear before his coming,
   The wild-cat glared, the viper hissed;
And died the long day's insect-drumming.
Where things of night began their humming,
   And witchly phantoms went to tryst,
   Was Herman exorcist.

" No land so tangled but my eye
    Can map its confines and its courses:
Yet on life's map who can espy
Where hides his foe — where he shall die?"
    So Herman said, and his resources
    Resigned unto his horse's.

All night the steed instinctive travelled —
    His weary rider wept for him —
Through unseen gulfs the whirlwind ravelled,
Up moonlit beds of streamlets gravelled,
    Till halting every bleeding limb,
    He stands by something dim,

And will not stir till morning breaks.
    " What is 't I see, low clustering there,
Beyond those broadening bays and lakes,
That yonder point familiar makes? —
    Is it New Amstel, lowly fair,
    And this the Delaware?"

VIII. — THE ECHO

Lord Herman hugged his horse with pride;
    He raised his horn and blew so loudly,
That more than echoes back replied:
Horns answered louder; horsemen cried,
    And muskets banged, as if avowedly
    On Stuyvesant's errand proudly!

" Die, traitor! fleer! though thou 'scape
    Our ambush on thy devil's racer,
Caught here upon this marshy cape,

Thy bones the muskrat's brood shall scrape,
   The sturgeon suck — Death thy embracer!"
   So shouts each sanguine chaser.

To die in sight of Amstel's walls,
   And gallant Joost to die beside him? —
O foolish blast, such fate that calls!
O river, that the heart appalls!
   Dear Joost may live. And *they* bestride him?
   "By hell! none else shall ride him!

"My steed, thy limbs like mine are sore!
   Few years are left us ere the billows
Roll over both. Come but once more,
And to the bottom or the shore,
   Bear me and thee to happy pillows,
   Or 'neath the water willows!"

He strokes old Joost. He bends him low.
   He winds his horn and laughs derision.
One spring! — they've cleared the bog and sloe,
And down the ebb-tide buoyant go —
   That stately tide, so like a vision
   Of home, to Norse and Frisian,

Where full a league spread Maas and Rhine,
   And in the marsh the rice-birds twitter;
The long cranes pasture and the kine
Loom lofty in the misty shine
   Of dawn and reedy islands glitter:
   Yet death all where is bitter.

Ere out of range a volley peals,
  But greed too great made aye a blunder.
His horse Lord Herman's self conceals,
Yet once his horse and he go under,
  And rise again.   No wound he feels.
  They hold their fire in wonder!

Short of the mark the bullets splash:
  "Now drown thee, wizard! at thy pleasure,"
The Dutchmen hiss through teeth they gnash.
He answers not; for o'er the plash
  Of waves he hears Joost's gasping measure
  Of breath's fast wasting treasure.

IX. — PEGASUS

The sighs when dying comrades fall,
  Struck by the foe, are only sad;
They leaped the ditch and climbed the wall,
And shared the purpose of us all;
  The fame they have; the joy they had:
  "Rest in thy tracks, brave lad!"

But thou, poor beast! unknown to fame,
  Whose heart is reached while ours is bounding,
Amidst the victory's acclaim —
By thee we kneel with more of shame,
  That bore us through the fight resounding,
  And dumbly took our wounding!

Lord Herman saw the blood drops seethe,
  The nag's neck droop, the nostril bubble,
And loosed the bridle from his teeth;

Yet swam the old legs underneath,
  Invincibly.   The gap they double;
But further swim in trouble.

And lovely Nature stretched her aid,
  Her sympathetic tow and eddy;
The oars of air with azure blade,
And silent gravities persuade
  And waft them onward, slow and steady —
  On duteous deeds aye ready.

High leaped the perch.   The hawk screamed joy.
  Under Joost's belly musically
The ripples broke.   Bright clouds convoy
The brute that man would but destroy,
  And all instinctive agents rally
  Strong and medicinally.

In vain! The gurgling waters suck
  That old life under.   Herman swimming
Seized but the horse tail.   Like a buck
Breasting a lake in wild woods' pluck,
  Joost rose, the glaze his bright eyes dimming,
  And blood his sockets brimming.

Then, voices speak and women cry.
  The treading feet find soil to stand.
Above them the green ramparts lie,
And 'twixt their shadows and the sky,
  The wondering burghers crowd the strand,
  And Herman help to land:

"Now to Newcastle's English walls,
  Hail, Herman! and thy matchless stud!"
Joost staggers up the bank and falls,
And, dying, to his master crawls,
  Yields up his long solicitude,
  And spills his veins of blood.

In Herman's arms his neck is prest,
  With martial pride his dark eye glazes;
He feels the hand he loves the best
Stroke fondly, and a chill of rest,
  As if he rolled in pasture daisies
  And heard in winds his praises:

"O couldst thou speak, what wouldst thou say?
  I, who can speak, am dumb before thee.
Thine eyes that drink Olympian day
Where steeds of wings thy soul convey,
  With pride of eagles circling o'er thee:
  Thou seest I adore thee!

"Bound to thy starry home and her
  Who brought me thee and left earth hollow!
An honored grave thy bones inter,
And painting shall thy fame confer,
  Ere in thy shining track I follow,
  Thou courser of Apollo!"

MECCA FROM OASIS

THE people of Mahomet
  In desert places dwell,
The palm tree is their fortress,
  Their citadel a well;
Once in their lives so lonely,
  They shall one city view —
Mecca! Mecca! Mecca!
  We pilgrims long for you!

(*Repeat Chorus.*)

We Arabs love to circle
  Around the Caravan,
Our hearts are ever social,
  We love our fellow-man,
But Ishmael, our father,
  No habitation knew:
Mecca! Mecca! Mecca!
  We pilgrims long for you!

Mahomet's mighty pity
  His lonely people gave
One chance to see a city,
  Around his holy grave, —
O, ope the golden wonder!
  The city let us view!
Mecca! Mecca! Mecca!
  We pilgrims long for you!

LATTER-DAY SAINTS

ALL evidences of a living church
  Are here, although imposture is its fame.
The angel who made for a prophet search
  And showed him Revelation to reclaim
Of his own hemisphere, that Christians smirch,
  But foreign superstition never blame;
  Miracles, portents, exodus and flame,
The Pentecost of tongues, martyrs, belief,
  Virtuous women to believers wife,
Disciples watching with their doomèd chief,
  Apostles *victrix* over pagan strife,
  A Promised Land, a strictly-ordered life.
Reason alone these evidences prods —
Reason, that is the judgment seat on Gods.
  UTAH, 1889.

PLAYING HOUSE

WITHIN me lay a little boy
  When I thought I was a man;
He was too poor to own a toy
  And many a toy would plan;
A mystic hole — some cellar once —
  Lay in his father's parsonage lot:
The fancy of this little dunce
  Built in the hole Aladdin's grot.

He saw a staircase there descend
  And he saw apartments rise —
Stone walls, bright halls, rooms for a friend

And the maid with bashful eyes;
And Cinderella's steeds did browse
    In fancy on that pasture ridge,
And fancy dropped from fancy's house,
    A road down to the springlet's bridge.

All fairy things the urchin planned,
    But Aladdin's uncle's lamp,
Yet that alone was in his hand —
    The friendless little scamp:
Inquiry, wistfulness, desire, —
    To find what *is* in what but seems, —
The tinder wick to turn to fire
    The rusty lamp of golden dreams.

What is it yonder on the mount
    Like a palace that I see? —
After the forty years I count
    In the caverns of mystery?
A King's highway drops down the steep
    To a bridge across a brook,
And I see a child who walks in sleep
    Descend with a lamp and book:

It is my bridge below my dome,
    My road, my steeds, I spy;
The hole in the pasture is my home
    And the little boy is I.
Oh cruel uncle, leave me not
    Without my lamp's bright spark! —
Though I am king of the golden grot,
    I am poor if it is dark.

Tomb at Gapland